SINFUL
HEARTS

USA TODAY & WALL STREET JOURNAL BESTSELLING AUTHOR
CHARITY FERRELL

Visit my website at www.charityferrell.com
Cover Designer: Lori Jackson
Cover Photographer: Wander Aguiar
Editor: Jovana Shirley, Unforeseen Editing, www.unforeseenediting.com
Proofreader: Jenny Sims, Editing 4 Indies

ISBN-13: 978-1-952496-91-2

SINFUL HEARTS

USA TODAY & WALL STREET JOURNAL BESTSELLING AUTHOR

CHARITY FERRELL

PROLOGUE

EMILIO

The woman walking down the aisle isn't who I agreed to marry.

The veil may hide her, but I *know*.

Her hips don't sway the same.

Her hair is thicker and darker.

I signed the contract for her sister.

Not her.

And when I lift the veil and the truth is revealed, there will be hell to pay.

1

LILIYA

Thirty Minutes Earlier

"No," I shout as Aleksy, my older brother and ruthless boss of the Morozova Bratva stares me down.

I shake my head, voice trembling. "I won't marry that monster."

He steps forward, invading my space. "Then tell me where she is."

"I don't know!" I throw my arms up in frustration.

He thinks I'm covering for my sister, Dasha.

His jaw clenches. "Put on your sister's wedding dress, Liliya. You're the bride now." He curses Dasha under his breath before storming out and slamming the door behind him.

"Liliya," my mother mutters before sighing. "We don't have a choice. Let's get you in that gown."

I rush to the trash can, ready to vomit the bile rising up my throat.

"I won't do it." I hold out my arms like a barrier to stop her from coming closer. "Over my dead body—"

"It'll be *all* of our dead bodies," she hisses, struggling to keep her voice low. "Stop being selfish. This isn't about your feelings. It's about saving this family." She swats my arms away. "Your sister ran. Now, you have to take her place."

Dasha climbed out of the bridal suite while I was in the bathroom.

I wish she'd told me about her plan. I'd gone with her.

She was smart to run.

Marrying Emilio Lastro is a death sentence.

He's a murderer, a capo in the Lombardi Mafia family, and a man who discards people who no longer hold value to him. The dark rumors about him are endless.

But worst of them all? He betrayed his own family, killing his father in cold blood.

"He'll know I'm the wrong bride," I say, more to myself than her.

She shoves the gown into my arms. "Quit thinking negatively."

I catch the dress before it hits the floor and scoff bitterly.

"He barely even looked at Dasha at the engagement party." She gives me an optimistic pat on the shoulder.

"He isn't stupid." I narrow my eyes at her. "He'll put a bullet through my head."

She says nothing, doesn't even flinch.

I splay the dress across the couch before kicking off my shoes and unbuckling my jeans. "I didn't wake up today thinking I'd be the sacrificial lamb."

All the pressure is on me.

Our lives now lie in my hands.

If we break this contract with the Lombardis, they'll kill us.

As I slip the dress over my head, it feels like a chain weighing me down.

Thankfully, Dasha chose a simple dress with a high neckline, dainty lace sleeves, with a flare at the bottom. While simple, it's tight and uncomfortable, clinging to my waist and chest.

I stare at myself in the mirror, fighting the tears threatening to spill down my cheeks.

"You look beautiful, honey," my mother says softly, stepping behind me to settle her hands on my shoulders before smoothing a hand over my arm.

I look away, refusing to meet her eyes.

As much as I want to kick her out of the room and be alone in my misery, I don't.

Being alone right now would be worse.

Dasha had no bridesmaids. I was supposed to be the maid of honor.

I don't even have one of those.

It's just little old me, about to stand at the altar with a heartless mobster, praying he doesn't kill me when he lifts the veil and finds the wrong bride.

2

LILIYA

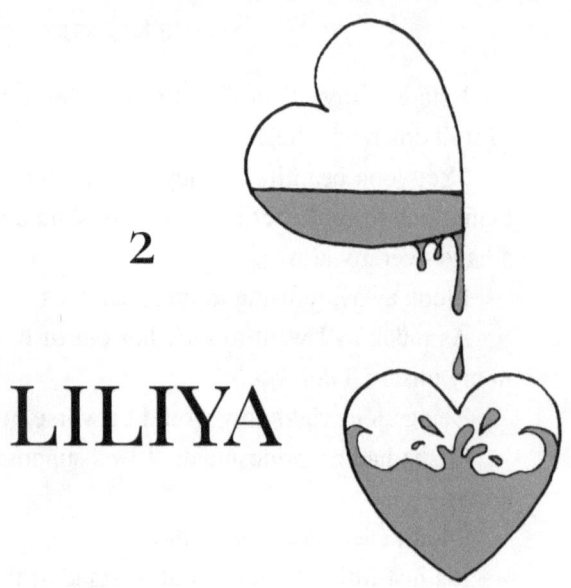

"She's ready," my mother tells Aleksy when he comes back into the room.

I look straight at Aleksy. "You need to tell Emilio. You're putting my life at risk if you don't."

"He won't notice." Aleksy drags a hand over his smooth jaw.

"Am I just supposed to let him call me Dasha for the rest of my life?"

He shakes his head. "Say your vows. We'll deal with everything else afterwards."

"You don't think telling him after will just piss him off more?"

He steps closer, clenching his fists at his sides. "Don't question me, Liliya. Just do what I say."

"Come on, honey," my mom says. "It's time."

It's time.

Time for me to be traded for peace, for power, for the Bratva.

Or die for it.

Aleksy walks me to the cathedral doors, and everyone turns silent when they open.

I claw at my throat, suffocating, as the "Bridal Chorus" begins.

For a moment, it's like time stops, and I can't move. My feet won't physically step forward.

"Don't do anything stupid," Aleksy warns, pulling me back into reality and extending his arm toward me.

I nudge him with my elbow, a silent *fuck you* that only the two of us sees, and then loop mine through his. If we weren't in public, I wouldn't dare do that. But Aleksy needs something from me.

I hold in my breath as we walk down the aisle, not even turning my head to look at the guests seated in the pews.

The priest stands at that altar.

A symbol of sanctity that I'm about to defile with lies.

When we reach him, Aleksy leans in to kiss my cheek. It takes everything I have not to push him away.

Aleksy offers his hand to Emilio.

Emilio takes it without even glancing in my brother's direction. He shakes it dismissively, and Aleksy takes a seat beside my mother in the front pew.

As I stand across from Emilio and stare at him through the veil, he watches me with suspicion.

I shut my eyes, feeling like I can read his mind.

This isn't the bride I signed on the dotted line for.

I keep my eyes closed, remembering the first and only time we've spoken.

It was two weeks ago at their engagement party. Emilio had hardly glanced or spoken to Dasha. When he did look in her direction, it was with cold glares, as if she were the one forcing him to marry her.

He wasn't just quiet with her. He was silent with everyone, ignoring all small talk, even with the Lombardis. He only spoke when words were necessary.

It wasn't until after dinner that he pulled Dasha aside. I crept toward them to eavesdrop. His tone was low, and I couldn't make out his words. Dasha looked terrified at whatever he was saying, though.

When he was finished playing bully and turned to leave, he walked straight into me.

The air left my lungs, like I'd slammed into a concrete statue.

I stumbled back, catching myself at the last second before falling on my ass. As I slowly lifted my gaze to his, my heart hammered in my chest as my eyes met wicked ones.

They were dark and narrow, like he was already reading my soul.

I gulped in fear while taking in every inch of him.

His face was heaven, and his heart hell.

He was made for art with his sharp jawline and high cheekbones, peppered with scruff.

Chills spread over my body, and I couldn't form words.

He didn't speak, just towered over me and stared with those unsettling eyes. I gulped again, begging myself to run away, but I couldn't.

There was something about his stare.

It was deadly, yes, but also different.

Emilio looked at me differently than he did Dasha.

He stared like I'd wronged him in another life and he'd been waiting for the right moment to punish me for it.

Since I couldn't seem to run, I stood there and glowered at him.

"Be careful who you glare at, *guaio*," he said, his tone low and lethal.

"What?" I asked—no, I *squeaked* out. "Is that a threat?"

His thick lip crooked up an inch. "Pray to whatever god you believe in that you'll never have to find out." He shook his head before moving around me.

I gasped when his shoulder collided with mine, pushing me back, and he charged out of the building.

While our conversation had been quick, it sparked a wildfire inside me.

There was also something more—relief that my sister was the one marrying him. Not me.

Being in the same room as him gave me chills. Hard pass on sharing a bed.

That night, I couldn't sleep as I replayed our exchange in my head. Grabbing my laptop, I searched what *guaio* meant.

Trouble in Italian.

Was he calling me trouble ... or warning me that I was already in it?

The priest speaking breaks me away from my thoughts. His voice sounds so distant since my ears are ringing. "We're gathered here today ..."

My gaze drifts to Emilio, standing tall in a black tux. His jaw is set, and his face is unreadable. He holds out his hand, stopping the priest, and immediately lifts the veil. To some, he may look like an eager man ready to see his bride.

But I'm no fool.

He knows I'm a fraud.

I take a breath so deep that it hurts. That deep breath slips through my lungs like smoke, and my heart races as recognition falls on his face. I brace for the chaos, for my possible death, for all hell to break loose.

But none of that happens.

At least not *yet*.

Emilio tips his head down, studying me and most likely plotting my murder in his head. The muscles in his jaw twitch, but his face reveals nothing.

I wait for him to announce I'm the wrong woman.

For him to call for my family's deaths for trying to play him.

But he doesn't.

Seconds pass, and I hear whispers around us.

The priest's gaze bounces between us as he waits for one of us to say something.

Maybe I'm just paranoid.

Maybe he doesn't know I'm not Dasha.

While I'll never forget our run-in at the engagement dinner, it could've meant nothing to him. For all he knows, I'm his bride. Though my gut tells me I'm wrong.

His stare is intense, like he can see *everything*. Every lie, every thought in my head, every feeling.

He signals for the priest to resume, who stutters the first few words as he does.

"And, Dasha," the priest says.

My heart stops, panic sweeping inside me.

"Liliya," Emilio quickly corrects.

The correction silences the room as people wait.

I don't dare look at my mother or Aleksy or anyone else.

The priest stutters again, studying us in confusion.

Emilio tips his head toward him, a silent *proceed*.

The priest clears his throat, nodding. "And, Liliya, have you come here to enter into marriage without coercion, freely and wholeheartedly?"

Freely?

Wholeheartedly?

Fuck no.

I hold in my scoff.

"Yes," I whisper, hating the sound of my voice and shocked that I could even get that word out.

My heart speeds as I repeat the priest's words, reciting vows that are nothing but lies.

Emilio does the same, his tone calm and deliberate, and his eyes never leaving mine.

When it's time for the ring exchange, Emilio reaches inside his tux pocket to retrieve a small black velvet box and opens it, revealing two rings.

The first is a simple black band.

The second is the opposite of simple. A large rose-cut diamond on a gold band shines in the light.

I don't have much time to admire the ring before he presses the black band into my hand. His rough fingers brush over mine, and goose bumps crawl over every inch of my body.

I nearly drop the ring in my unsteady hand. My throat tightens as I slip the band over his thick finger. He doesn't let me off that easily. Right before I can release him, he curls his free hand around mine. I shudder as he keeps his hand on mine there for a moment. My skin burns hot at his touch.

He immediately tightens his hold.

A warning.

You belong to me now.

I own you.

I tense when he abruptly releases me. He snatches my hand to firmly shove the diamond ring on my finger, officially branding me as a Lastro. I stare down at my hand and admire the ring that sits on a spiraled pair of bands, fused into one.

It's a ring for true love.

For fairy tales.

Not unions born on lies for power and money.

And then it happens, the moment I've been dreading since I made it past our vows alive.

The priest finally says, "You may now kiss the bride."

All eyes are on us.

My body tightens, as I'm unsure of what Emilio will do.

No way in hell am I making the first move.

Everyone is quiet as his hateful eyes lock on mine.

Then, slowly, he steps closer.

I hold in a breath, close to fainting, when he cups the back of my head. His hand is large, nearly spanning my entire skull. He digs his fingers into my hair to yank me closer and then settles his hand along my cheek to hold me in place.

I shut my eyes for a moment but hurriedly open them just as his lips brush against mine.

My body relaxes as he kisses me.

That warmth I felt when he touched me turns into burning flames.

I moan into his mouth when he slips the tip of his tongue into mine. For a moment, I think there's romance. But that doesn't last long when he pulls away.

My eyes flash open, and I raise my head.

That wicked smirk from the engagement party is back on his face.

It's a smirk that confirms I'll face the consequences for this betrayal.

I am so fucked.

3

EMILIO

"What the fuck?" I roar to Aleksy when we're in a private room inside the cathedral. "You can't just throw a random woman in front of me at the altar."

My pulse hasn't slowed since the moment I lifted the veil and saw *her*.

Not Dasha.

Liliya.

The wrong fucking bride.

The wrong fucking sister.

I played along with their game long enough to recite our vows, to tie her to me for the rest of her life. All of it was a part of my strategy to completely fuck Aleksy and the Russian Bratva.

I did what I had to do and then sealed my scheme with a kiss.

Then, I pushed Liliya away as if her kiss had poisoned me, turned to our guests, and told all of them but Aleksy to get the hell out.

Liliya stared at me, speechless, her green eyes wide in shock.

I'm not a man who plays games.

I'm the one who cheats in them.

Luckily, our guests, along with the priest and my bride, did as I'd demanded.

Antonio, the boss of the family I work for, also stayed. So did his underboss, Damien, and a capo, Julian. As did the mother of the dishonest bride.

Aleksy, along with his underboss, Lev, and Antonio, Damien, and Julian, followed me into this office that I'm positive belongs to the priest.

Aleksy stands in front of the door and leans back on his heels. "Technically, she's still a Morozova."

I smirk at his lack of concern, pull my fist back, and punch him square in the jaw.

He stumbles back, slamming into the door, and his skull makes a *thud* against the wood.

"Technically," I sneer, shaking out my hand, "that was just a love tap, you mouthy motherfucker."

Aleksy lunges toward me, which I happily welcome, but Antonio steps between us. Aleksy stops in his tracks, refusing to break through Antonio.

I square my shoulders, staring Aleksy down in a silent dare.

Do it, you dumb motherfucker.

Give me an excuse to break every bone in your fucking face.

"All right," Damien says, stepping to my side, as if ready to intercept me if Aleksy gets mouthy again. "Let's work this out before someone ends up dead."

"I don't mind a few dead Russians." I keep my glare on Aleksy.

Aleksy spits blood from his busted lip on the ornate rug. His jaw is already swelling, and I clench my fist, wishing I could punch the fucker again. My knuckles still tremble from the first blow, and it's like they're begging for a second go at him.

I shove aside a stack of paperwork on the desk, lean against it, and cross my arms while waiting for Aleksy's pathetic excuse.

He wipes the corner of his mouth with his sleeve. "Dasha ran off."

"Ran off where?" I pop my knuckles.

"We don't know." He slaps his lanky arms to his sides, looking too weak for my liking.

"Then why the fuck are you *here*, playing Swap the Fucking Bride, instead of tracking her down?"

"We found out she was missing only thirty minutes ago," Aleksy explains. "Liliya was here, so we made a judgment call. It's a small change."

"A small change?" Julian repeats with a dry laugh, shaking his head. "Jesus. You're talking about a woman like she's a lunch order substitution. *Sorry, we're out of Dasha. How about a Liliya instead?*" He grins. "Good thing my wife isn't listening to this conversation. She'd tear you a new one."

I shoot him a death glare.

He chuckles in amusement. The fucker clearly isn't as pissed as I am about the situation, which only frustrates me further. I'm ready to punch him next.

"Look," Antonio says in an all-business tone. "We can make this work." He shoots me a *work with me* look. "She's a Morozova woman. Be glad we found out the other was a runner before the wedding."

"I won't let Dasha get away with this," Aleksy bites out. "When I find her, I'll kill whoever helped her run off. Then you can wed her to any man of yours." He presses his palm to his heart. "We'll make this right, Antonio."

I work my jaw, knowing I won't let Aleksy off the hook for this.

But Antonio's right. It's not that big of a deal.

The issue is, he doesn't know why I wanted the other sister.

Dasha was the safe option.

When I looked at her, there was nothing but disinterest. In

the short conversation we had, I knew she wasn't a bride I'd care about.

But her sister?

She's a different story.

The moment I saw Liliya, she captured my attention. I'd never seen such a beautiful woman before. Her red dress clung to her every curve, and her heels brought her closer to my height. When she glanced at me, her green eyes burned in my direction. Her dark curls fell down her back, and I clenched my fist every time I thought about gripping those strands in my hand.

I wasn't the only man who noticed her either. A stab of jealousy hit me anytime another man looked at her—an emotion I'd never felt before. Liliya was trouble—everything I shouldn't want—and I was thankful she hadn't been chosen as my bride.

I wanted to touch her, to fuck her, to possess her.

That's not indifference, so I couldn't have that.

I only agreed to the marriage contract for the sake of business and peace.

"You want to make this right?" I ask.

Aleksy nods.

I let the silence hang for a moment and run my tongue over my front teeth.

"A change for a change," I finally say. "Your ploy will not go unpunished, Aleksy."

"What do you want, Lastro?" Aleksy raises a thick brow.

Antonio cocks his head to the side. He didn't expect me to follow through with Aleksy's offer.

"My new wife moves in with me *tonight*." I stare Aleksy down. "No more surprises. I'm not in the business of chasing runaways or tracking down wives."

Aleksy steps forward. "That wasn't part of the contract—"

"Neither was me marrying the other sister," I interrupt before grabbing the closest notepad, yanking off a page that looks like it belongs in a sermon binder, tossing it over my shoulder, and tapping the pen against the fresh sheet. "You broke the deal, Aleksy. That means, I get to rewrite it. Liliya moves in with me, or I nullify this wedding. And your little empire?" I use my hand to create a slashing motion across my throat. "Dead. No more Bratva influence in this city for the next thousand fucking decades."

Aleksy pinches the bridge of his nose in frustration. "Liliya won't go for that."

I scoff. "Are you not the Bratva boss?"

His face hardens at my disrespect.

In the first contract, where I married Dasha, I didn't press the issue of her moving in with me. Cohabitating with someone sounded like a fucking nightmare, especially with a woman I didn't care about. Liliya and Aleksy both knew this. I'm sure it's one of the reasons Liliya agreed to even walk down the aisle.

Aleksy hesitates, fumbling for the right words, like a lost puppy in a new home.

He's a new boss, and the Bratva will crumble under his rule.

Some men are born to lead.

Aleksy isn't one of them.

He's bound to fuck up early and get himself killed.

Liliya should be grateful she'll now be under my protection instead of his.

"Tell her to pack her bags." I scribble words onto the paper, rip it off the notepad, and fold it before slipping it into my pocket. "After all, it's just a minor change, right?"

Aleksy runs a hand through his buzzed hair, his face red and rigid.

I jerk my chin toward the door, holding back the urge to say *chop-chop*. My patience won't last long with my new brother-in-law.

"Fine," Aleksy says, jabbing a finger in my direction. "That's the only fucking change."

I shoot him a cocky smile. "Pleasure doing business, Aleksy."

He opens the door and stalks out of the room with a huff.

Lev follows him. A few seconds later, Julian, Damien, Antonio, and I do the same.

I almost instructed him to pass my note to Liliya, but I don't trust him not to open it. When I return to the nave, I spot their mother sitting nervously in the pew. Liliya is nowhere to be seen.

I step closer, sliding my hand into my pocket, and pull out my note.

"Give this to Liliya," I tell her. "You open it, I'll chop your fucking fingers off."

"Excuse me—"

I talk over her. "You played Switch It with the wrong man. Now, you play by my rules."

4

LILIYA

L iliya Lastro.
I don't like the sound of it at all.
It sounds fake.

Doesn't roll off the tongue well.

At least, that's what I'm trying to tell myself.

I'm back in the bridal suite, trying to collect my thoughts after Emilio kicked everyone out.

While I hope they don't kill Aleksy, fingers crossed he at least gets punched once.

Hard and right in his smug, controlling face.

He needs a good blow to knock some of the arrogance out of him. He's never had power like this before, and he's relishing it. It's getting rather annoying.

The Morozovas run the Russian Bratva in New York City. My *dedushka* started it in Russia before sending my Uncle Yaroslav to the States to run a sector of the crime organization here. His son and my cousin, Dima, wanted the boss title for himself and recently killed Yaroslav.

Dima's run as boss didn't last long. He was killed shortly after by a woman he'd kidnapped.

Karma's a bitch.

With Uncle Yaroslav and Dima dead, the only man in the States with Morozova blood was Aleksy.

He's gone from being a mere foot soldier to boss, making life-and-death decisions for a dangerous crime organization. His new position has made him reckless and cruel.

Aleksy's first *power move*, as he called it, was setting up an alliance via a marriage contract with the Lombardis. A peace offering on their end since Dima died at the hands of a Lombardi capo's wife.

I plop down on the sofa in the bridal suite and touch my lips, remembering how Emilio's felt against them.

I liked it more than I should've. For a moment, when his mouth was on mine, I felt peace. I convinced myself that his gentleness meant I was safe from murder.

It was all just a mind game for him.

The door flings open, and my mother walks inside the room. She's breathless, like the walk to the bridal suite was miles long, and clutches a folded paper against her chest.

She shuts the door and eyes me uneasily while holding out the note in my direction. "Emilio told me to give you this."

I stare at the note as if it contains anthrax.

She thrusts it closer, so similar to how she had the wedding gown earlier.

I slowly take the note from her and unfold it. My head grows dizzy as I read it.

Pack your bags, my deceitful wife.
You're mine now.

This note is so on-brand for my new husband.

Of course, he'd send a threat as our newlywed present.

"What does it say?" my mother asks.

I hand her the note without a word. Let her read it herself.

"Wait," she says in alarm while reading, lowering the note to look at me. "Does this mean ..."

"I'm not moving in with him," I declare, standing to snatch the note back and march across the room. "Absolutely fucking not."

I refuse to live under Emilio's roof like some prisoner.

Especially after his little note.

The door opens again, and Aleksy stumbles inside, clutching a bloody tissue to his lip. His blazer is gone, his shirt now wrinkled, and blood speckles the collar. He shuts the door. Mom winces when he kisses her cheeks, and his eyes lock on me.

"No," I immediately say, already knowing what's coming.

"Liliya, we have no choice," he says, his voice nasally. "He's pissed we didn't tell him Dasha ran off."

"Oh, he's pissed about that?" I seethe, shaking with rage. "What a shocker. It's almost like I warned you something like this would happen. I begged you to listen to me."

"We did what we had to do." His voice turns harsh. "For the family."

I violently shake my head.

"Don't make this harder than it already is, Liliya." His glare darkens. "It's happening whether you like it or not. But you will pretend to like it when you're with Emilio."

I take deep breaths to stop myself from crying.

"What if I refuse?" I ask as my mother takes my abandoned seat.

"Then Emilio kills you," he replies with no hesitation, no softness. Just the truth, stabbing me like a knife to my throat. "He made that crystal clear. You think *I* changed the deal? It was him." Aleksy steps forward, sweat dripping down his forehead. "If we refuse, he said he'll kill all of us and hunt down Dasha."

A shiver rips down my spine.

"Change into the reception dress," he instructs before turning on his heel and leaving the bridal suite.

It's done.

My voice doesn't matter.

I don't matter.

I flip off the door, wishing it were to Aleksy's face and Emilio's.

As I rip the wedding gown over my head, I know what I have to do.

I'll go to this reception dinner and pretend to be a good wife, and then, like Dasha, I'll run.

5

LILIYA

E milio yanks the wineglass from my hand. "That's
enough."

I attempt to grab it back, but he presses his cold
palm against my forehead and shoves me back into my chair.

Those are the first words he's said to me since we arrived at
the reception dinner. He's spent most of the night acting as if I
were invisible.

Not that I'm angry about that. I'd prefer he ignore me
forever.

"Rude," I mutter when he places the glass out of my reach.

The alcohol has given me a bravery I shouldn't have.

Emilio sets a full glass of water where my wineglass was.

I harden my gaze on him in disapproval.

"Drink," he demands. "Sloppy drunks are distasteful."

I inhale the smell of his breath. It's a sharp mix of mint and
bourbon. I bite down the urge to say *rude* again … or something
worse.

Normally, I'm not much of a drinker.

A glass of wine here. A margarita on occasion.

But tonight? Bring me the entire bottle.

I cast a glance at Aleksy and my mother, sitting at their table, and struggle to resist the urge to pick up the water glass and hurl it at them. All night, they've laughed and toasted—and without even checking on me once.

Aleksy dropped another bomb on me during the ride here. After this, I'm leaving here and going straight to my new home with my new husband.

I don't get to pack my own bags. They'll be waiting for me when I get there.

I look away from them to Emilio. He raises a brow as I lift the water to my lips and take a drink. I hold it in my mouth for three seconds before spitting it back into the glass.

It's so unladylike.

The look he gives me could freeze hell.

My lips twitch into a smile.

He leans back in his chair, studying me like I'm a puzzle.

A puzzle he wants to rip apart.

Staring back, I fake a confidence I most definitely don't have. I gulp, making the mistake of taking my husband in, remembering how gorgeous he is.

Before coming to the reception dinner, he ditched his tux jacket, now only wearing a black shirt with the top three buttons undone, sleeves rolled to his elbows.

Why can't my monster husband have horns growing from his head like the devil he is?

They do say the devil is alluring.

It's how he draws you in.

This dinner is a snoozefest and reminds me more of a funeral reception than one for a wedding. It's nothing like the weddings I grew up attending.

There's no dancing, karaoke, or speeches. We haven't even had a first dance. However, I won't complain about that one. I'd rather dig my own grave with a spork than dance with Emilio.

I've texted Dasha a few times with no reply.

All she did was leave a note that said, **Sorry, I won't marry him** in the bridal suite before hightailing it.

Aleksy tracked her phone. It's at the bottom of the Hudson River, hanging out with the fish, litter, and bodies people have forgotten about.

I grab the glass, my eyes on him, and pour the water into my mouth, not swallowing it again.

"Swallow the fucking water, Liliya, or I'll pour it down your throat and watch you choke on it," Emilio warns.

I count to five before spitting the water in my glass again, not caring if anyone is watching.

His jaw tightens as he scoots his chair closer to mine. "Don't fucking test me."

"I'll drink more water …" I pause for dramatic effect and tap my French-manicured nails against the glass. "*If* I can sleep at my own home tonight."

"You will sleep in your own home. Your *new* home." Without breaking eye contact, he snatches the wineglass he confiscated from me earlier, raises it in a mock toast, and knocks it back. He smirks before licking his lower lip, slow and teasing.

Tingles shoot between my legs, and I press my thighs together.

"The home *I grew up in*," I say tightly.

"Oh, that home?" he says with a cruel laugh. "No."

"You had that arrangement with Dasha."

"Are you Dasha?" He raises a thick brow as his gaze mockingly trails down my face to my cleavage.

"Obviously not." I cross my arms and lean back, scowling. "She was smart and ran. Unfortunately, I didn't."

"Exactly." He flashes a cold smile. "You're still here, and my arrangement with her is irrelevant now."

Stretching his arm along the back of my chair, he snaps my dress strap. I flinch at the sting and shove my shoulder forward to put distance between us.

He cups my shoulder to stop me, pressing me into the chair, and digs his fingers into my bare skin. "While some grooms teach their brides to fuck on their wedding day, here's my first lesson for you."

I attempt to pull away again, but he tightens his hold on me.

"I make the rules here, Liliya." He lowers his head so that his lips are at my ear. "Every single thing you do from now on will be controlled by me."

As he rears back, another grin tugs at his mouth. It's one I imagine he gives his victims before he snaps their necks.

"It's unfortunate I must inform you that I'm not a dog and I don't follow commands," I fire back.

"I'll break that out of you. Trust me." He snaps my strap again. Standing, he motions toward the server who's kept my glass full all night.

The server scrambles toward us. "Do you need a refill, sir?"

Looking at him, Emilio juts a finger toward me. "If you serve her another drop of alcohol, I'll break this glass and slit your fucking throat with it."

Oh great.

Another trait of my husband: threatens innocent waitstaff.

"Uh … yes, sir," the server murmurs, his tray now shaking above his trembling hand.

Emilio's gaze hardens. "Good."

He doesn't pay me another glance as he walks away and heads straight to a round table draped in white linen. Antonio and his wife, Gigi, greet him, pretending they weren't watching our exchange.

I offer the server an apologetic smile.

He nods stiffly, turns on his heel, and flees.

Shutting my eyes, I run Emilio's words through my mind. *"I'll break that out of you."*

There was a reason Aleksy chose Dasha to marry Emilio at the beginning. Prior to her running off, she was the obedient sister. Even when Aleksy told her about the engagement, she cried, but didn't argue.

But me?

I'm the opposite.

Emilio is about to find that out.

———

Before we leave the reception dinner, Aleksy tells Emilio he'd like to speak with me privately and say his goodbyes.

Yes, he told Emilio, as if my new husband must grant permission to who I can speak to now.

Instead of taking me to a room, Aleksy leads me outside. We walk through the rain, straight to his black Bentley.

It's new. A promotion gift for himself.

For a sliver of a moment, I have hope in my brother as we slide into the Bentley.

Maybe he'll take me home.

Ha. Who am I kidding?

Aleksy locks the doors before peering into the back seat, checking if the coast is clear. "Liliya, I need to tell you something very important."

I turn in the leather seat to stare at him. "What?"

"*The family* needs something from you."

"Nope." I shake my head so hard that I'm surprised my neck doesn't snap. "I'm all favored out."

"Not a favor," he corrects, the words gritted through his clenched teeth. "A demand."

"I'm all *demanded* out as well. Try again next year *if I'm still alive.*"

Leaning in closer, he levels his elbow on the console to get into my face. "It's a demand from *Dedushka.*"

I force down a breath, meeting his gaze, but not saying a word.

Our *dedushka*, Rurick Morozova, is only mentioned in serious conversations. He's not like your typical grandparent.

He started the Morozova Bratva family decades ago. While he rules in Russia and rarely comes to the States, he still controls most aspects of the family affairs here. He told Aleksy he had a year to prove he could run the family successfully or he'd replace him.

"He said it's your duty to do as the family says. As *he* says," Aleksy adds.

I turn my head, creating distance between us, and stare out the window. My throat turns dry. "What's *my duty*? Is marrying a murderer not enough for you men?"

"You're going to kill Emilio," he states with no bullshit in his tone.

I turn my head, staring at him in shock. "You want me to *murder the murderer?*"

His lip slightly lifts as he slowly nods.

I wait for him to laugh.

To tell me he's messing with me.

But he doesn't.

He looks just as serious as when he told me I was the new bride.

"Have you lost your fucking mind?" I hiss. "That's a death sentence."

"Not if you're careful."

"Aleksy, did you forget who the Lombardis are? They're not stupid. If *I* or *anyone* kills Emilio, they'll hunt down whoever is to blame."

Aleksy sighs in annoyance, as if I were saying no to letting him borrow a jacket, not freaking murder. "Listen, I know this is asking a lot. But look at it this way: Murdering him is your ticket out of the marriage. You become a widow, who will then choose her own husband. All we need from you is this one *simple* favor."

I stare coldly at him. "No."

"You don't have a choice in this. It's final." He kisses my forehead, as if that seals our deal. "Make the family proud. You're the future matriarch of the Bratva, Liliya. Make your husband happy. Get his guard down. Then, kill him."

6

LILIYA

Aleksy's demand replays in my head as if on a loop.
"Get his guard down. Then kill him."
Not only am I suddenly supposed to be a Mafia wife, but I also need to become an assassin.

I sink into the cool leather seat and glance out of Emilio's SUV window.

Thunder rolls, and a bolt of lightning zips across the sky. For a split second, I consider throwing open the door and making a run for it.

Dread has etched itself in the pit of my stomach over what happens when we get back to his—no, *our* home.

We haven't spoken the entire ride. The only sound is the screech of the windshield wipers and the storm.

Emilio finally slows at a black iron gate with pointed tips and stone pillars. Blinking, I attempt to see beyond it, but the rain makes it too blurry.

Water spills into the car when Emilio rolls down his window. He punches a code into a rusty speaker box. Craning my neck, I attempt to see it, but he blocks me.

The gate opens like a mouth ready to swallow me whole.

Emilio rolls up the window and drives up the sloped driveway. Darkness and trees surround us.

My jaw drops when the headlights land on the all-stone estate home. It's stunning and nothing like what I expected from Emilio.

The home is a fortress, fit for billionaires and regals. I don't know how much the Lombardis pay their capos, but in the Morozova Bratva, only bosses have homes like this.

I turn to look at Emilio. "Did you grow up here?" That has to be the only explanation.

He tightens his hand around the steering wheel. "Yes."

We park in the circular driveway, not in a garage. He cuts the engine, and without a word, steps out into the rain.

Sighing, I unbuckle my seat belt and trail him. The rain relentlessly soaks my dress and hair. By the time I walk inside, I'm drenched.

Emilio flips on a dim light, and a chandelier with cobwebs overhead casts a golden light in the grand entry.

For a long second, neither of us says anything.

Silence is our main form of communication.

Arguing seems to be the second.

The air is stale and thick with traces of dust. The interior reminds me of an old castle that's been vacant for too long. But beneath the dust and cobwebs is architecture art.

Soaring ceilings that make me feel short, arched windows, dark walnut trim, and stained glass bleeding with assorted colors, create its beauty.

Whoever built this home spent time perfecting every detail.

Whoever lived here doesn't have good lasting memories.

I can feel it in the air.

When I peer back at Emilio, his emotionless gaze roams over me. My soaked hair. My wet and now-see-through white dress. I shiver beneath his stare.

I clear my throat. "How long has it been since you stayed here?"

"Years." He slams the door shut before wandering to the iron staircase, collecting a coat of dust with his finger.

"Where did you stay before?"

"My place in the city." He shakes water droplets from his hair.

"Why are we here then?"

He doesn't reply.

I roll my eyes. "So, what? Do I pick a random room and claim it as mine?" Stretching out my arms, I force myself to yawn. "I'm tired, tipsy, and possibly three seconds from puking."

I don't need to puke, but it's my attempt to turn him off.

Surely, no one wants to consummate a marriage with a wife claiming they need to vomit, right?

He turns without a word and starts up the stairs. Pausing for a moment, he peers over his shoulder, as if waiting for me to follow.

"Hopefully, there's somewhere for me to puke up there," I say loudly while following him.

If only I'd been able to pack my bags.

I'd have snuck some weapons in there.

When we reach the second floor, he leads me to the first bedroom on the right. A queen-size bed with a white headboard trimmed in gold sits along a wall. The wallpaper is blush and gold, giving the room a soft and feminine feel.

The white comforter that was on my bed this morning is now here. A folded stack of my clothes is on the bed, and my suitcase is on the floor.

"You'll sleep here," he says.

I spin to face him. "Whose room is this?"

"Yours."

"Not *yours*?" The question slips out before I can stop it.

Here I am, giving him ideas. Stupid.

Again, he doesn't respond.

My new husband doesn't give words or information freely. Not a great match for a blabbermouth like myself.

He leaves the room, shutting the door behind him. I swear, I hear a lock click on the other side.

I kick off my wedges, sweep my gaze over the room, and take in my new space. There's an en suite bathroom and an empty walk-in closet.

I collect my clothes from the bed and shove them back inside the suitcase. I'm not unpacking because I'm not staying.

Sitting on the edge of the bed, I wring out my hair before digging in my purse for my phone when a thought hits me.

"Her Instagram," I mutter, opening the app. "I'll message her on there."

I slump my shoulders, ready to throw the phone across the room when I find Dasha's profile deactivated. She knows she can never show her face here again without consequences and will have to hide from Aleksy, the Bratva, and the Lombardis for the rest of her life.

Both of us are stuck in a shitty life, either way you look at it.

I toss my phone on the bed, wander to the bookshelf, and pull down a notebook.

Someone wrote *Aurora loves Edward Cullen* on the first page and glued magazine clippings of *Twilight* characters. They also drew hearts and scribbled *Team Vampire*.

Poor Aurora. She caught the *Twilight* bug too.

All of us thought pale, stalky men were the rage then.

I shove the notebook back onto the shelf and check the door, seeing if Emilio actually locked me in. He didn't, thankfully.

I slowly open the door, cringing as it creaks, and tiptoe out of the room. Voices float through a closed door down the hall. I creep toward the door, pressing my ear against it, and attempt to listen to Emilio speaking on the other side.

"I don't trust her." He goes quiet for a moment, as if listening to someone on the other end of a call. "She means nothing to me."

I squeeze one eye shut, like it'll help me hear better, as he pauses again.

"I'll visit soon. Okay?" Another pause from Emilio. "I love you too. Goodbye."

Footsteps come closer from the other side of the door. I spin on my heel and bolt in the opposite direction toward the stairway. I'm halfway down the stairs when the door creaks open.

When I hit the landing, I turn right, in search of the kitchen. I pass through a dining room with long maroon drapes and an old table that could easily seat twenty people.

Again, something fit for kings and queens.

My shoulders slump, and I bend at the waist when I reach the chef's kitchen with outdated appliances. I open the fridge to find bottled water, ginger ale, and a basket of strawberries and blueberries.

Weird combo, but no judgment.

I grab a water, shut the fridge, turn, and slam straight into a hard chest—so similar to how I did the night of the engagement dinner. I gasp, losing my balance, and fall back against the fridge.

Emilio stands only inches away from me, his face hard and brimming with anger. His gaze sharpens as he stares me down. My heart pounds, ready to lurch out of my chest, when he pulls a switchblade from his pocket.

He crowds me so close that I can't move, and I shrink against the fridge when he flips open the blade and slowly glides it along my jawline. As fucking terrified as I am, I refuse to look away from him.

Don't beg him to stop.

He adds pressure and lowers the blade to my throat. Cold steel brushes along my skin. I gulp, and his smirk says he heard it.

"Don't eavesdrop on me again." He nudges the blade's tip into my throat just deep enough to break the skin.

I grip the water bottle, wishing I had something to use as a weapon so I could smash it against his face. "If you don't want me eavesdropping, then let me go home."

"This is your home." He slowly drags the blade down the curve of my neck before leaning in closer, his cold breath brushing my cheek. "Get used to it."

A shiver crawls down my spine.

"Why me, but not Dasha?" I whisper. "Why did I have to come here?"

The blade leaves my skin as he steps back and slips it back into his pocket. The water bottle falls from my fingers.

Emilio captures my face in his hand, brushing his thumb over the skin he punctured with the knife. "Because Dasha never made me feel this alive."

My mouth drops open, unable to form words.

He doesn't give me a chance to respond before turning on his heel and charging out of the kitchen.

I double over to catch my breath, resting my hands on my knees as I draw air into my lungs.

Seconds later, the front door slams shut.

I creep from the kitchen, my heart hammering, and into the foyer to find Emilio gone. Peeking out the window, I spot taillights fading down the drive.

This is it.

My time to run.

Jack-freaking-pot.

I open the door, and an alarm shrieks through the house.

My chest clamps tight when the taillights bleed brighter and then reverse, coming closer.

He's coming back.

Do I hide? Make a run for it?

I have no money. No shoes. Nothing.

"Fuck it." I run.

I run faster than I've ever run in my life in the opposite direction of the driveway.

I'll sleep on the street if I have to.

Or under a bridge or in a ditch. Anything is better than living with this knife-wielding psycho.

My lungs burn, my feet pounding against the pavers, and I glance back to see the SUV stopped.

I sprint faster, ignoring the brutal rain and strong wind.

Don't stop.

Run, Liliya.

Run like Dasha.

When I reach the backyard, I pass a pool, a pond, and head straight for the wooded area. Every few steps, I glance back, expecting Emilio to suddenly appear behind me.

I plunge deeper into the trees, branches hitting my body, and the lack of light makes it hard to see. My legs feel weak, and my body hurts.

Then it happens.

Crack!

"Fuck!" I scream.

Pain shoots through my foot, and I collapse to the ground. I clasp my ankle to find a jagged stick stuck through the arch of my foot. I sink my teeth into my lip to stop myself from screaming again, biting so hard that I taste blood, and yank the stick free.

The wound isn't deep, but the pain radiates through my leg. As badly as I want to stop, I can't.

My freedom is on the line.

I force myself up and stumble forward, limping through the trees and praying I find a road soon.

Air leaves my lungs when a crushing weight slams into my back.

I hit the ground hard. Hands seize my wrist, pinning them to the ground so tight I'm positive he wants to break my bones. He shoves my face into the dirt.

I try to fight him off as his heavy breath grazes the back of my neck.

Emilio's mouth drifts to my ear. "You'll pay for this, my deceitful wife. No one runs from me."

7

EMILIO

I should punish Liliya for running.

Leave her out here alone to suffer in the dark.

That was my one of my father's favorite punishments.

If I lost a fight, or my aim was off, or if he was just having a shitty day, he'd drag me out into the woods. I wasn't allowed to come back home until sunrise.

That bullshit stopped when I turned fourteen, punched him in the face, and broke his nose.

Rain pelts down on us harder, and anger seeps through my veins as I keep my weight on Liliya. Pulling my head back, I can see her shaking beneath me.

She's scared. *Good.*

"I'm going to stand," I warn sharply. "If you run, you'll fucking regret it."

She doesn't say a word.

I press her wrists deeper into the dirt. "Confirm you won't fucking run."

"I won't run," she says, forcing the words through hitched breaths.

I slowly release one hand, then the other, before standing.

The moonlight filters through the tree branches, giving me a low-lit view of Liliya as she flips onto her back.

Her breasts move in sync with her heavy breathing. Dirt covers her dress and skin, and leaves are tangled in her hair.

She grunts while pulling herself to her knees, careful not to put any pressure on her right foot. I cock my head to the side in confusion.

"A stick jammed through my foot," she explains like I care.

My only concern is that she gets her ass back inside the house.

I glance at her foot, fighting back the urge to say that's what she gets for running.

She attempts to pull herself up again but winces in pain, falling back down.

Even though my little runner doesn't deserve it, I offer her my hand.

She stares at it like it'll bite off her finger.

I stretch it out farther, leaving it hang for a few seconds, and just as I'm about to tug it back, she takes it. Leveling her palm to the ground, she lets out a painful gasp as she lifts herself.

"You pull out another switchblade, I'm running again," she warns. "I don't care if I die doing it." She drops my hand the second she's stable. "You'll have to drag me back to that house."

I scrub my hands together. "Would you prefer I drag you by the hand or hair?"

She lets out another huff and then staggers toward my child-hood home in defeat. With every step, she hisses in pain.

I follow a few paces behind her, giving her space. When she nearly face-plants, I grab her arm and drape it over my shoulders. She stiffens for a moment before giving me her weight, no longer having the energy to fight me.

The smell of her floral perfume trails up my nostrils. It fits in with the rain and trees around us.

Bringing her here was a mistake.

Before tonight, I hadn't set foot inside my family home in years. I pay caretakers to tend to the maintenance, but I want nothing to do with it.

People have tried to purchase the estate. I turn down every offer. Even the ones double its worth.

My mother's great-great-grandfather built the estate, and she inherited it after my grandparents' deaths. She made the mistake of putting my father's name on the deed. He made it clear she'd lose it if she ever tried leaving him.

I help Liliya inside, up the stairs, and to her en suite bathroom. She shivers as I settle her onto the vanity stool, kneel in front of her, and take her filthy foot in my hand. I've seen enough wounds to know she'll be fine. It just needs to be cleaned and wrapped.

"I'm a nurse." She attempts to pull out of my grasp. "I'll fix it myself."

I clamp my hand around her ankle. She should consider herself lucky I'm not wrapping it around her fucking throat for running off.

I almost didn't chase her, but the last thing I need is for her to go missing. With my reputation, people would believe I killed her.

I'm known as a ruthless killer.

They're not wrong. I'm ruthless, and I've killed.

But I'm not guilty of all the rumors.

I allow people to whisper and don't bother correcting them.

I prefer men to flinch when I enter a room.

Fear keeps people at a distance.

Liliya sits silent as I pull the first-aid kit from a drawer.

Tonight, I won't be my father. Liliya won't tend to her own wound, no matter how capable.

She watches as I clean her foot, dry it, and rub antibiotic ointment over the wound.

A tense silence fills the room, but neither of us says a word.

I wrap her foot and smooth a hand over it when I'm finished.

"You try running off again, and I'll cut off your fucking feet." I secure the bandage and press my hand around her ankle.

Her gaze rises from her foot to my face. "Why are you keeping me prisoner here?"

"I'm not keeping you prisoner."

"You threatened to cut my feet off if I left. Those are words for prisoners."

I must give it to my new wife. She's fucking brave.

Very few men would speak to me like that, let alone in that tone.

"Fine, I'll take a toe. How's that?" I tighten my hold on her ankle. "But each time you attempt to run, I'll take another— because I'll always fucking catch you."

"That leaves me ten tries then."

"Depends on which day you get me."

Her shoulders slump. "Why did you go through with the wedding?"

"Why did *you*?"

"I had no choice. You did."

"That's where you're wrong."

"You have more say than I do."

"You're my wife," I say. "And you'll be my wife until the day you die."

"What if I don't want to be?"

"Too fucking bad." I drop her foot and stand.

"Told you!" She throws up her arms. "I *am* a prisoner."

"Are you behind bars? Shackled to the wall?" I snatch her wrist, raising it to show her free use.

She jerks out of my hold. "Give me the freedom to come and go as I please then."

"You have to earn that privilege."

She tilts her head up to meet my eyes as I step closer and loom over her.

"Follow the rules, Liliya. Don't fuck with me, and I won't make your life miserable." I jab my finger in her face. "But if you spy on me or try to run again, I'll bury you in those woods so fucking deep that not even your ghost will be able to escape."

"You can't kill me. My brother will start a war with you."

"Your brother sold you to me." I raise a brow and pet the top of her head. "I'd also gladly welcome a war. Killing men is my favorite pastime." I rap two knuckles against the door and leave the room.

———

It's after midnight when I enter the back door of Lucky Kings Casino, the business run by the Lombardi family. As far as the IRS knows, Lucky Kings is my employer and only source of income.

As soon as I left my home, I called a meeting with the others to discuss my shit show of a wedding.

Before entering the boardroom, I power off my phone, toss it in the basket with the others, and walk inside. Everyone is already here, and Antonio sits at the head of the table.

When the Lastros immigrated from Sicily with nothing but desperation and the clothes on their backs, Antonio's great-grandfather took mine in and gave him work. Our loyalty to them was born from that.

My father was a capo, but he fucked up that loyalty when Antonio's father died. Instead of accepting Antonio as the new boss, he sided with Antonio's Uncle Sonny and died for it.

I was there when he died.

Saw the light leave his eyes and the last breath leave his lungs.

And I didn't do or feel a goddamn thing.

Damien and my fellow capos, Julian and Leo, are also seated at the table.

These men are all I have.

We've shed blood and gone through wars together. They have my back as much as I have theirs. It's why I chose Antonio over my father. Loyalty is thicker than blood in my veins.

"There's the groom." Julian smirks. "Celebrating his wedding night like a true romantic."

I shut the door and then lift my middle finger in his direction. "Fuck off."

Damien chuckles, leaning back in his chair. "I've spent three hours this evening explaining to *my wife* why you didn't mention it was the wrong bride."

I ignore their amusement. Fuckers wouldn't be joking if the roles were reversed.

Strolling to the bar cart in the corner, I pour myself a glass of whiskey and then take the chair beside Julian. It's a rarity for me to drink this much, but it's been a fucking night.

"I don't like this," I say. "The Russians are playing games."

"Aleksy isn't smart enough to play games," Julian argues.

"Aleksy isn't smart enough to fucking lead," Antonio chimes in.

I point my glass at Antonio. "Which is exactly my concern. I don't want us affiliated with his fuckups."

I never wanted to marry, but we ended up in a tricky situation with the Russians. In exchange for clearing his debt, Carlisle Astor had agreed to marry off his daughter, Genesis, to Dima Morozova. Julian went to Dima's father, Yaroslav, and brokered a deal behind his back, making Genesis his.

Dima lost his shit, *allegedly* murdered Yaroslav, and abducted Genesis. The problem was that Dima didn't know Genesis was as batshit crazy as Julian, and she murdered him.

Now, Aleksy is the boss, and he offered us a peace deal and a cut of the Russian businesses if we signed a marriage contract. That was the only smart decision he's made since becoming

Bratva boss. He wants a seat at the big-boy table, an *in* with the Mafia families who run New York.

Four mob families run New York City: Lombardis, Marchettis, Cavallaros, and O'Connors. The Morozovas aren't even on the list.

"What do you want to do with the runaway sister?" Antonio asks me.

"I have a wife. I'm not interested in hunting down another." I shrug and take a drink. The whiskey is cool as it slides down my throat.

"If a man helped her run, he's dead," Damien adds. "We won't tolerate that level of disrespect."

This isn't about Dasha.

We couldn't give two fucks about her.

I scrub my hand over my face. "I'm aware. We'll start looking into it tomorrow. I'd rather Aleksy do the heavy lifting with this problem. It's his sister who fucked him over and made him look like the idiot he is."

Damien studies me, flicking his Zippo lighter open and closed. "I don't think you have a problem with the wife swap. In fact, you prefer this one." He opens the Zippo again, staring at me through the flame. "I saw the way you looked at her at the engagement party."

I shake my head, not responding.

He's not wrong, but that's not the point.

"Next order of business." I down the whiskey. "How do we fuck over the Russians and take every dollar their businesses bring in? I want to know every outside deal they have and steal it from them. Their income. Every-fucking-thing."

Antonio leans in, resting his elbows on the table. "Let's proceed."

8

LILIYA

At 9:38 a.m., my phone rings.

Unknown Number.

I know it's Dasha because that's *our time.*

Even though Dasha and I were born two years apart, on different days, we entered the world at the same minute—9:38 a.m.

Every year on our birthdays, we eat our cake at that time. It became a ritual with us. We even have matching *9:38* tattoos on our wrists.

I hurriedly hit the Accept button. "Hello?"

"Liliya," Dasha breathes out on the other line.

"Where the hell are you?" I grip the phone to my ear, pull myself out of bed, and limp to the bedroom door to make sure it's locked. "Are you okay?"

"I'm fine. I'm fine," she rushes out, as if on a time limit. "What are they saying there … about me?"

I drop back onto the bed, crossing my legs, and my pulse races. "Aleksy is losing his absolute shit. I'm sure he already has people out looking for you." A chill runs over my skin when I think of what they'll do if they find her.

Last night, after Emilio left, I locked the door, got into bed, and checked my phone to find ten texts from Aleksy.

Six ordered me to keep Emilio happy.

Four asked if I'd heard from Dasha.

None asked me how I was doing or thanked me for my fucking service of marrying a fucking killer and possibly dying.

There were no texts or calls from my mother.

"How mad is he about canceling the wedding?" she asks.

My blood turns cold. "They didn't cancel it."

"What do you mean?"

"You're talking to the new Mrs. Emilio Lastro."

"Oh, Liliya," she says, guilt clear in her voice. "I'm so sorry."

I don't doubt her guilt, but she knew this would happen. Aleksy would never have just canceled the wedding.

I'm not angry with her though.

I sigh. "Where are you?" I say, hating that my voice shakes.

"Liliya," she says around a longer sigh, "you know I can't tell you that."

"Who are you with?"

"I can't tell you that either."

"Can you at least promise to stay in touch?"

"Of course."

I perk up at the sound of a voice in the background.

A *man*'s voice.

I press the phone harder against my ear. "Who is—"

Dasha speaks over him and me. "I have to go. Talk soon." She ends the call.

I toss the phone to the side and roll my neck as tension tightens every muscle. Shutting my eyes, I wonder if she'd known about Aleksy's murder plan or if he'd sprung it on her like he did me.

Maybe that's why she ran.

Now, I have to decide whether I'll run … or do as my family said and kill him.

———

I've never plotted to kill anyone before.

In less than twenty-four hours, I married a killer and then was told I needed to basically become a hit woman.

I've never even considered killing someone.

Not even the doctor who ruined my career and got me fired.

I spend another two hours in bed, hating every second of my new life, before getting up to change my foot bandage. Emilio thankfully left the supplies in the bathroom before storming out last night.

Sitting on the closed toilet seat, I unwrap the dressing and clean my wound. The pain has eased, and there's no sign of infection. I rewrap it, stand, and start unpacking my toiletries.

When I'm finished, I change into a black romper and make my way downstairs to explore my new prison.

It's quiet and empty. A yellow sticky note is on the front door, and I grab and read it.

There are alarms and cameras everywhere.
Try to run, and I'll catch you.

Another romantic note from the hubby.

I crumple the note in my hand and shove it inside my pocket before checking out the window for Emilio's SUV.

It's gone.

Good riddance.

My new home may be quiet, but it's not peaceful. An eeriness follows me with each step.

I peek into the parlor room, where there's intricate wallpaper, a stained glass Tiffany chandelier, and a sofa covered with a dust cloth.

As I keep walking, I pass a bathroom and a billiards room with a pool table.

I don't stop my search until I reach a library. Standing in the doorway, I take in the room with awe. Moss-green walls and shelves of the same color take up most of the space. Crown molding traces the ceiling.

As I inch deeper into the room, I inhale the smell of dust and leather. An outdated computer sits on the desk in the center of the room.

I walk around, running my fingers along the book spines.

So many classics.

There's even a shelf of books I spent my childhood reading.

Junie B. Jones. The Baby-Sitters Club. *Anne of Green Gables. Twilight. The Sisterhood of the Traveling Pants. The Hunger Games.*

I laugh softly while grabbing a Junie B. Jones book before collapsing on the faded green sofa, curling my legs beneath me. I flip through the pages and make myself comfortable.

All my troubles fade as I read. I forget about Emilio, my marriage, murder, Dasha.

It's just me and fiction.

When I'm finished, I grab another book and sit back down.

"What the hell do you think you're doing?"

My heart races as I slowly drag my gaze toward the doorway.

Emilio stands there, jaw clenched, with revulsion on his face.

He's pissed I'm in here, and I'm about to pay the consequences for it.

9

LILIYA

E milio stares me down, his nostrils flaring wider with every second. "Stand up."

I didn't hear him come inside.

Though I'm sure he'd win an Olympic medal in the sport of sneaking up on people and hitting them when they least expected it.

My father spent years trying to teach Aleksy that skill. He always failed. It's probably why he's passing the whole *murder Emilio* task to me.

Emilio clears his throat, snapping my attention back to him.

He's wearing another sleek black suit—no tie, the collar loose, and a few buttons undone. His thick hair is messy, a single strand falling over his right eye.

"I'm only reading." I hold up the book to partially shield my face. "I'm not hurting anything. Geesh."

"Stand the fuck up, Liliya."

I sigh, dropping the book beside me to show I mean business. "Last night, you said this was *my* home. And in my home, I'd like to read in peace, without being bossed around."

I settle back, grabbing my book with a dramatic huff and

opening it like a fan. I still peek over the top to watch his reaction.

He pushes himself off the doorframe and walks toward me.

Don't be stupid, Liliya.

Drop the book and get up. Don't provoke him.

Easier said than done.

When he reaches the sofa, he looms over me like a high-rise.

I pretend he's not there and start reading the book aloud.

He snatches it from my hands and flings it across the room. Before I can react, he clamps his hand around my wrist.

I attempt to break free, but his grip is too tight.

He yanks me upright, and I hate that I whimper as pain shoots through my injured foot.

Surprisingly, his hold loosens, and he steadies me. His touch suddenly has a sense of gentleness.

My new husband, so hot and cold.

So brutal yet tender.

It's like the villain and hero are waging a war inside him.

His handsome yet stoic face is only inches from mine.

Whiskey-colored eyes with irises so dark that I can almost see my reflection in them. Olive skin with not one flaw. His face, carved with sharp lines and perfect symmetry, like something you'd see in an ancient Greek god sculpture. Days-old stubble dusts his jaw and cheeks, adding to his raw masculinity.

Emilio is built like a man created to make chaos.

Molded into a world with no moral compass.

"Stay out of this room." He backs me up against the wall and releases me.

My body collides with an oil-painted family portrait. "Why?"

"This room is evil."

I blink at him. "What does that even mean?"

"Don't come in here again." He grabs my wrist and drags me out of the library.

I wave goodbye to the books, mouthing to them that I'll be back.

We go straight down the hallway and toward the kitchen. When we walk in, a petite woman with silver hair framing her wrinkled face shuts a cabinet door and stares up at us. She smiles, and then her gaze drops to Emilio's grip on my arm.

She shoots him a hard look, and he releases me.

Emilio gestures to her. "Liliya, this is Maggie. She's the home caretaker."

I smile awkwardly at her. "Caretaker?"

"Chef. Housekeeper." Maggie shrugs. "I'm here for whatever you need, dear."

Before my father's death, we had live-in staff. But then when he was gone, Uncle Yaroslav cut our monthly allowance, claiming Aleksy wasn't worth the same salary.

Maggie tucks a pen behind her ear and clasps her hands. "I'm off to the grocery store. Anything you'd like me to pick up? Do you follow any special diets?"

"I'll go with you," I quickly offer, sounding almost a little too desperate.

"No," Emilio immediately says. "You can make a list for Maggie."

I slump my shoulders. "Anything is fine. I'm not picky."

"Emilio will give you my number," Maggie offers. "Text me if you think of anything." She circles the island, stands on her tiptoes to kiss Emilio's cheek, waves goodbye, and leaves the kitchen.

Emilio motions to the two-person table. "Sit."

I don't move. "Where have you been?"

"That's not your concern." He pulls out a chair and gestures for me to take a seat.

I reluctantly sit.

He takes the chair across from me.

"If you can come and go as you please, then I should have the same freedom," I say.

He leans back, stretching his legs under the table. "No."

"How's that fair?"

"You're a runner. Just like your sister."

I glower at him.

He snaps his fingers before knocking his knuckles against the table. "Speaking of your sister, where is she?"

I shrug. "No idea."

He narrows his eyes skeptically. "Have you heard from Dasha?"

"Nope."

"Why are you protecting her?" He draws his head back. "She fucked you over."

"No, *Aleksy* fucked me over." I bite back the urge to add his name to that as well.

He scratches his jaw, probably thinking of all the ways he'll murder her.

"Don't hurt her, please," I plead. "She ran because she was scared for her life."

He's quiet for a moment, running his tongue along his front teeth. "Are you scared for your life, Liliya?"

"Does someone run through the woods barefoot in the middle of the night if they're not?"

His shoulders relax an inch. "You don't need to fear me." He levels his elbows on the table, erasing the distance between us. "But like I told you last night, if you try to run again, that'll change. Am I understood?"

I hold his stare. "What do you expect me to do all day then?"

"What did you do all day before?" He stands, and the chair squeaks as he pushes it back beneath the table.

"Not be held hostage—that's for sure," I reply with a huff.

"Be good, and *maybe* I'll grant my *hostage* some freedom." He walks toward the doorway before stopping to glance back at me. "Stay out of the library. If you want books, I'll have one of my men take you to the bookstore."

I perk up in my chair. "With an unlimited budget?"

He shrugs. "Sure."

"That's a very dangerous statement."

He cocks his head to the side, as if not understanding. "I said you'd have a lack of freedom. Not a lack of funds to buy whatever you want. If you want books, I'll buy you every damn book in the store."

"That's very *Beauty and the Beast* of you."

He comes closer, lowering his head so his haunting eyes are level with mine. "Unfortunately for you, your life won't become a fairy tale, and I won't turn into Prince Charming. I'm the villain, day in and day out. There's no getting rid of the beast inside me."

I suck in a breath, and he leaves me there, speechless, with not another word.

10

EMILIO

I haven't set foot in my father's office in years.

That room is a fucking curse.

It's full of haunted memories that deserve to stay in the past.

I slide into my SUV, and the horn blares when I slam my hand against it.

"Should've stayed with the fucking plan." I drag my hand through my hair.

I need to treat Liliya with the indifference I planned with Dasha.

I had no problem with Dasha staying at her home and me sleeping at my condo in the city. This place would sit here and rot.

But when I saw Liliya standing across from me at the altar, something changed inside me.

I wanted her here, to breathe life back into these walls and give back a warmth that had been stolen. I wanted her to re-create the happiness my mother had prayed for, but never got.

I shift the SUV into drive and leave. Just as I reach the gate, Maggie texts me.

Maggie: Don't forget our deal.

I roll my neck until it cracks and then reply.

Me: I won't.

Maggie worked for my family for decades and left the day after my mother's and Aurora's deaths. She'd wanted to quit before that but stayed, refusing to abandon them. She was always there to help my mother with the blood and bruises after my father unleashed his temper on her.

She only came back to work for me because I told her I'd be present and renovate the home. I also promised I'd be a good husband. Not all promises are meant to be kept, though.

I toss my phone in the cupholder.

Some people believe I'm like my father.

That I was involved in my family's deaths.

Julian's call interrupts my thoughts, and I answer.

"I emailed you everything I'd found," he says through the speaker.

"Thanks." I hang up and open his email.

Julian is the best at background checks. He goes beyond credit checks and background history. He pulls every detail from the minute someone took their first breath to their last.

I put the car in park and read through his report.

Liliya Morozova, the middle daughter of Susannah and Armen Baranov. Armen worked for the Morozovas in Russia and moved to the States to help Yaroslav get his operation in order. Him and Susannah married.

Neither Susannah nor the children took the Baranov last name. Instead, they took Susannah's maiden name. Years later, when Liliya was ten, Yaroslav murdered Armen, claiming he was a rat.

Liliya graduated from high school and got a degree in nursing. She worked in the city hospital until six months ago, after she was fired for reporting the chief ER doctor for sexual harassment.

My jaw gets tighter as I read the last sentence. I toss my phone into the passenger seat and make a U-turn.

Change of plans. I suddenly need to see a doctor.

The bastard's shift ended ten minutes ago.

The sun bleeds into the horizon, casting shadows across the hospital parking lot. I crack the tinted window of the black BMW coupe I boosted earlier. I parked in the corner of the lot, just close enough to keep my eye on the doctor's shiny red Mercedes.

There he is.

The smug prick waves goodbye to a nurse and strolls straight to the Mercedes. I roll up the window, push my Ray-Bans up my nose, and slide the BMW into drive. As the Mercedes reverses, I fall behind him.

The route is short, but I curse when he makes a right into a gated community. He rolls down his window to talk with the security guard, who then nods and waves him forward as the gate opens.

I follow, slow and steady.

The pudgy guard approaches my window, blinking, as if trying to recognize me. "Good evening, sir. Do you have ID?"

I smile and hold up five crisp hundred-dollar bills.

His eyes dart left and then right. His hesitation doesn't last long. Greed thankfully wins, and he snatches the cash from my fingers. He hurries to the booth, and seconds later, the gate opens.

I give him a salute as I roll past him and into the neighborhood of multimillion-dollar homes with manicured lawns and luxury cars in the driveways. The Mercedes is parked at the home on the end of a cul-de-sac. I park a few houses down and wait.

Time feels like it's crawling, but when it comes to a plan, I'm a patient man.

I reread Liliya's harassment report so many times that I have the thing memorized.

When the sun sets, I step out of the BMW and break into the doctor's home. Julian emailed me the floor plan, so I know exactly where I'm going. I climb the stairs and head straight for his bedroom.

The door is ajar, and I let myself in. The TV plays the news in the background as I pass it. I follow the sound of the shower running and ease the bathroom door open.

The doctor is singing a shitty rendition of "We Will Rock You."

Steam fogs the mirror and glass shower.

I waste no time before ripping open the shower door. The doctor freezes, his fingers tangled in his shampooed hair. His eyes lock onto mine, and he blinks, thinking he might be imagining me.

I step into the shower, water hitting my back and soaking my shirt. It's roomy enough for the two of us.

"Hello, Dr. Oswald," I greet.

He backs away, his feet slipping against the wet tiles.

I don't bother looking down his body. My eyes are on his face. I always like to look a man in the eyes before I kill him.

I'd like to say it's a sign of respect, but it's not.

I just enjoy watching the life drain from their eyes.

It's so fucking poetic.

"What the hell?" he yells, falling against the tiled wall.

His gaze slips to the shower door.

The only way he'll make it through that door is by fighting me off.

Given his slender frame, he won't make it far.

I pull my gun from my blazer pocket, and he cowers against the wall.

"Please," he begs. "Whatever you want, you can have. Is it money? I'll give you the combination to my safe in my office. Five-five-six-six."

I click my tongue against the roof of my mouth and hold my gun out, as if inspecting it. Shaking my head, I return it to my pocket.

He slumps forward, releasing a breath of relief.

Fucking idiot.

I reach into the other pocket for my knife.

No gun for this fucker.

No quick death.

I want him to feel every moment of me taking his life.

"Why are you doing this?" he cries out, staring at the knife.

"You touched someone who didn't belong to you." I crowd closer, getting in his face.

He shakes his head violently. "I … I don't know what you're talking about."

"Liliya Morozova."

Recognition dawns on his face.

Oh, yeah, the fucker did it.

"I didn't rape her, I swear."

"No one mentioned rape, you fucking sleazebag."

He pales, and his foot slips. He crashes down on his knees, his body collapsing onto the hard tiles. A groan rips from his throat as I crouch down beside him. I grab a fistful of his wet hair and slam his head against the tiles.

He fights me, pleading and squirming like a pathetic fish out of water.

I bash his head against the tiles, lowly humming the lyrics to "We Will Rock You."

He screams for help. Blood sweeps across the tiles, paling

with the water. I grin, watching it swirl around the drain. I don't stop beating his head until he's nearly unconscious.

A gurgle releases from his throat, and he's lost all his strength to fight.

But I'm not done with him yet.

I pull his head back again, jerking it toward me, and shove the blade to his throat. "Doctor, did you stop when she said no?"

He opens his mouth but can't speak.

"Did you corner her like I did you in here?" I sink the tip of the blade into his neck, drawing blood. "It's not so fucking fun, is it?"

He somehow manages to get a, "Please," out. His body trembles, on the verge of shutting down.

"You touched what's mine." I slice the blade clean across his throat.

Blood sprays across my hand and along the shower floor.

His body twitches as he bleeds out. Blood gushes from his throat, and I relish his suffering. I watch the life drain from his eyes with pleasure and not an ounce of guilt. His mouth is slack, and water still beats down on his body.

When he's good and dead, I slowly rise and rinse his blood from my hands. I step out of the shower and text Marco—one of our soldiers—to come clean up the mess.

I leave the room to find the safe and key in the combination.

It unlocks, and I grin, collecting the ten grand in cash, a Rolex, and a gold bracelet from inside.

I might not have wanted this wife, but that doesn't mean I won't protect her.

That I won't kill for her.

I leave, ready to visit my new idiot brother-in-law, but Julian calls.

"Leo's dumbass got stabbed," he tells me. "We need a doctor."

I might not have a doctor, but I have a nurse.

11

LILIYA

Most brides know their husbands before they marry them.

Hell, most brides aren't *forced* into saying *I do*.

But now that we've tied the knot, I want to know more about Emilio.

About his home. His history.

Oh, and the easiest way to murder him without him killing me first.

Every time I think of Aleksy's murder plot, I want to jump out the window.

When Maggie returned from the store, I tried picking her brain. All I got from her is that she loves Emilio, she's known him since he was three, and she was also in the room when Emilio's mother, Evalina, gave birth to his sister. Maggie also said she once lived here in a private wing but moved out after Emilio's sister's and mother's deaths.

When I asked her if she planned to move back into that wing, she shook her head in sadness and said, "This will never be my home again."

Maggie offered to make dinner before she left, but I told her I was fine. She waved goodbye and said she'd be back in the morning.

Now it's just me, all alone in this creepy home.

I grab another bottle of water, walk upstairs, and sit on my new bed. Dragging out my MacBook, I decide to research Emilio's family myself.

Mr. Google always has the answers I'm looking for.

The search produces article after article, most of them about the car accident that took his mom's and sister's lives. According to sources, his mom drove straight into Lake George like she had a death wish.

They claimed it was suicide, but not everyone believes that. There are tons of comments blaming Emilio's father, Nuncio, for their deaths and then setting it up to look like a suicide. After days of searching the lake, they only found one body and eventually stopped looking at Nuncio's request.

No one was charged with any crimes.

I shudder, glancing around the bedroom.

Aurora's bedroom.

Goose bumps cover my arms, as if her ghost just whipped past me.

Is that why Emilio hates this place?

Does he believe his father is responsible for their deaths?

Did Emilio help him?

Even though I know her phone is gone, I text Dasha.

> Me: I miss you.

I send it before typing another.

> Me: At least Emilio didn't set up a honeymoon for us, in case you were curious.

I text my next message with a long sigh.

> Me: Love you.

I drop my phone to the side, and to stop my mind from racing, I binge-watch old *American Horror Story* episodes before falling asleep.

I'm woken up by screaming downstairs.

Cursing.

Banging.

"Liliya!"

My heart pounds as loud footsteps thunder up the stairs, closer and closer.

Get out of bed!

Hide!

I stretch across the bed, reaching for my phone, when the door flies open. The room is dim, and the only light source is the show playing on my MacBook. I curse, dropping my phone, as Emilio moves into my room.

"Get up," he snaps. "I've found a way for you to be useful."

Drawing back, I place my hand against my chest. "Um, excuse me, Mr. Rude."

Reaching down, he closes his hand around my wrist and yanks me to my feet.

I twist, attempting to break free, but he's too strong. "Let me go."

He drags me into the hallway, downstairs, and straight to the dining room. The screaming and cursing grow louder.

I gasp when I see Leo sprawled across the table while Julian and Damien stand on each side of him. Inching closer, I notice blood soaking through his white shirt.

"You son of a bitch," Leo hisses through his teeth when Julian raises his shirt and presses a towel to his bloody wound.

Emilio finally releases me. "He needs medical attention."

"No shit," I grumble, resulting in a glare from him.

Julian turns around. "He was stabbed."

I move toward Leo, squeezing between Julian and a chair to get a better look. The wound is deep, and he's losing a lot of blood.

"Stitch him up," Emilio demands, coming up behind me.

I shake my head. "You need to take him to the hospital."

Emilio scoffs, crowding against me closer. "You're the hospital, Liliya. You said you're a nurse. Tend to his fucking wound." He pushes me forward, causing my stomach to ram into the table.

Technically, I *was* a nurse, but I'm no longer employed.

I want to help Leo, but the way Emilio is speaking to me pisses me off.

I whip around, pushing his chest, and he takes a step back.

"You want me to help him?" I cross my arms and point at him. "Then you need to speak to me with respect."

Swear to God, I hear Julian laugh.

Emilio leans back on his heels. "Or what?"

I tilt my head sideways and carefully enunciate each word as I say, "Or he bleeds out."

Everyone in the room freezes.

They go quiet.

Even Leo has stopped his panting and yelling.

Seconds later, he groans and attempts to raise himself to his elbows.

All their attention is on me.

The woman who told a group of murderous mobsters no.

If you bring me into a heartless world, expect me to lose some of mine, too, assholes.

I don't say that aloud, obviously.

I'm already digging a few inches of my grave by back-talking Emilio in front of these other men.

"You won't let him bleed out." Emilio smirks, so sure of himself. "You're too nice for that."

I match his smirk, mine a bit more dramatic. "Care to test me on that?"

"Emilio, what the fuck?" Leo screams behind me. "Can you two save your marital issues for later and stitch me the fuck up?"

I glance over my shoulder, and Leo curses as Damien applies more pressure to his wound.

"Be nice to your wife so she'll fix the fucking hole in my side!" Leo screams.

My eyes return to Emilio's. He taps his foot, checking his watch, and then shakes his head in annoyance.

He waits for me to cave.

One second. Two seconds. Three seconds.

I'm caught off guard when he grips my shoulders, turns me to face Leo, and shoves me toward him. I hiccup at the feel of his heavy chest against my back again and inhale the scent of his cologne.

Reaching around me, Emilio smacks Leo's side—*right on his wound.*

"You fucking asshole," Leo screams.

"You say one more negative thing about my marriage, and I'll add another stab wound," Emilio warns him.

Leo does his best to flip off Emilio in response.

"Stitch him the fuck up, Liliya," Emilio hisses in my ear.

"Apologize first." I stare straight ahead, refusing to look back at him.

"What the fuck?!" Leo screams in agony. "I'm dying over here, in case anyone forgot!"

Emilio grabs a fistful of my hair. "Fuck off with that attitude and help him."

I shake my head, trying my best to ignore the slight sting of pain when he pulls on my strands. "Apologize, or he bleeds out."

"I'll pay for the fucking counseling!" Leo yells. "Isn't this against some HIPAA bullshit? I thought you nurses had a duty to help!"

"HIPAA is privacy, idiot," Julian comments.

Leo tries to pull himself up. "Hand me the fucking first-aid kit then." He crouches in pain, sweat dripping down his forehead as the bleeding worsens. "I'll stitch myself up."

"You're going to let a man die?" Emilio challenges. "His blood will be on your hands."

I shake my head. "No, it'll be on *yours*. He's not *my* man. Not my friend."

"Well, that's pretty fucking rude," Leo grunts as Damien opens the first-aid kit. "I'm taking back my wedding gift. No fucking panini maker for you."

"You think I care about blood on my hands?" Emilio asks coldly.

No, I don't think he does.

But unfortunately for me, I do have a heart.

Unlike him, I have compassion. Apology or no apology, I won't watch Leo suffer without trying to help.

"Fine." I swat at his hand on my hair.

He releases me, stepping back.

I turn to stab my finger in his face. "But this isn't for you."

"Obviously. I'm not the one stabbed," he comments as I roll up my pajama sleeves.

Damien steps out of my way, giving me the space I need.

"First-aid kit," I say, waving my fingers forward.

Damien drops it beside me.

Everyone watches as I cut Leo's shirt to get a better view of the wound and collect the supplies I need. I can feel Emilio's eyes on me with every move I make.

A wave of guilt washes over me at the realization of how much blood Leo has lost. I shouldn't have spent time arguing with Emilio.

I'm surprised the Lombardis don't have an on-call doctor or

nurse. I was Uncle Yaroslav's. It's the only reason he paid for my nursing school. If one of his men was injured, it was my job to tend to them.

I snap on a pair of latex gloves and get to work.

"Motherfucker!" Leo hisses as I disinfect his wound. "Some warning would've been nice."

"The peroxide was in her hand," Emilio states with irritation. "Be respectful and open your fucking eyes."

Ah, so he's the only one allowed to act like an asshole to me.

"My apologies, Liliya," Leo says, relaxing his shoulders as I fan my hand over his wound, attempting to dry it.

When it's time to stitch him up, the men cater to my every request without argument. Emilio stands close behind me as I thread the needle through Leo's skin. With each pass of the needle, the bleeding slows down.

"All right," I say when I'm finished. "You need to make sure you keep this clean, okay?"

Leo nods.

Julian and Damien help Leo off the table.

"Thanks, Liliya," Leo says before winking. "Keep the panini maker. I was only bullshitting."

I offer him a gentle smile. "You're welcome."

He gives me a salute, and the other two men thank me before assisting Leo out the front door. As soon as they're gone, I whip around to glare at Emilio.

I inch closer, putting my finger in his face the same way I did earlier. "Let me make this clear, mister. If you want a favor from me, acting like a jerk isn't how you get it. Be nice for once in your mean-face life."

He narrows his dark eyes at me. "I'm never nice, *guaio*."

"I'm not trouble. I'm your *wife*."

He inches closer, clasping my chin in his hand. "If you weren't trouble, *wife*, then you wouldn't be here."

"*Contracted* wife," I huff out. "Not by choice."

"In case you forgot, you weren't my first choice either."

I attempt to jerk out of his hold for that comment, but he tightens it. He sweeps his cold, callous thumb over my cheek, and my teeth chatter.

"You're easily replaceable, just like your sister." He taps my cheek before pulling away. "Who knows what Aleksy would do with you after? No man wants a *disposed-of* wife."

12

EMILIO

I'm already a shit husband.

Though not for the same reasons as most men.

Not for another woman, a drink, or gambling.

More along the lines of murder and business.

We took Leo home, and while Damien stayed with him to make sure the idiot didn't bleed out, we disposed of the two men responsible for his stabbing.

I gave them quick deaths. Not out of mercy, but because I was fucking exhausted and gave no fucks about them.

It was Leo's fault that he had been stabbed. We'd banned the men from Lucky Kings, and they snuck into the casino. Instead of calling for backup, Leo decided to handle it on his own.

Lesson fucking learned for him.

My phone rings when I slide into the Range Rover, and Antonio's name flashes on the screen.

"Hello?" I answer.

"I haven't received your RSVP to Gigi's birthday brunch."

"I didn't know we formally RSVP'd to shit," I grumble.

"I expect you to be there."

"Can't. I'm a newlywed."

"Fuck off with that shit. Liliya can meet the other wives. Maybe it'll make her feel better since the man she married most likely acts like she doesn't exist."

Antonio knows me well.

"Unlike you, I wasn't given a choice on my wife."

"I almost died for marrying mine. I don't recommend it. Be there. If you don't bring Liliya, I won't be happy."

He ends the call, and I drop my phone in my lap, massaging my temples.

Defying a mob boss is dangerous. While Antonio is a killer, we grew up together and were friends before he became the boss.

Some bosses treat their men like shit. Those bosses either die at an early age or their men hate them. Loyalty is easier to break when your boss is a cunt.

When you don't trust him.

I trust and respect Antonio.

When my phone rings again, I debate throwing it out the fucking window.

This time, it's Maggie.

"Hey," I answer.

"Liliya isn't eating," she tells me. "I've tried *all* day. The same yesterday. She'll drink water, but that's it."

My wife starving herself is the last fucking thing I need.

"Keep trying," I tell her. "I'll be home in a few hours."

If she hasn't eaten a bite by then, I'll force it down her throat if I have to.

I won't have my new wife starving on my watch.

———

At first, when Aleksy approached Antonio about a marriage proposal, Antonio rejected the idea.

But then Aleksy sweetened the deal, offering peace with the Russians *and* a portion of their New York–based businesses.

That second addition is why Antonio said yes.

He didn't give two fucks about peace with the Russians. They aren't strong enough to beat us in anything—not power, not wealth, and sure as fuck not street smarts.

We also don't *need* the money. Lucky Kings, along with many of our illegal ventures, brings in plenty of revenue, but who doesn't want *more* money?

We're men. We're fucking selfish.

So, Antonio agreed, knowing the Russian businesses would give us more avenues to funnel our illegal money through as well.

We also knew if the Russians owed us something, they wouldn't come after Genesis for murdering their boss. Though Dima's death was his own fault. The idiot made the mistake of kidnapping a batshit crazy woman and then letting his guard down with her.

Play stupid games, win stupid fucking prizes.

We celebrated Dima's death and would much rather have Aleksy in charge than him. While Dima was reckless, he was at least qualified to run the Bratva. Aleksy is far from that. I wouldn't trust him valeting my car, let alone running an empire.

The Bratva will fall under him, and we'll have one less enemy to worry about. Our plan is to suck them dry financially, steal their businesses, and then either kill or force them out of the city.

Some say the more allies you have, the better.

But not when those allies are fucking idiots.

Aleksy's upgrade to boss also meant an upgrade in living conditions.

I brake at the wrought iron gate in front of the estate where Yaroslav once lived. Two Russians stand guard, holding AK-47s.

Rolling down the window, I make myself known, and they open the gate before waving me forward.

The drive is around half a mile before I reach the front of the

Morozova estate home. As a man who grew up around architecture enthusiasts, I can confirm Yaroslav had good taste. I'd guess the square footage is around the same as my family home. Sculptures and fountains surround the front of the home.

Aleksy and Lev stand at the top of the porch steps. I park and duck out of my SUV, and they walk in my direction. When we meet, Aleksy holds out his hand, offering it to me as if we're about to make another business deal.

I reluctantly shake it, wishing I could tear the scrawny limb off his body.

"I'm surprised to see you here," he says. "Not warning a man before you come to his home could result in death."

He says this like a threat.

I cock my head to the side. "Is that your way of saying you're going to kill me for this?"

He blinks, taken aback by my response.

"Uh ..." He retreats a step, his hand falling limp to his side. "It was just a ... comment."

"Words of advice: don't mention something resulting in death to another man unless you intend to kill that man."

He takes a second to come up with a response before deciding to just nod. "Come on. We can talk in my office."

I follow him and Lev inside the house and grimace at all the gaudy gold embellishments. It's like someone gave a golden shower to every inch of this place.

We pass a room where a half-naked woman is snorting a line of coke. Another woman is beside her, and she squeals when they notice us.

She lifts her hand in a wave and shimmies her chest toward me. "That one is cute."

"The fuck, Monica?" Aleksy asks. "I thought I was your favorite mob guy?"

Mob guy?

Jesus Christ.

Was his training watching the fucking Sopranos?

Monica giggles, scurrying over to us to cozy up to his side.

I scratch my cheek, annoyed I have to stand here and witness this bullshit.

"We need to talk *now*," I say, breaking up his little party.

"Sorry, babe." Aleksy smacks her bare ass. "Got business to do."

I snarl my lip in disgust.

She stands on her tiptoes to kiss his cheek, kisses his cheek, and yells for the girl to save her some coke while hurrying back into the living room.

Aleksy chuckles.

I follow him further through the foyer and into a large office with gold panels and expensive artwork. Lev trails behind me and shuts the door behind us.

"Are you here about Dasha?" Aleksy asks. "We're still working on her whereabouts, but we know she ran off with some guy we had grown up with. I have one of my men working on finding his family. We can probably torture some information out of them." He smirks, strolling to the bar cart, and pours himself a glass of whiskey.

I shake my head when he holds a glass in my direction. "What's your plan with her?"

"What's *your* plan, Lastro? She was supposed to be *your* wife. Not mine."

The fucker doesn't have a plan.

He wouldn't know what a plan was if it punched him in the mouth.

So, he wants me to figure it out for him.

"Correct. She was *supposed to*," I reply. "You never fulfilled that contract, making it void *for you*, meaning her running off is your responsibility."

"She defied"—he pauses to gesture back and forth between us with his glass—"us."

"She defied *you*. She fucked *you*." I straighten my cuff links. "I still got a wife out of it. I'm happy either way."

He downs his whiskey and pours another. "Lev, leave us."

Lev pays me a glance, nods, and then disappears from the office.

"We need to talk," I say as soon as the door shuts behind Lev.

Aleksy walks behind the desk and collapses into the leather chair. A framed Sylvester Stallone photo is on the wall, and an AK-47 is displayed above it.

That's new.

Yaroslav didn't have that when I last visited his office.

It was a painting of his old-as-fuck parents, who looked miserable.

But I don't have time to give a shit about Aleksy's decor choices. I need to get this over with so I can go home and force my wife to eat something before she starves to death.

"Why didn't you kill Dr. Oswald?"

"Who?" Aleksy props his feet on the desk.

"The doctor who sexually assaulted Liliya. Why didn't you kill him?"

"That wasn't my business."

"Someone hurting your sister wasn't your business?"

If someone hurts my damn pinkie toe—let alone my own blood—I want to bash their fucking head in.

Aleksy goes quiet for a moment, as if contemplating every word he wants to say before allowing it to leave his mouth.

Smart.

"Where's your sister, Emilio?" A sudden cockiness is in his tone. "Did you protect her?"

And he turned stupid real fucking quick.

I take a moment, rub my jaw, and wait for him to take back his words.

He only smirks, proud of himself.

Too sure that I won't put a bullet between his eyes.

I stride to the corner bar.

Aleksy doesn't take his eyes off me while I pour myself a glass of whiskey.

I raise the rim to my lips but don't take a drink.

He taps his lips as I shrug and walk back toward him with the glass in my hand. "Emilio—"

I smash the glass against his desk, and the whiskey splatters, soaking his paperwork. Drops of liquid hit him in the face.

"What the—"

I stop him from finishing his sentence again as I race around the desk with a shard of glass in my hand and hold it against his throat.

He gasps for air and makes out a rasped, "Lev."

I pin him against the chair with my free hand and dig the glass into his jugular. "I know you're new to this boss thing, Aleksy, but I owe you no loyalty. You are *nothing* to me, and I do not fear you, boss or not. I suggest you watch your mouth when speaking to me."

I toss the shard onto the desk and release him.

He hunches forward, inhaling deep breaths as I return to my place in front of his desk.

"Don't worry." I knock my knuckles against the desk. "I took care of your light work. Dr. Oswald is dead. You're fucking welcome."

He runs his finger along his throat, a faint glimpse of blood on his skin. "Putting your hands on me was a mistake."

I pick up the Stalin bust—which *what the actual fuck?*—from his desk, throw it on the ground, and stomp on it. I grin in satisfaction as it breaks.

"Was it?" I ask.

He shoves back his chair and stands. "I'm a Bratva boss. You're merely a capo, barely above a soldier. Do you need me to educate you on ranks within our world?"

"I don't give two fucks about rank or who you are." I crack my neck. "Titles mean nothing to me. I only care about the safety of my wife."

"Wife?" he huffs out. "You don't care about Liliya."

"It may be hard for a man as self-centered as you to understand, but when I said my vows to your sister, I vowed to protect her. It's what *real men* do—boss, capo, fucking peasant." I pound my finger on his desk. "Don't forget that."

"You don't want to cross me, Lastro."

"I don't care about you, Aleksy. But one thing I do care about is respect. Not for you since you don't deserve it. But respect toward *me*. You speak to me like that again, I'll cut out your fucking tongue and make your sister eat it for dinner." I salute him. "Pleasure speaking to you today, *brother-in-law*."

He doesn't try to stop me as I leave.

Neither does Lev nor the men at his gate.

———

Maggie shakes her head when I walk into the kitchen. "Still nothing."

This new wife will be the death of me.

I won't die at the hands of a murderer.

It'll be from a heart attack from the stress she gives me.

"Son of a bitch." I snatch the plate of food from the island, storm out of the kitchen, and march up the stairs to Liliya's bedroom.

I don't bother knocking on the closed door before walking in.

"Why the fuck aren't you eating?" I pause at the empty room.

My gaze immediately shifts to the open window.

It's cracked, a slight breeze flowing in from outside.

No fucking way did she squeeze through that and jump from the second story.

But after everything she's pulled, I wouldn't put it past her.

I set the plate on the nightstand and walk toward the window but stop at the sound of water running.

The bathroom door is shut, and I jiggle the handle.

Unlocked.

Again, I enter without knocking.

Privacy is a privilege, which my runner has yet to earn.

She's lucky I haven't taken her damn door off the hinges.

The fogged-up shower door reminds me of killing the doctor.

I smirk, remembering the perfect sight of him bleeding out.

Instead of "We Will Rock You," Liliya hums a song I don't recognize.

I lean back against the vanity, crossing my arms and ankles, and listen to her. My throat turns dry at the view of her naked body moving behind the steamed door. Every few seconds, she swings her hips to the beat of whatever she's humming.

I make out the hourglass curves of her body.

The swells of her breasts and ass.

This is fucking porn-worthy, and I can't even fully see her naked.

My cock jerks when Liliya runs her hands down her breasts.

She pauses her humming, and I swear, I hear her call me a smug asshole.

I have to stop myself from stripping out of my clothes and joining her.

I want to fuck my wife in there.

I want to make her *mine*.

Just when I can't take it anymore, the shower shuts off.

Like my wife subconsciously knew her big, bad husband was contemplating coming in to take what was his.

I grab the towel hanging on the hook when she opens the shower door.

Liliya comes into view, her naked body dripping wet, and blinks away water droplets.

I hand her the towel at the same time she reaches toward the hook.

Her eyes flash open, and she screams. She holds the towel tight against her body to cover herself.

"What the?" She staggers backward. "What the hell do you think you're doing in here? Get out!"

So brave, my new wife.

She should know I'm not tolerant of attitude.

"You're not eating," I say simply, returning to my spot against the vanity.

I may want to fuck the shit out of my wife, but I'm not a fucking creep who'll take her against her will.

She stares as wet hair sticks to the side of her face.

Seconds pass, and I wait for her to answer.

"Get out," she says again. Her body shivers as she points at the door.

"You're not eating," I repeat.

"That's none of your concern."

"My wife starving herself is my business."

I can't stop myself from licking my lips while taking her in.

Even covered up now, she's still sexy as hell. My mind floods with thoughts of all the ways I could pleasure her.

And all the ways I could punish her.

Water drips from her tan skin onto the stone shower floor.

Her breasts move as her chest heaves in and out.

I bite into my tongue, fixating on her shaven pussy glistening with water.

My face would fit so well between those toned thighs.

My mouth waters as I think about it.

Her gaze rises to mine in an almost slow motion, and a low whimper releases from her thick lips.

Adrenaline rushes through me.

I push myself off the vanity, and the swift movement snaps her back to reality.

She clears her throat. "I think we need to set some boundaries in this marriage."

I stop at the shower door, looming over her. "I think you need to drop your towel."

She draws back, glowering at me. "I think you've lost your ever-loving mind."

"Oh, I lost my mind a long time ago, *guaio*."

I crowd her inside the shower. She backs up against the wall, and I lightly tug on her towel. It drops at our feet. Goose bumps coat her skin, and when she attempts to reach for the towel, I grip her wrist, stopping her. She flattens her back against the wall, splaying her hands to each side of her, and sucks in deep breaths.

My body is on fire as I brush my thumb along her chin, tracing it over her jawline.

She quivers, opening her mouth, but no words come out.

I've never felt a pull like this toward anyone before. It's like I lose all my willpower and control around her.

Lowering my hand, I brush it down her stomach, straight between her legs.

So fucking close to her pussy.

I give her a second to stop me.

To smack my hand away.

She slightly parts her thighs farther.

I'm fully dressed while she's completely nude.

This is my way of still having power.

I always like being in control.

That's all the invitation I need.

I cup her pussy tight, showing my ownership. She gasps, clawing her nails against the tiled wall. Opening my palm, I rub her warmth.

God, she's soaked.

Her wetness nearly drenches my hand.

"*Guaio*," I whisper, skimming my finger along her slit, "would you like me to play with your pussy?"

She whimpers again, dropping her hand to dig her nails into my arm through my shirt.

I tip my head forward, running my lips along her jawline. "Say yes, Liliya." I press a kiss along her soft skin and run my thumb over her clit. "Give in to your husband. Let me make you feel good."

"Yes," she moans, shifting her head so that her lips brush against mine.

My moan is loud and travels straight from my chest. I suck and then bite on her bottom lip before dropping to my knees. My mouth waters as I raise her toned thigh, settling it over my shoulder. The heel of her foot digs into my back.

Then, like a starved man, I eat my wife's pussy.

I devour, suck, and lick her—losing myself in her sweetness.

While my wife may be trouble, her pussy tastes like pure heaven.

I thrust one, then two, then three fingers inside her.

Groaning, I love how wide I'm stretching her—prepping her cunt for my cock.

Speaking of cock, mine aches, and I know blue balls are in my near future.

There's not a number high enough to explain how fucking bad I want to drop my pants and fuck her against this wall.

Liliya pants above me, her fingers now digging through my hair, scratching at my scalp.

Moans and curses leave her lips like secrets she never wanted to confess.

This is the second time I've been in the shower with someone in the past twenty-four hours.

The first time was for murder.

This time, it's to pleasure my wife.

While I enjoy bloodshed, I'd much prefer to taste Liliya.

"Please," she begs. "I'm … oh my fucking Gooood."

Her body shakes, her limbs trembling.

I sink another finger inside her, my pace moving faster, thrusting as hard as I fucking can. Even though I hardly know her—don't even know her middle fucking name—I one hundred percent know when she's about to come on my tongue.

Her thighs squeeze around my head, pressing against my ears, while her hips buck against my face.

I relish the taste and aroma of her cum on my tongue as she lets herself go.

I peek up, taking in every second of her orgasm.

How she shuts her eyes, how her lips pinch together, her fucking beauty.

I hold my palm against her waist, pushing it against the wall to stop her from collapsing to her knees. Her thighs fall limp, loosening around my body, and I ease myself back.

I wait until she's fully come down from her high before standing tall. Staring her down, my standoffish demeanor returns.

I wipe my mouth with the back of my hand, my lips only inches from hers. "I ate, and now it's your fucking turn, *guaio*."

13

LILIYA

My head spins as I try to collect my breath.

Emilio makes sure I'm steady before stepping out of the shower.

Goose bumps prick my skin as I bend down to grab the towel and wrap it around myself.

I count to ten, praying Emilio leaves the bathroom, but he doesn't.

Sighing, I step out of the shower, holding the towel tight, and search my brain for the right words to say.

You can leave now.

Thanks for the orgasm, but I still don't like you.

Luckily, he starts the conversation for me.

"Your dinner is on the nightstand," he says, suddenly back to business.

Like what happened in the shower was nothing to him.

"You need to eat." Without offering me another glance, he leaves the bathroom.

I hurriedly dry myself before shrugging on my pink cashmere robe. Tying it around my waist, I stomp into the bedroom. Emilio is seated on the edge of my bed, typing on his phone.

He stops when he notices me, slips his phone into his pocket, and jerks his head toward the nightstand. "Eat, Liliya."

"I'll eat when I damn well please," I snarl.

He massages his temples. "I already drew blood from one Morozova today. I don't mind doing the same with another."

"What?" I suck in a breath. "Did you hurt Dasha?"

"Negative." He gives his temples another stroke before dropping one hand and rubbing his dark brow with the other.

"Then which *Morozova* did you draw blood from?"

"Your dumbass brother."

I inch closer. "What'd you do?"

"Relax, *wife*." He says the last word as if he'd just tried my sandwich and it was nasty.

"Did you hurt my brother?"

"It was a small nick." He makes a show of scratching his neck. "If I were you, I'd be happy every time something negative happened to your brother, considering he sold you out."

"He didn't *sell me out*."

"He sold *you* to *me*."

"Buying a woman isn't the flex you think it is."

"It's a better flex than being the *purchase*." He stands from the bed. "Now, why are you making me waste my time, coming up here to make sure you don't starve yourself like a fucking child?"

"I don't have an appetite."

Since moving into my new home, I've yet to eat anything.

It's not from stubbornness—okay, it's *somewhat* out of stubbornness—but mainly from my nervous system in overdrive. When I'm stressed, I don't eat.

"Too bad." He motions toward the plate. "Eat."

I stay in place.

"Fine, have it your way." He sits back on the bed. "I'm not leaving this room until you eat. And I'm a fucking night owl, Liliya."

I glare at him before stomping toward the nightstand and snatching the plate. Instead of sitting on the bed, I plop down on the floor, sitting cross-legged. Emilio's gaze stays glued to me as I pick up the turkey sandwich.

When I told Maggie I didn't want dinner, she made me a turkey sandwich, saying it was there in case I got hungry.

I cup the sandwich tight in my hand before pointing it toward Emilio. "I don't like people watching me while I eat. Look at your phone or something."

He makes a show of intensely watching me. "That's your own damn fault. Eat when you're supposed to, and I won't have to waste my time watching you."

I pretend to mock him before taking a massive bite of my sandwich. I finish the thing in just four bites. Bites so big that it takes me a couple of tries to swallow them down.

When I'm finished, Emilio stands. "Good girl." He taps my head as if I were a dog while walking past me. "It seems that if I want you to follow my authority, I just need to make you come. Duly noted."

He leaves the bedroom, and I flip the door off.

————

Two hours later, my phone rings.

Unknown Number.

I hurriedly answer. "Hello?"

"Liliya," Dasha says on the other line. "I need your help."

14

EMILIO

I hold many job titles and perform many tasks.

Some I enjoy. Some I don't.

Killing men I don't like is one I enjoy.

I consider it a release—like what some find from a morning workout.

Tonight, I'm in our industrial warehouse. It sits in an alley near a waste management site outside of the city.

Royal, a low-ranking soldier, sits tied up in the chair across from me. His right eye is swollen shut, his lip bleeding onto his white T-shirt. The light above him flickers—a reminder that I need to rip Klide, our maintenance man, a new one for not changing it.

That shit gives me a goddamn headache.

Now, back to Royal.

We added him to our roster six months ago. Unless men were born into the family via the Lombardi bloodline or brought in young from their father, it takes at least a decade to even move up the ladder in the Lombardi family. We trust very few.

Which is why we kept Royal on security detail, giving him

side hustles here and there, and we also wanted his connection to a well-known cyber hacker, Hack-Bob.

Lame-as-fuck name, I know.

Hack-Bob firmware attacked our slot machines, programming them to win at certain times when he and his friends were gambling. They didn't win much before we caught on and were easy to find on camera. We put a million-dollar bounty on his head with the stipulation that we wanted him alive.

Royal came to us, saying Hack-Bob was his cousin. He didn't want the money. Instead, he wanted us to give him a job, a role within the family.

We agreed so long as he brought Hack-Bob to us and took every piece of hardware from his home. Royal followed through. We murdered his cousin and, as promised, gave Royal a job.

While he always remained an errand boy, we'd have let him live if he hadn't gone bragging about his new job and how he helped us murder his cousin.

Talking like that is a death sentence in our world.

And that's what he shall receive.

I told Antonio from the beginning not to trust a fucker named Royal.

When he was hired, he referred to himself as Royal Flush before slapping his hand on the table and saying, "Get it?"

I wanted to shoot him in the head just for that comment.

I'll add an extra bullet tonight now that I remember how annoying it was.

"Emilio, come on, man," Royal begs, trying to press his restrained hands together in a pleading gesture. "You know I ain't no snitch."

I roll my neck until it pops.

"I only told my nana and friends about my new job!" His voice hitches, the fear rising with each word. "That's it! None of them are cops! No feds! I swear!"

I pull my gun from my pocket and turn off the safety. "Loose lips sink ships, Royal."

He spits blood at my feet. "Fuck you! You kill me, that shows you have no loyalty to anyone."

I raise my gun. "Not to you."

The bullet flies from the gun barrel, zipping through the air, and glides straight through Royal's forehead. Blood immediately starts squirting through his skin, little dribbles at first before growing thicker.

His eyes are wide open, his tongue half out of his mouth.

The idiot is as good as dead.

I flick my finger against the trigger again, firing off another bullet. "This is for that stupid *Royal Flush* name."

And for shits and giggles, I walk closer, careful not to get blood on my shoe, and place my gun beneath his chin. With one swift jerk, I push his head forward and put another hole in his throat.

Leo whistles behind me before taking a long chug of his energy drink. "Thank you for keeping that short. I hate when guys go *on and on* with some bullshit loyalty speech. It's a waste of time and breath." He's been on chair duty with his new wound.

"It depends on the man. Some need to know why they're about to die." I slip my gun into my pocket. "That their action led to a consequence. If you're giving a man a death sentence, let them know why they earned that bullet."

My phone rings, interrupting us, and I rip off my leather glove before fishing my phone from my pocket.

My security guy's name flashes across the screen.

"Yeah?" I answer.

"I'm watching the cameras at your place," Ned starts.

"No shit. That's what I hired you to do."

"You may have a runaway bride *again*."

I can tell the fucker's trying to hold back his laughter.

"Explain." I grip my phone tight.

"She ran out the front door one minute ago."

"Did you follow her?"

"As far as the cameras would reach on the property. Once she stepped twenty feet into the woods, I lost sight of her."

I grind my teeth, digging my molars together. Stupidly, I didn't leave Liliya with a babysitter. Right now, with us allowing few men into our circle, using one to sit in a home is a waste of resources. I also thought I'd made myself clear after her last runaway attempt.

"Keep an eye on the property, in case she comes back into view," I tell Ned before ending the call and glancing at Leo. "Clean the scumbag up. Apparently, Antonio knows a guy who needs a fucking gallbladder. They'll be here in the next thirty minutes."

Leo salutes me. "You want me to take his heart before you go? Maybe give it to your new bride since you don't have one to give her yourself."

"Why don't I give her yours then?" I pull my gun from my pocket and quickly fire a shot only a few inches above his head. "I'll give you another fucking hole in your body."

"You motherfucker," he says, smirking and not flinching once.

I hear him chuckle a few times before muttering something about how good gallbladders are hard to come by as I leave the warehouse.

It seems Morozova is synonymous with running the fuck away.

What my new little bride doesn't know is that I put a tracker in her purse.

If I have to hunt her down in the woods, there'll be hell to pay.

I've survived a traumatic childhood, a Mafia war, and more bullets than I can count, only for the possible death of me to be caused by the woman I just gave my last name to.

15

LILIYA

Darkness surrounds me, and I use my phone's flashlight as a guide. I sigh every time I step on a twig, remembering what happened the last time I ran through these woods.

Sneaking out is stupid, but it's a risk I have to take.

Dasha said she needed my help.

Emilio thought he had me held as a prisoner, but he forgot about the advancement of technology. All it took was the Find My Location feature on my phone to learn the address of my new home.

I shared my location with Dasha and told her I'd start walking and that we'd meet somewhere in the middle. It's not like she can drive right up to the front door and pick me up, and Uber isn't an option.

I glance back over my shoulder at the sound of an animal howling in the wind.

Is it a wolf?

Coyote?

Keep going, Liliya.

I nearly drop my phone when it rings.

A number I don't recognize flashes on the screen.

While Dasha's calls have been coming up as *Unknown Number*, maybe she's calling me from a different phone.

I immediately answer the call. "Dasha?"

"You'd better get your fucking ass back to the house."

I stop dead in my tracks at the harsh voice on the other line. The hairs on the back of my neck stand, and a breeze knocks through the air, causing leaves to fall around me. It's like Emilio's command was a threat to everyone and everything around me.

"I'll be at *our home* in ten minutes, and your ass had better be there," he sneers.

I release a shaky breath, hoping I sound more confident than I feel. "I don't know what you're talking about. I'm sitting in bed—"

"Bull-fucking-shit," he hisses.

"I'm sitting here, journaling about how much I don't like you." I inhale another breath and change my tone, sounding almost whiny. "*Dear Diary, I feel like a princess locked in a tower. Maybe I need to grow out my hair to escape this place.*"

"Get your fucking ass back in the house," he says, each word leaving him slow and clear in warning.

"I *am* in the house," I huff out.

"You're in the woods."

I do a circle, searching as if he were looking down on me from somewhere. "Honey"—I force a laugh—"did you have a little too much to drink tonight?"

"What did I tell you would happen the next time you ran off?"

Fuck, the toes.

He threatened the little piggy that went to the market.

He's also made, like, a hundred other threats, so it's hard to keep track. I should make a list, starting with the one he made at Dasha's engagement party.

I decide not to reply. If he did forget, don't want to give him any torture ideas.

"The house *now*, Liliya."

"I am in the house, Emilio."

My phone beeps, another call coming through.

"Crap," I mutter, pulling the phone away from my face to find *Unknown Number* flashing.

It has to be Dasha.

"Hold that thought, sir." I switch the call over without waiting for his response.

Emilio may know I'm not at the house or that I'm in the woods, but he doesn't know *where* in the woods. It'll take him a while to search it, and hopefully, I'll be long gone.

"Dasha," I say into the speaker. "Where are you? Did you get my location ping?"

"Yes, but we're having a little delay."

"What?" I shriek and keep walking.

There's a road up here soon. I'm almost sure of it.

"Don't worry," she says, along with a heavy sigh. "Our ETA is thirty minutes."

Thirty minutes?

I could be toe-less or dead in that time if my husband finds me.

"I'm in the middle of the woods, waiting for you!" I grip the phone, feeling my throat tighten. "Emilio knows I left and is looking for me. Now isn't the time for delays!"

Dasha had called because she needed help *ASAP*, and there was no mention of any delays. She told me I needed to go now and there was no time to waste. I threw on my sneakers, grabbed my purse, and took off through the woods with no plan in mind.

She said she needed money. I told her I could give her the cash in my wallet and then we'd go to the ATM to empty every penny I had.

I also have *another* plan I'm keeping to myself until I see her.

I'm tagging along wherever she's going.

She escaped Emilio, and now, it's my turn.

"I'm trying to hurry, Liliya," she replies, sounding annoyed. "Give me some patience here. I'm a girl on the run."

"Yeah, and right now, so am I. We're both running from the same psychopath."

I bend at the waist in relief when I reach the road. It's pitch-black, not a streetlight, car, or home in sight. I pause, giving myself time to catch my breath and recollect my thoughts.

I stumble backward as a set of headlights appears out of nowhere. A vehicle speeds down the road. I flatten myself against a tree, watching the headlights come *closer and closer.*

When the vehicle reaches me, I wait for it to pass.

It doesn't.

It slows for a second before jerking straight toward me.

Fuck!

I turn at the same time the driver's door opens and take off running.

And just like last time, I don't make it far.

A heavy body tackles me from behind. I cry out in pain, fear, and frustration.

I was so close—so damn close.

But also so stupid.

The smell of Emilio's cologne rolls up my nostrils. He doesn't pin me to the ground this time. One second, I'm in the dirt, and the next, he pulls me to my feet, jerking me upright. He snatches my purse, drapes it over his forearm, and then grabs my phone.

Fear trickles down my spine as he grips my elbow and tugs me forward. I dig my heels into the dirt, using all my strength to stop him from pulling me toward the vehicle.

Emilio curses, and with hardly any effort, he quickly releases my wrist to wrap his arm around my waist. I gasp when he hauls me over his shoulder.

I beat my fists against his back and kick my feet as he walks us out of the woods and back to the road.

There are no other headlights or cars.

No one else to save me.

Just me, my murderous husband, and an owl hooting in the background.

All that's around me are predators, always prepared to scoop down on their prey and rip them apart.

Emilio carries me like I'm light cargo, almost weightless.

Is this how easily he carries dead bodies around before he buries them?

Surely, that's how he disposes of them, right?

Is that how he'll dispose of me?

He grunts when we reach his SUV, yanks the passenger door open, and tosses me inside. I'm out of breath as he slams the door in my face.

I immediately try opening the door, but it's locked.

Scooting back, I attempt to kick it.

Nothing.

I kick the window next.

Same result.

So, I keep trying.

Persistence is always key.

I stop kicking when the driver's door opens. I glance over my shoulder to find Emilio slipping behind the steering wheel and shutting the door.

"You kick my door again, and you'll ride home strapped to the hood," he warns. "I'll be sure to drive fast and swerve too."

His eyes lock on me, and he works his jaw, waiting for me to tell him how I'd like my ride back to my prison.

"Home?" I huff. "That isn't my home."

He takes my response as not wanting to ride on the hood and

shifts the SUV into drive. I grip the seat belt, ready to wrap it around my body, but I am thrown forward when he punches the gas.

My head nearly whacks into the dashboard, and he only tsks as he veers back onto the road.

"Rude," I grumble under my breath before strapping myself in.

"You say that isn't your home," Emilio starts.

"It isn't." I cross my arms as my back relaxes against the heated leather seat.

"Where is your home then?" He keeps his eyes on the road.

I recite the address of where I slept before my life was taken away from me and I was sold off.

"That house sold yesterday. Below asking price." He shakes his head and tsks again. "Someone really wanted to let that place go."

I rear back, pressing my hand to my chest. "No way. I've lived in that house my entire life."

"Someone else will live there now. Your mother sold it." His attention returns to the road, and he lowers his speed. "Looks like *our home* is *your only home*."

I shut my mouth, the energy to argue dying inside me.

I never thought of my childhood home as sentimental. It hadn't been passed down through several Morozova generations. I didn't help my mother design or remodel it. But that home was all I ever knew. It was somewhere I felt safe, where I had a room and a bed, where I had my sister.

Now, that's gone.

Another piece of me chipped away.

Another piece shoving me straight to Emilio.

Why would my mother sell our home and not tell me?

She's growing more and more suspicious by the day.

"Whose call did you switch over to earlier?" Emilio asks.

"No one's," I blurt out.

"Whose, Liliya?"

"It was some solicitor." I wave my hand through the air. "He was trying to sell me a new vacuum or something."

Emilio doesn't reply, only taps his fingers along the leather steering wheel as we drive back to *our home*.

The one I just tried to escape.

But what will happen when I'm back there?

Rumors have said my husband kills his enemies.

He took the life of his own father.

Will he do the same with his disobedient wife?

16

EMILIO

M y father used to say, "A threat without action is just noise."

       He also used to say, "Talk is cheap, and pain speaks louder."

I was raised on both of those mentalities and use them regularly.

Threats and violence get you what you want.

But it's not so simple when it comes to my new wife.

So far, she's given no fucks about my threats, even when they've included violence. I've also not followed through with a single one—a rarity for me.

What happened tonight further proves my threats aren't working.

It doesn't matter how many toes I threaten; she'll run on nine if she has to.

Neither of us speaks for the rest of the ride home as I consider what I'll do with her when we get there. I've checked to make sure her door is locked a few times. I don't trust her not to attempt to roll out of the SUV and flee, and I'm not in the mood to chase her down again.

She chews on her nails as I turn into the drive and open the gate.

I park near the front door, and she jumps at the sound of the door unlocking. With no hesitation, she steps out of the SUV.

I'm quickly behind her. Her body straightens when I hold my Glock barrel against the back of her head.

Maybe the problem is, my wife doesn't believe how merciless I can be.

That I'm all bark and no bite.

"Go inside." I shove her forward.

I follow close behind, our strides matching, and we climb the steps.

She opens the door she stupidly left unlocked during her escape. All the lights are on as we enter the foyer.

I push her toward the stairs, and she walks up them with caution. When she stops at her bedroom, I tug her back, stopping her from going inside.

Digging my fingers into her shoulder with my free hand, I guide her away from the doorway and jam the gun harder against her skull, pushing her away from it.

"Keep walking," I demand.

Her shoulders hunch as she tiptoes forward.

When we reach the last door on the left, I collect the key from my pocket and unlock it. I open the door, and she sucks in a gulp of air as I shove her inside the room.

I release her, flip on the light, and slam the door shut behind us.

She shakes her head, as if needing confirmation that the gun is gone before sweeping her gaze over the bedroom.

I take her in, seeing dirt on her white shirt, jeans, and sneakers. Two twigs are stuck between strands of her thick hair.

With my Glock, I motion toward the chair in the corner of the room. "Sit down."

She glances from me to the door, to the chair, and then back at me. Just when I think she's about to give me shit, she exhales a long breath and plops down on the chair.

I lower the gun and take a long stride so I'm standing over her. "Let's play a game."

She settles her hands in her lap. "Can I take a hard pass on that?"

I don't know if I want to shoot her in the mouth or fuck it.

No one has ever spoken to me like this, apart from my father when I was younger. People don't defy me, for fear I'll strangle them with my bare hands.

I crack my neck, unsure of what to do with her.

"Who were you talking to on the phone?" I ask.

She doesn't reply.

I retrieve her phone from my pocket. "What's your passcode?"

"Tell me the code to the gate, and I'll tell you."

I narrow my eyes before kneeling in front of her and holding the phone up to her face. She attempts to swat it away so it doesn't face unlock, so I grip her face tight in my hand to keep it in place.

As soon as it unlocks, I stand and start going through her phone log, seeing multiple calls from an unknown number.

"Who's the unknown number?" I ask.

She half shrugs. "I told you, a solicitor." The words leave her mouth as if she's bored with this conversation.

I hold up the phone, showing her the screen. "A solicitor you've spoken with multiple times?"

If I were having this conversation with some Joe Schmoe, they'd have already had a few punches to the face or bullet holes inside them.

She opens her mouth, most likely to spew some bullshit response, so I exit the call log and go to her texts.

"Hey!" She tries to stand from the chair, but I push her back down. "You can't go through my phone. That's an invasion of privacy."

I keep my eyes on her phone as I speak. "I either go through your phone or I grab a pair of pliers and take off your pinkie toe. Which do you prefer, *guaio*?"

"C.) None of the above."

The last person she texted was Dasha, and I open their text thread. I read the messages. She's sent her countless texts the past few days with no reply. I reread the texts sent on our wedding day before returning to the call log.

As if on perfect timing, the phone vibrates in my hand.

Unknown Number flashes across the screen.

Liliya lunges out of the chair, and again, I shove her back onto it.

"Hi, Dasha," I answer.

"Oh shit," the woman says before ending the call.

I hold the phone in Liliya's face. "It's your sister, isn't it?"

"I don't know who it is." She gives me another one of those half shrugs.

"Don't die for her."

She slams her mouth shut.

I throw the phone over my shoulder and hear it hit something. "Frankly, I don't care if you talk to your sister."

"Okay," she mocks, rolling her eyes.

"I'd just be careful not to let your brother know since he wants to kill her and all."

She blinks at me. "You *also* want to kill her."

"Am I a Dasha fan? Fuck no. But I got a wife. One I'd prefer not to hunt down all the goddamn time." I inch closer, standing over her again. "*But* if you're plotting anything with her, I'll kill her *and you*."

She bites into her lower lip, nibbling on it.

"Listen," I say, sounding the calmest I have in my life. "I'm your husband, and you're my wife. Neither of us wanted it, but it happened. Now, it'd be much easier if we learned how to cohabitate and if you'd stop running off every second I left you alone."

She clips a strand of ratty hair behind her ear. "Well, here's an idea: don't put a gun to my freaking head."

"You ran prior to that, so nice try." I crook my finger. "Now, come on. Let's get your shit. Because you and me? We're sharing a room now."

She winces, pulling herself back in the chair. "I'm not sleeping with you."

"Too fucking bad. I'm tired of chasing you."

17

LILIYA

Sharing a room with a killer who just shoved a gun to the back of my head?

I'd rather have him take a toe.

I've now learned I make a better prisoner than escapee. Both attempts I've failed miserably. Though neither time was I given much of an opportunity for a plan.

After the first try, I told myself I wouldn't make another run until I was prepared. But Dasha sounded desperate when she called me, begging me for money and saying she needed it by tonight.

I did what any sister would do. I said *fuck it* and ran to help her.

Emilio easily found me in the woods, which means I need to search my purse for a tracker. Hell, at this point, he could've snuck into my bedroom in the middle of the night and implanted one in my body.

I groan when he pulls me up from the chair.

"What the—" I attempt to wrangle free from his hold as he drags me from the bedroom and down the hallway.

Geesh.

He should just hook me to a leash the way he likes to jerk and drag me around.

When we reach my bedroom, he releases me. "Grab your pajamas, toothbrush, whatever you need for tonight."

I cross my arms, not moving. "What if I don't want to sleep in your room?"

"What if I don't give a fuck?" He moves closer, causing me to stumble backward. "The more you misbehave, the more I feel like locking you in this bedroom and throwing away the key." He thrusts out his arms to push me toward the dresser. "Now, get your stuff."

I catch myself before falling. "What if I sleep naked?" My mouth slams shut the second the last word leaves my mouth. I hold back the urge to face-palm myself at my stupid comment.

I whip around on my heel and hurriedly collect my pajamas and robe from my packed suitcase and scramble to the bathroom for my toothbrush. As I leave the bathroom, I glance at the window, another escape plan coming to mind.

You are no Harry Houdini, Liliya.

Plus, you're supposed to unalive this man.

Emilio makes a show of tapping his foot at my slowness.

I shove my pajamas beneath my armpit, stick my toothbrush in my pocket, and stomp toward him. When I reach him, I expect him to snatch me up like a rag doll again.

Instead, he retreats a step, signaling for me to go ahead.

As I pass, I peer over my shoulder and catch him checking out my ass.

To further mess with him, I sway my hips from side to side.

I'm playing with fire, doing this.

No, I'm playing *with death.*

When we return to the bedroom, I try to grab my phone from the floor. Emilio returns to his wrangler-self and snatches it from my hand, throwing it farther out of my reach. He snaps his long fingers before making a gesture toward the bathroom.

I trail behind him like an obedient dog, stepping into the bathroom. The layout is nearly identical to mine with a double vanity, the granite top outdated but still beautiful, and a glass shower. Except this bathroom has a claw-foot tub, which mine doesn't.

My focus is on taking in the space, so I don't even process Emilio being Emilio.

One second, his back is turned to me. And the next, his hand clamps around my arm, and he drags me toward the radiator against the wall. My pajamas fall from my hold during the scramble.

Something cold and heavy snaps around my wrist.

Click.

My arm jerks down, suddenly weighted.

"What the hell?" I twist my wrist instinctively, trying to tear away from him.

Did this asshole seriously handcuff me to the radiator?

I tug at the cuffs, rattle the chain, try to wedge my finger into the lock, but nothing works.

"I need to shower," Emilio says, casually retreating a step, as if cuffing people to things is the norm for him. "You stand or sit there and be a good girl."

Be a good girl?

Chills roll up my spine.

His saying that shouldn't cause tingles to shoot between my legs.

He empties his pockets, including his gun, walks into the closet, and I hear a safe open and close.

When he returns, I watch him, slack-jawed, as he unbuttons his shirt. Mud is smeared along the right side.

There's no stopping my lips from forming a smirk. I'm the result of the mud. My run might not have gone successfully, but at least it messed up his designer shirt.

I gulp.

Change the subject, Liliya.

Stop him from stripping.

Because Lord knows, if that shirt falls from his body, revealing his chest, I'll go from wanting to run for the hills to wanting to run straight into his arms to touch every inch of him.

This has never been me—a woman lusting over a man at just the sight of him.

His shirt drops to the floor. His stomach is all muscles and a six-pack. A single tattoo runs up his side.

The handcuff clinks against the radiator as I try to move closer and get a better look, but he's too far away.

He stretches inside the shower to turn on the water.

I tug at the handcuffs again.

"I wouldn't waste my energy doing that if I were you," Emilio says dryly.

His stank attitude reminds me that he isn't a man nice enough to be eye-fucked.

Killers should be feared, not desired.

He unbuckles his pants, acting as if he doesn't notice me gawking as he slides them off. He's not undressing striptease-style. More along the lines of a man just wanting to shower and get clean.

He might not be trying to look sexy, but he is.

Sex appeal just oozes off him.

"You'd think you'd let *me* shower first," I spit, trying to get my mind on something else. "I am the dirtier one, given you tackled me to the ground. It'd be the gentlemanly thing to do."

His eyes, cold and unreadable, pin on me. "Have I not made it clear that I'm no gentleman?" He pushes down his pants, revealing his boxer briefs. "It's also your own fault that you're dirtier. Haven't you learned that most escapees are always caught?"

"Am I just supposed to sit here and watch you shower?"

He turns to open a cabinet and pulls out a towel and a washcloth. "You don't have to watch me. You can no longer run free, nor do I trust you. Now, you get to wear handcuffs. This is your own doing, Liliya."

I try to raise my arm to flip him off and obviously fail.

"You can shower after I'm finished or join me."

"Do the handcuffs stay on if I join you?"

He pauses, thinking about it for a moment, and without replying, he drops his briefs.

I rear back, gulping, but he doesn't give me much time to admire him before stepping into the shower. The glass steams, but I can make out his silhouette through the door. I sigh, slumping down against the radiator, and the reminder that I need to murder this man hits me.

Glancing around, I look for something to use as a weapon.

Well, first, I need something to pick this lock *and then* a weapon.

I pull my toothbrush from my pocket, turning it in my hand and wishing it'd morph into a knife.

Even if it did, do I even have the balls to kill him?

Knowing me, like everything else I've done so far, I'll fail.

Then, he'll kill me.

Positive that killing him isn't in my plans for tonight, I turn my focus back to the shower.

I can't kill him right now. So might as well enjoy the view.

I lick my lips, unable to tear my eyes away as the muscles in his arms tense while he washes his hair. It's like I'm in some daze, and I feel like a total creep that my mouth is practically salivating for him.

I'm so wrapped up in him that I'm not sure how much time passes before he turns off the water. He steps out of the shower and tugs the towel off the hook, and I pretend to block my eyes from the view, peeking through my fingers.

I perk up, telling myself this isn't ogling. This is surveillance.

I'm studying my target for weak areas.

Though one weak area is definitely not what's between his legs.

Holy shit.

Even with his cock not fully erect, he's huge.

The longer I stare, the harder and thicker it gets.

He knows I'm checking him out.

I'm a wife, attracted to her husband; that's not out of the ordinary.

The problem is, my husband is crazy, and we want to kill each other.

He hurriedly dries off and ties the towel around his waist. "Your turn."

I jerk my arm up. "I can't exactly shower with cuffs on."

He grabs his pants from the floor and pulls a key from the pocket. Taking two long strides in my direction, he kneels in front of me and unlocks the handcuff. I dramatically shake out my hand and rub it like it's in pain.

As I stand, he does the same, taking a step back to give me room to walk around him. He backs up against the door, as if blocking it, as I turn on the shower.

Crossing my arms, I glare at him. "Do you plan to stay in here and watch me?"

"You watched me," he fires back.

"Is that you giving me permission to handcuff you to the radiator as well?"

He motions for me to get in the shower. "I'll get dressed while you shower. Don't worry, I won't eye fuck you like you did me."

"That wasn't eye fucking. That was *murder glaring* for being held captive."

I swear, for a moment, I notice him fighting back a smile, like the idea of me killing him is hilarious. He clicks his tongue against the roof of his mouth, but doesn't move from his spot blocking the door.

With a groan, I turn off the shower, step inside to undress, and throw my clothes out.

The water is already steaming hot when I turn it back on.

I jump and shriek when the door opens.

"Forgot this." Emilio throws a washcloth inside, and it smacks me in the face. He shuts the door.

I take my sweet time in the shower but also keep my eyes on my surroundings. I watch his profile move around the bathroom, but he never lingers too close. When I'm finished, I open the door.

He holds out a towel for me, and when I step out of the shower, I notice he's changed into gray sweats and a white V-neck tee. It's the first time I've seen him casual. As I dry off, he walks to the vanity and starts brushing his teeth.

I keep the towel tight around me as I snatch my pajamas and bring them back into the shower, not caring that the bottom of my pants gets wet. When I step out, he doesn't pay me any attention as I join him at the vanity.

My side brushes against his, but he doesn't move.

I steal his toothpaste, waiting for a reaction, but he continues to ignore me. As I brush my teeth, I jerk my elbow around, hitting him a few times. The man doesn't even flinch.

When he's finished, he takes a step back.

I do the same, not even concerned about my skin-care routine for the night.

"Come on," he instructs. "Time for bed."

As if his voice is a trance, I follow him.

My phone is no longer on the floor. I'm sure the thief stole it while I was in the shower.

The bedroom has dark gray walls, and deep chocolate-brown bookshelves line one wall. Half the shelves are filled with books.

There's a framed photo of Emilio with his mother and sister. A long dresser, the same wood as the bookshelf, runs along the wall opposite the bed. A few bottles of cologne are on there.

"Do I need to handcuff you to me tonight, or will you keep your ass in bed?" he asks.

"I'll stay in bed." I hold up three fingers in a Scout's honor sign.

"I'm a light sleeper," he warns.

"*You're* sleeping in here too?" I don't know why my brain didn't put two and two together before this. It was too clouded at the sight of him naked.

"It's my bedroom, and I don't trust you." He signals for me to get in bed.

I pull back the covers and slip underneath the crisp gray sheets. He doesn't move, only stands on the other side.

I turn my back to him, then face him, then turn my back to him before peering over my shoulder, seeing him still standing there. He's lurking like I did when he was showering.

"I don't like you staring over me." I dramatically shudder. "It's creep city."

"And I don't like you being a runaway hazard, but here we are, Liliya." He turns on the bedside lamp, punches a code into the nightstand, and opens a drawer.

I blink as he pulls out a silver MacBook, then heads to the door to switch off the ceiling light. He strolls across the room, sits in the corner chair, and opens his MacBook. All I hear next is the *tap-tap-tap* of his fingers hitting the keys.

I flip on my side to face him. "Can I go get my laptop?"

He stops typing. "No."

"Why do you get yours then?" I huff out, tightening the gray comforter around me as cold air suddenly hits my body.

"Go. To. Sleep."

"Jerk," I mutter under my breath before turning my back to him again.

I shut my eyes, knowing it's stupid to turn my back to him, but if he hasn't killed me already after everything I've done, the chances are, it's not that high on his priority list. At least not *yet*.

I'm sure if I keep acting up, that may change.

I try to brainstorm possible ways to kill him before slowly drifting off to sleep.

I wake up to silence.

No tapping of keys.

The lamp is off.

No sign of Emilio.

I slip out of bed and carefully tread toward the door.

It's shockingly unlocked.

I tiptoe downstairs.

Hearing his voice, I focus on staying quiet and following the sound.

He's in the parlor room, and the door is closed. I place my palm and ear to the door, trying to listen the best I can.

"I'll come there as soon as I can," he says, keeping his voice low. "She's hard to keep an eye on right now." His tone is sad yet frantic at the same time. "Yeah, I know." A deep sigh. "Love you too."

The moment he ends the call, I dash back upstairs to bed.

Last time he caught me eavesdropping, he held a knife to my throat and made it a point to nick me with it. My entire body tenses as I hear him walking up the stairs, getting closer to the bedroom.

I turn to the side, facing the chair.

When the door clicks open, I slam my eyes shut and pretend to sleep.

The sound of his footsteps is heavy as he comes closer. I wait for another knife, a gun, something to punish me for my nosiness.

That docsn't happen.

He turns on the lamp again and settles back into the chair, and as I open one eye, I notice he has *my* laptop.

I grit my teeth, holding back the urge to say, *What the fuck?*

He attempts the password once, and I expect him to set it aside in failure.

No chance in hell will he guess *Imliterallyjustagirl101*.

Under the dim light, he wipes his brow and keys in another attempt. A smirk twitches at his lips as he glides his fingers over the trackpad.

The asshole got in.

I have two options—confront him or feign sleep and allow him to snoop.

I snap my other eye open, fake a yawn, and lift my arms in the air. I wait a few seconds, as if slowly waking up, and peer at him. "Are you on my computer?"

"Yes," he says, not stopping. "You've been watching me on here for the last ..." He pauses to check his watch. "Six minutes."

I lift onto my elbow, using the pillow for support. "How'd you get my password?"

"I know everything about you." He types something.

"You know nothing about me."

"Liliya Morozova. Daughter of Susannah and Armen. Your uncle murdered your father, claiming he was a rat but there was little evidence. You attended an all-girls' school—Grave Prep School. Growing up, you had a dog named Sparky, who died at the old age of sixteen. Your father hated him. You've had one boyfriend, Kale, which makes me question your sanity to date a man named after food. You've also taken it upon yourself to become a detective of my family's history, and you play Wordle every day."

"Stalker alert," I mutter, yawning as I sit up in bed. "Now that you know so much about me, tell me about *you*. It's only fair." I ease back, resting against the wooden headboard.

No response. Just more clicking of keys.

"Can you please get off my computer?" I plead in frustration. "That's an invasion of privacy."

Still, he doesn't look up.

Groaning, I swing my legs off the bed. It takes me a moment to find my footing before I stomp over to him. Just as I touch my laptop, he pulls it away.

"Give it," I snap, crawling over his lap to grab it.

Our eyes meet, his stare burning deep.

For a heartbeat, it softens.

Not for long though.

Using his free hand, he snatches my wrist to restrain me.

I struggle to break free.

"Fight me for it, *guaio*," he grits out.

I get in his face, ignoring the awkward position I'm in. "I'm not as weak as you think."

He leans in until his lips nearly brush mine. "Then, *fight me for it*."

I try to reach forward, but he holds me firm. As I slide against his lap, I feel the jerk of his cock beneath his pants. I freeze, my breath hitching as heat warms beneath my skin. He shifts—an effort to hide his excitement for me—but I keep my weight steady.

This time, *I'm* pinning him in place.

Tingles race through my veins as I lock eyes with him.

His gaze heats as he licks his lips.

I relax against him, sinking deeper onto his lap, and his hold on the laptop loosens.

A loud ring cuts through the air, and his pants vibrate.

I jerk back, and Emilio glances down at his lap. He tosses my laptop over his shoulder, not a care in the world that it's expensive and could break. Grabbing my waist, he lifts me off his lap.

And just like that, whatever *that was* is gone.

I back away as he stands and fishes his phone from his pocket.

"Yeah," he answers, nodding a few times before ending the call.

He waves the phone at me before using it to gesture toward the bed. "Go back to bed."

I furrow my brow at him. "Are *you* going to bed?"

"Yes," he says, surprising me before pulling his tee over his head.

I stomp around the bed and crawl back in, dragging the covers over myself and letting out a dramatic sigh. He slides out of his pants, draping them over the chair, and climbs into bed.

We stay turned away from each other, strangers forced to share a bed.

I hate that I wonder what he'd do if I turned around and reached for him.

Would he touch me back?

Would he want to have sex with me?

Or would he remain the same cold and distant husband?

Before the wedding, I was terrified of him wanting to consummate our marriage.

But now, even though I'm still scared of him, it's all I can think about.

I thought I could survive a loveless marriage, so long as Emilio didn't kill me.

Lying beside him now, the thought of that sounds worse than death.

I want more from our marriage.

Love. Connection. Intimacy.

All things Emilio will never give me.

Aleksy said I can have that *if* I kill him.

A husband who will love me.

One of my choosing.

My body softens as Emilio's breathing grows steady. And like a lullaby, it lulls me to sleep.

18

EMILIO

I wait until Liliya is asleep before sneaking out of bed and walking downstairs for a glass of water.

I down it in seconds, refill the glass, and leave the kitchen. Taking the glass with me, I walk around my home—something I haven't done in years.

My father infected this home when he moved in forty years ago.

Even after his death, the evil lingered like a ghost, the dark memories kept hostage between these walls.

I stop when I reach the library and flip on the light. It flickers a few times before the chandelier brightens the room. I walk across the room, and the old leather office chair squeaks under my weight as I sit behind the desk. Leaning back, I close my eyes, cursing this room and my father.

A sound breaks the silence, and I snap upright, just in time to find Liliya trying to sneak past the doorway.

"What did I tell you about spying?" I call out.

I hear footsteps, and then she peeks into the room.

"Technically," she says, drawing out the word, "you only warned me against *eavesdropping*."

She enters the library, inviting herself in. Her hair is tangled and knotty, like she was fighting with the pillow all night.

"Am I allowed in here if you are?" she asks, running her hand along a bookshelf before whipping around to face me. "Hey, is there some secret bookshelf that leads to a hidden room?" Stopping again, she pouts her lower lip before pointing toward me. "Though I doubt you'd tell me if there was."

My new wife is a rambler.

She can't ever seem to keep up with her thoughts.

I massage my temples, ignoring her.

"This library is beautiful." She glances around, taking the room in. "Did you read in here when you were growing up?"

I shake my head. "My sister did before my father took it over as his work office."

She raises a brow. "Are you not a reader?"

"I can read. I didn't have time to read as a hobby."

"What did you do instead?"

"I'm sure my father raised me similarly to how yours did Aleksy."

She snaps her mouth shut for a moment before saying, "Oh," in understanding. Her face softens as she peers down at the floor, as if searching for her next words but struggling to come up with them.

While Liliya and I grew up somewhat differently, we share many similarities in the sense of how children are raised according to their sex and the ranks of their fathers. We're put through hell to find our weaknesses, and then they use those against us.

I'm thankful for her moment of silence.

Unsurprisingly, it's only temporary.

"You grew up in this home?" She sits on the same sofa I kicked her off days ago, staring at me with deep, prying yet tired eyes.

I nod, providing the simplest answer I can.

"Was the home passed down through generations?"

"My mother's family. She grew up here." I motion toward the room. "Her father built the library for my grandmother, who loved to read. She and my mother would spend hours in here. My mom did the same with my sister until it became his office."

My father took this special place away from them.

The fucker ruined our family in so many ways that I'll never forgive him for.

She drums her fingers along the armrest. "Will this become your office now?"

"Fuck no," I huff out.

"Do you have an office somewhere else?"

"Lucky Kings."

"The casino?"

I nod, forgetting that my wife really doesn't know much about me. The people I normally surround myself with already know these things. I don't want anyone else to know where I come from or what I'm up to.

"Is that office your only one?" she questions.

I nod. "I'm not much of a sit-behind-the-desk kind of man." My response is ironic, given that's exactly what I'm doing at the moment.

"What kind of man are you, Emilio?"

"One who likes variety."

She glowers, as if that were a personal insult.

"Monotony and I aren't friends," I go on, surprised at myself. "I usually bring my laptop and work in different places."

She's still staring, untrusting. "By *variety*, you mean *for work*. Correct? Otherwise, those words aren't something a new bride wants to hear from her husband."

"Aren't you supposed to be sleeping?"

"Aren't *you* supposed to be sleeping?" she fires back before standing.

She walks to the bar cart in the corner, where a lone bottle of whiskey sits. Grabbing it, she blows off the dust and holds it up. "How old is this thing?"

I shrug. "Not sure."

"Want a drink?"

"Nah. I'm good." I motion toward the bottle. "Have at it yourself."

"Eh, I'm okay." She returns the bottle to its place. "I only drink when I'm nervous."

"Yes, I learned that at the reception dinner."

"Otherwise, I'm not much of a drinker." She sighs before slumping down on the couch. "My father liked the bottle a little too much. I saw the destruction alcohol caused from a young age."

"Same." I chug the rest of my water, wishing it'd give me a buzz that liquor does.

Maybe I should've accepted that drink.

She pulls her legs up on the couch. "What did your father do when he got drunk?"

I'm quiet for a moment.

Her question is personal.

Too fucking personal.

My wife is trying to get to know me. The opposite of what I want.

I sullenly stare straight ahead at her. "He used to beat my mother."

She winces at my honesty before releasing a deep breath. "My father didn't put his hands on my mother. I'm sure that's only because he knew Yaroslav would kill him for it. To get his anger out, he'd break things. Our belongings, never his." She shuts her eyes, as if reliving the memories. "He didn't beat us with his fist, but he was violent with his words."

I nod in too much understanding.

My father always threw out harsh words with every violent punishment.

Liliya picks at her nails, glancing down at her lap. "Every month, we'd have to replace TVs and remotes from his anger fits. It was so weird that after his death, we didn't have to buy a new TV for three years." Her eyes grow heavy. "I've forgotten so many things about my father—his voice, his favorite things— but I'll remember that about him until the day I die."

A combo of anger and sadness—an emotion I rarely feel— whips through me. I clench my fist, pissed that my wife had to endure that. I plant my feet on the ground to stop myself from standing and wrapping her in my arms.

We can't have that.

This needs to be a loveless marriage.

"Was your father a rat?" I ask, needing to change the subject.

"I have no idea. Yaroslav told us that and expected us to believe him, so that's what we did." She pushes tangles of hair away from her face. "How'd your father die?" The question leaves her mouth slowly.

I pause, deciding how truthful I want to be with her.

"He was murdered at a strip club." I lean back in my chair, a *there you have it* expression crossing my features.

Her eyes widen in shock. "Who murdered him?"

I scratch the side of my head. "I don't know."

She knows I'm lying.

Her shoulders tense, and her gaze slips to the doorway.

"I didn't do it," I quickly say to put her at ease before muttering, "Sometimes, I wish I had though."

There's an urge to tell her more, but I stop myself.

She may be a Lastro now, but she has Morozova blood. Her father was possibly a rat. She's also tried to run from me numerous times. She can know some of my past, but never all of it.

She smiles at me. "Thank you for opening up to me."

I grab my father's Montblanc pen and point at her with it. "Now, please stop googling me. Half of what you read is lies, and the other half will give you nightmares. It's in your best interest not to know all my demons."

She crosses her arms. "Speaking of that, how'd you get into my computer?"

I drop the pen and stand. "Never question my ability to find out information. Now, let's get you back to bed—*again*."

She thankfully listens, and I take a once-over of the library before shutting the light off. My cock hardens as I follow her upstairs.

I'm not sure if she's doing it to fuck with me, but with each step, she sways her hips. I bite into my lip, watching her ass jiggle in my face. I inhale deep breaths, telling myself not to bend her over the stair railing and fuck her from behind.

I thought I didn't want to desire my wife.

But the more I'm around Liliya, the more I want to touch her.

Fuck her.

Own her.

19

LILIYA

I n bed, I suddenly pause doomscrolling social media.
  A nurse who worked with me at the hospital reposted a
news article.

High-Profile Surgeon Murdered in New York Home.

My mouth turns dry as I read what she typed: *Rest in peace,
Dr. Oswald. You were a great doctor and friend, and you will
forever be missed.*

Great doctor? Yes.

Friend? No.

Forever be missed? Not by me.

Sorry, not sorry.

I bite my nail while reading the article about Dr. Oswald's
murder—the man who cornered me in a supply closet and stuck
his hand down my scrubs. Also, the same man I kneed in the
balls until he dropped to his knees, and then I called him an
asshole before running out of the closet.

They found him murdered in the shower. The detective

emphasized that it was a violent, bloody murder. His safe was cleared out, so while they think the attack was personal, they ruled it as a robbery gone wrong. They have no suspects, no fingerprints, and the home cameras were disabled an hour before the crime.

Robbery gone wrong?

They literally went out of their way to murder him.

Someone has the police on their payroll.

I peer over at where Emilio slept, but he is now gone.

Is my husband connected to Dr. Oswald's murder?

No way. There's no way.

Emilio's words replay in my head. *"I know everything about you."*

The more I learn about my new husband, the more it wouldn't surprise me if he were responsible. He could've easily found the report I'd filed. My complaint, the board meeting I attended, my firing—all of it is on record.

Did he kill for me?

The thought shouldn't make me feel all warm and fuzzy inside, but it does.

When I told Uncle Yaroslav and Aleksy about Dr. Oswald, they did nothing. When I was growing up, my mother always said that no one would dare lay a hand on a Morozova woman out of fear of Yaroslav. Turned out, that was nothing but a lie.

I close out of the article and toss my phone on the nightstand. As I slide out of bed, I think about last night in the library. Emilio opened up about his father. From what I'd read online and rumors I'd heard, I knew Nuncio was a bad guy.

But after seeing the pain on Emilio's face when he talked about his father, I wish he'd come back as a ghost so I could punch him in the face.

Look at me, wanting to protect the hubby I'm supposed to kill.

I shuffle to the bathroom to brush my teeth and hair before stopping by my old bedroom—*is that what I should call it?* After changing into leggings and a red tank, I walk downstairs.

My plan today is to pick Maggie's brain.

To learn more about my husband.

She's in the kitchen, squeezing oranges into fresh juice when I walk in.

"Good morning, Liliya," she greets. "What would you like for breakfast?" She offers me a hopeful smile that I'll actually eat today.

The turkey sandwich Emilio forced me to eat is all I've had in days.

I know I need to eat, but my nerves find food as appetizing as maggots at the moment.

My cheeks burn red at the reminder of what he did before forcing me to eat that damn sandwich.

His facial hair against my wet thighs.

His tongue inside me.

I shudder, squeezing my legs together.

When my gaze flicks back to Maggie, she's staring at me curiously.

I shake my head, snapping myself out of it.

Resting my elbows on the counter, I lean toward her. "Will you talk to me while I eat?"

"Of course." She perks up, pushing the juicer aside to give me her full attention. "What would you like?"

"What's your favorite breakfast?" I release one elbow and tap the counter. "I want you to eat with me."

Her brown eyes soften. "If it gets you to eat, I'll share a meal with you every day, honey."

I grin, understanding why Emilio's mother and sister loved her so much.

Maggie is a good person with a good heart.

I pull back. "After we eat, are we allowed to leave? Maybe

have a girls' day?"

Maggie has a car, which means she has the means to break me out of this place. Even if it's just for a few hours.

She slowly shakes her head.

I frown.

"We can talk to Emilio about it," she says, sounding hopeful again.

I pout my lip.

"He's only trying to keep you safe."

"No, he's keeping me hostage."

"Maybe if my hostage didn't *run*, she'd get more freedom."

My back straightens, and I slowly peek over my shoulder to find Emilio standing in the kitchen doorway.

He looks well rested even though I know he got only a few hours of sleep. There isn't one wrinkle in his black suit. Blinking, I wonder if he irons his clothes himself.

He fixes his stony stare on me while walking deeper into the kitchen.

Not wanting to get a neck cramp, I slowly turn to face him.

"You're spending the day with me, Liliya," he says.

There's no question in his tone.

It's a demand.

I cross my arms. "What if I don't want to?"

He inches closer until he's nearly in my face.

My breath hitches, and I place my hand against my chest to level it. "Maggie and I were about to eat breakfast."

He checks his watch. "It's almost noon."

Yes, I slept in.

Well, I slept in until ten and then spent almost two hours scrolling in bed.

Unlike him, it seems I do need my beauty sleep.

I inch back a few steps and am grateful he doesn't follow. "Maggie was going to make us *brunch*."

"We'll brunch tomorrow, honey," Maggie says behind me.

I rub my stomach. "I'd better eat now. I get pretty hangry when I haven't eaten. I also have a strange urge to put on running shoes and go for a jog."

Emilio's eyes narrow at me.

I do the same in return, though I doubt I look nearly as intimidating. "On second thought, I'd prefer to stay in my hostage situation. I'll return to my room now." I start to move around him.

He snatches my wrist, jerking me back. "There'll be food where we're going."

"They have food in hell?" I attempt to wrangle out of his hold.

This seems to be a common occurrence for us.

Maggie snickers behind me, and Emilio glares in her direction. She breaks into a full-blown laugh, as if wanting to push his buttons.

When he releases me, I rub at my wrist. "Can you at least tell me where we're going so I can change?"

"L'ultima Cena."

My jaw drops open. "The restaurant?"

"No, the fucking graveyard." He rolls his eyes. "Yes, the restaurant."

"Then I definitely need to change."

He checks his watch *again*. "You have five minutes."

"I need ten."

"Seven."

"Eight." I walk past him, and he doesn't try to grab me this time. "You should've given more notice."

He rubs at his temples. "You were sleeping."

I pause, wasting valuable get-ready minutes in favor of arguing. "You could've woken me up."

"You make less trouble when you're sleeping."

I wait until I'm out of the kitchen and around the corner

before mimicking him. *"You make less trouble when you're sleeping."*

Wait until he learns that I sleepwalk sometimes.

That'll really throw him off his game.

As I trek up the stairs, I decide that'll be my next excuse if he catches me running.

I change into a black maxi dress and tan wedges before fixing my hair into a half-up, half-down hairstyle and applying winged eyeliner and black mascara. It's simple, but with my time constraint, it'll do.

While I've heard of L'ultima Cena before, I've never been to the Italian restaurant.

Uncle Yaroslav said it was Mafia territory that we shouldn't intrude on. He was certain they'd poison his pasta if we were to ever set foot inside. He also called the back private rooms slaughterhouses and said L'ultima Cena translates to *the last supper*.

Let's hope it won't be mine.

Emilio is waiting for me at the base of the stairs when I come down. I hold back a grin as I watch his gaze travel down my body in appreciation. It gives me that same warm and fuzzy sensation I felt when thinking about him murdering the man who'd hurt me.

I hitch my black purse over my shoulder. "Bye, Maggie!"

"You two have fun!" she calls from the kitchen.

Emilio grunts at her last word.

I hold back the urge to mimic his grunt.

My husband wouldn't know fun if it kicked him in the balls.

I follow him outside and block the sun from hitting me in the face as I walk toward the SUV.

Surprisingly, my hostage keeper becomes a gentleman and opens the passenger door for me.

I keep my eyes on the ground as I sink into the cool leather. He slams the door shut and slides behind the wheel.

As he turns the key in the ignition, I smooth a hand over my dress and peer over at him. "Why are we going to L'ultima Cena?"

"You'll see when we get there." He shifts the car and drives through the gates.

I'm finally breaking free from this place.

Though my keeper is still beside me.

20

EMILIO

I haven't set foot into L'ultima Cena in years.

It was once my mother's favorite restaurant. Their braciole was her favorite dish. That changed when I was eleven. During her birthday dinner, she made a comment about my father drinking too much. He stood from his chair and dumped his bowl of spaghetti over her head. After that, she refused to go back.

That was the day I lost the little respect I'd had for Nuncio Lastro.

It was also the day I decided I didn't care if he died. Deep down, I hoped for it and knew there was a possibility it'd be at my hands.

Today is Gigi's birthday brunch. I try to opt out of these events as often as I can.

I'll volunteer to do the worst job if it gets me out of a social situation.

Birthday party or bury a body? Where's the fucking shovel?

Family dinner or scrub brains off the floor? Pass me the gloves.

Usually, I get away with this. In our line of work, there's

always a job that needs to be done and someone who'd rather socialize than do it. But Antonio made it clear. Today, I had to attend and bring Liliya with me.

Attending a party *and* spending quality time with my wife? Sounds like my personal hell.

Or that's what I keep telling myself.

That plan has been unraveling from the start.

I was supposed to keep my distance from my wife, not care, and keep her locked up like a prisoner while I went about my daily business. Sure, I'd check on her every so often, but I had Maggie there for the day-to-day, *make sure she doesn't die* bullshit.

Instead, I keep returning to the place I once wanted to burn to the ground. Whether it's to stitch a man up, to force her to eat, or to stop her from running through the goddamn woods.

One of us men could've easily stitched Leo up. It'd have been sloppier work, but we would've managed.

I keep putting myself in situations to be near her.

Last night, I took it too far.

We shared a bed. Something I'd never done before.

Have I fucked women and made them come? Yes.

But I always leave after. No cuddling or spending the nights together. I normally tell them thanks and toss a few hundred on the bed.

As I lay in bed beside her, I regretted not giving her time to grab her own body wash. She smelled like my soap, but I wanted her to mark herself on my sheets. I dreamed of her. Another rarity for me.

My wife is getting under my skin.

She's consuming me in every way.

Liliya's stomach growling breaks me from my thoughts.

"Maybe if you hadn't starved yourself these past few days, you wouldn't be so *hangry*, as you called it," I comment, stopping at a red light.

She crosses her arms. "It's my silent protest to this marriage."

"Look at how far that's gotten you. You're still married, at my mercy, and hungry." I hit the gas when the light turns green.

She glares at me, turning back to look straight ahead, but her lips morph into a smug smile. "Actually, look at how far it's gotten me. I'm breaking free of my prison *and* being fed at one of the nicest restaurants in the city."

"Trust me, this isn't out of the kindness of my heart *or* me caving in to your games."

She slaps her hand against her thigh. "Of course it isn't. There's no kindness inside you. As with all men in this world, any shred of kindness in your heart was eaten up by cruelty—like Pac-Man chomping up every last bit of your humanity."

I have to fight back a smile at her comment. Another fucking rarity for me.

"Do they teach you how to make terrible analogies in nursing or Russian Bratva school?"

She turns in her seat to glare at me. "This kind of humor can't be taught. You're either born with the gift or you're not." She waggles her finger in my direction. "You, my forced husband, were not born with that gift."

"Good thing I was born with plenty of others." I half smirk.

Her cheeks redden, as if her mind went to the dirtiest thought she could imagine.

Maybe that'll shut her up.

She stays quiet for the rest of the short drive and perks up in her seat when I veer into L'ultima Cena's back parking lot. I swerve into the spot between Antonio's and Damien's vehicles.

The sun beats down on my back when I step out of the SUV and circle to Liliya's side to open her door. She takes her sweet time getting out of the vehicle, as if trying to punish me.

"For someone hungry, you sure are moving slow," I say stupidly, because it only causes her to move slower.

When she's finally outside, I slam the door and check the time, finding we're ten minutes late.

I push Liliya forward. "Straight to the door. You run, and I have a room full of people in that building ready to hunt you down."

She mutters words I can't make out—most likely talking shit —and shuffles forward.

After a few moments, her walk turns more into a strut. She swings her hips and twirls a strand of hair around her ring finger.

Sometimes, I think this woman actually wants me to strangle her.

I stare at her, my eyes moving with the sway of her hips, like a man who wants to fuck his wife. I tug at my collar, noticing sweat building up there, while not taking my eyes off her until we make it to the door.

Her body has become my new obsession.

The dress clings to her perfect curves and full ass. With each strut, her ass jiggles in my face.

I bite into the corner of my lip, hoping I don't have to punch a man if they look at my wife with lust in their eyes.

She hesitates when we reach the door, not knowing what to do.

I notice and salute the two-armed guards standing on the roof. My guess, that's Cristian's doing, and probably the only man who could get away with having armed men here.

Liliya glances back at me, biting into her lip while waiting for my next move.

Not so bold when you could be entering a slaughterhouse, huh?

I brush around her and hit the bell on the door. The door swings open moments later, and Oliver—the owner's grandson who was recently promoted from server to general manager— stands in front of us, wearing the L'ultima Cena uniform.

Liliya falls back a few steps, hitting my chest.

Oliver tilts his head, squinting in my direction. "Emilio? Is that you? *Cavolo!* Long time no see!"

He waves us forward, grinning like we're old friends.

We're not.

While we're the same age, the only time we've spoken is when I came here for dinners and he bussed tables for his family.

The smell of fresh-baked bread, Parmesan, and garlic lingers in the air. A thunder of memories of my family hits me.

"And who's this lovely lady?" Oliver asks as the door shuts behind us.

"My wife," I reply, completely emotionless.

"Does your wife have a name?"

"Liliya," she answers for me, offering her hand to him. "Don't mind my husband. He forgets I exist sometimes. Matter of fact, this is the first time I'll have eaten in days." She drops his hand, turning to look at me smugly. "He prefers to keep his hostage hungry."

Oliver glances from her to me before raising a bushy brow. "Newlyweds, I take it?"

I nod while grabbing Liliya's half ponytail and jerking it back.

She hisses in pain.

"Explains it." He tips his head, half bowing toward Liliya. "It's nice to meet you, Liliya. I hope your husband brings you here for plenty of date nights. The rest of the party is in the burgundy room. You two enjoy your meals." He smiles at Liliya, then me, before walking down the hall.

Oliver knows how this world works.

His family isn't in the Mafia, but they cater to us.

For decades, the restaurant has provided us with a place to talk business with other families or the privacy to kill another man who's crossed us. I was fourteen when my father told me they charge extra for cleaning blood off walls and any cold bodies must be removed within the hour.

Liliya winces while tugging away from me.

I wait three seconds before I release her hair. A punishment for her little attitude.

She rubs at her scalp while turning to glance at me. "Burgundy room?"

"That way." I motion toward the hallway lined with photos and doors that lead to private rooms. "Third room on the right."

The same room where I killed my first man.

I slit his throat with my dinner knife and sat next to him, eating dessert while he bled out. He held his neck, begging me for a bullet to the head, a quick death of mercy. I stabbed my fork through his eye for asking such a disrespectful question.

My father said I'd never made him prouder.

All Liliya's confidence is gone as she takes slow steps toward the room. As we grow closer, I hear commotion on the other side of the door.

Ignazio, one of our foot soldiers, stands guard at the door.

"Emilio," he greets, stepping to the side before nodding toward Liliya. "Liliya."

She smiles at him nervously, staying behind me as I push open the door into chaos.

We're barely inside when I hear her mutter, "Holy shit. I'm in Mafia hell."

She has no damn clue what's coming.

21

LILIYA

oly fucking shit.

Literally every New York Italian mobster who haunts people's dreams is here.

The private dining room is quiet with no music, and all talk stopped at our arrival.

Before the wedding, Dasha and I researched the Lombardis, which led us into learning more about the other crime families that run New York, including the Marchettis and Cavallaros.

Scanning the crowd, I recognize faces from all three families.

I'm in a damn Mafia summit.

In our research, we learned that not too long ago, the Lombardis were at war with the Marchettis and Cavallaros. It all started when Vinny, Antonio's older brother, kidnapped his ex-girlfriend. Cristian Marchetti murdered him for it.

Cristian, also known as Monster Marchetti, is the boss of the Marchetti Mafia family. If there's one man to fear in this world, it's him. He's the cruelest mobster in the country.

In retaliation for Vinny's murder, Vincent Lombardi—Antonio's father—planned to kill Cristian's son, Benny. The plan went wrong, and they shot Benny's wife, Neomi, instead.

That's what brought Severino Cavallaro, boss of the Cavallaro mob family and Neomi's father, into the war. No one dare touch his daughter and get away with it.

It also didn't help that after Vincent's death, Antonio kidnapped Gigi, Cristian's daughter.

Yes, my brother contracted me to marry into a family that makes even the Bratva seem functional.

Everyone expected Cristian to torture and murder Antonio when he found him, but surprisingly, that didn't happen. Behind closed doors, Gigi and Antonio had history. Antonio saw his *kidnapping* more as protection for Gigi during a civil war within the Lombardi family.

Gigi told Cristian to accept her relationship with Antonio or lose his daughter.

It took time and convincing because Monster Marchetti doesn't give up easily.

But eventually, he chose Gigi and even walked her down the aisle at their wedding.

Mercy like that is rare in our world.

No Morozova man would've done it.

I flinch when Emilio shuts the door behind us, snapping me back into the reality of where I am. I peer back at the group of men, counting eight of them. Some faces are unfriendly, some uninterested, and others look ready to murder at any second.

Goose bumps spread over my skin like armor as I stand there.

Aleksy wants me to kill Emilio and then what?

Face the wrath of these crazies?

I think the absolute fuck not. They'd slaughter me in two seconds.

He'd better have a good escape plan before I play executioner.

My gaze coasts from the men to across the room. Clusters of birthday balloons are spread around the room, and a birthday banner hangs along the wall. The wallpaper is a deep maroon. I shut my eyes, my imagination getting the best of me.

It's to mask the color of blood, isn't it?

I shake my head, my attention shifting to the group of women seated at the end of the long dining table, a white table-cloth draped over it. All of them are staring straight at me.

A short, dark-haired girl stands and settles her wineglass on the table.

I immediately recognize her. Gigi Marchetti-Lombardi— a.k.a. New York's Mafia princess.

Two other women do the same, and they walk straight to us.

Out of instinct, I scoot closer to Emilio's side.

"Aren't you going to introduce us, Emilio?" Gigi asks when they reach us. She rests her hand on her hip, staring him down.

"You were at our wedding," Emilio says flatly. "No need."

I glare at his rudeness.

What kind of husband doesn't introduce his wife?

It's the least he could do.

None of them even wince at Emilio's cold indifference.

"Yes," Gigi says, drawing out the word. "But we expected a different bride that day. As we all now know, she isn't Dasha."

She smiles at me. I return the smile, deciding I like her.

"She can speak." Emilio's face tightens. His nostrils flare as he fixes his glare on me. "She had no problem introducing herself to Oliver only minutes ago."

Gigi playfully elbows the petite woman to her right. "Is that jealousy from him?"

Her friend repeatedly nods. "Never thought I'd see the day when Emilio had *emotions*."

Emilio clenches his jaw and shakes his head as he walks away without a word. His shoulders are tense as he heads straight to the group of men.

While the Bratva and Mafia may be different crime syndicates, this has the same outdated seating chart as the parties I grew up attending. Men on one side and women on the other.

Gigi rolls her eyes. "I swear, sometimes, I wish these men would pop some pharmaceuticals to relax. Eat a fucking gummy. Enjoy a Xanax. Or hell, go get hypnotized."

The petite woman nods. Her thick black hair is pulled into a tight French braid. "I suggest therapy to Damien on a regular basis. Does he listen? *Nooo.* He tells me he's going to the freaking gun range."

"Men love to talk a mean game about how women are *so emotional*, but they'll literally join the Mafia and murder instead of going to therapy," says the dark-haired woman standing on Gigi's opposite side. She holds out her hand toward me. "I'm Neomi."

I shake her hand. "Liliya."

Gigi slaps her hand to her chest. "I'm Gigi." She motions toward the girl with the braid. "And this is Pippa."

I politely wave at them, suddenly feeling shy.

If anyone ever looked the part of Mafia princess, it's Gigi, dressed in high-waisted black trousers, a crisp white button-up with a Chanel brooch, and stiletto heels. Her long curls fall over her shoulders, and her tan skin glows with hardly a touch of makeup.

Pippa's style is more playful in a flowing emerald-green dress and glittery pink ballet flats. With her hair pulled away from her face, her dimples and pink cheeks are put on display.

Neomi looks the most laid-back and comfortable, dressed in a black leather jacket and dark jeans. Her sleek, straight hair hits her shoulders.

Suddenly, I feel so *plain* in only my cotton maxi dress.

I love dressing up for events. Emilio will get a lecture about giving me plenty of notice before parties going forward.

"Come on, Liliya." Pippa taps my arm. "Let's get you a drink, and you can meet everyone."

Hopefully, *everyone* excludes the murderers in the corner.

We join four other women at the table. They all smile and wave at me.

"Is it someone's birthday?" I ask while taking the open chair beside Gigi.

"Mine," Gigi replies before grabbing her wineglass.

"Happy birthday," I say, my cheeks blushing in embarrassment. "I'm so sorry. Emilio didn't tell me where we were going. Otherwise, I wouldn't have come empty-handed."

"Girl, no worries," Gigi replies with a kind smile. "I told everyone to donate whatever they planned to spend on a gift to Safe Hearts. Emilio already wrote the check."

"The women's shelter?" I ask.

A few years back, I heard my uncle complaining that one of his mistresses was hiding at Safe Hearts. A week later, I saw her on a missing persons bulletin board.

"Yep," Pippa says as the other women nod. "Safe Hearts is Genesis's baby, which makes it our godchild."

The table turns silent at the mention of Genesis.

Pippa slams her mouth shut, realizing what she did.

Genesis not only murdered my cousin, but also his underboss, Yuri.

A woman with long, glossy jet-black hair dressed in a colorful halter top raises her hand. "In my defense—"

"You have no reason for a defense," I say, instantly realizing she's Genesis. "Dima's actions earned his death."

Genesis is gorgeous, so it's no surprise Dima was obsessed with marrying her.

My cousin made his own bed when he kidnapped her. If Genesis hadn't killed him, he'd have committed even more atrocious crimes and murdered more people.

On the other hand, if she hadn't, maybe I wouldn't be married to Emilio.

Genesis lowers her gaze and voice. "Thank you. I appreciate that."

"Phew," Pippa says, faking swiping sweat off her forehead. "Glad we got that over with. Genesis was worried it'd be weird between you two."

Genesis pushes Pippa's shoulder.

"But you're family now," Pippa continues. "I told her, sooner or later, we'd all be in the same room. Might as well do it now." She shrugs before grabbing her glass and taking a sip.

Genesis groans. "There's not a non-weird way to say, *Sorry I murdered one of your family members.*"

"Trust me, it's not that weird in this world," Neomi says. "Gigi's father-in-law almost killed me. Yet here I am, brunching with the Lombardis when I wanted them dead not too long ago."

"And that's why I love you, dear sister-in-law," Gigi says, raising her glass toward Neomi.

Their honesty surprises me.

In the Bratva, women don't talk like this. Everything is hush-hush. They pretend their husbands work boring desk jobs and don't come home bloody.

The three other women introduce themselves.

First, Natalia.

Even though I've *heard* of her, since she's Cristian's wife, I've never seen her in person. They didn't attend the wedding. It's no wonder two Mafia men started a war over her. She could've easily passed on the *Mafia wife* life and become a model with her olive skin tone, piercing brown eyes, and high cheekbones.

Natalia also became talk in this world since she was Gigi's best friend before marrying Cristian.

Then there's Isabella and Bria, Neomi's sisters. There's no mistaking that they're all Cavallaros. Not only do they have similar hairstyles—though Isabella's is pushed back with butterfly clips—but they're all wearing similar clothing. Bria's leather jacket is red, and Isabella's is pink. Bria's face is makeup-free, and Isabella has sparkly eye shadow and long black lashes.

Our conversation stops when a blond server enters the room. She takes the men's orders first before coming to us.

I order a mimosa. Genesis and Pippa do the same.

Gigi orders another glass of wine.

Bria and Isabella order margaritas.

I relax in my chair as we chat. They welcome me like I'm one of them, and I laugh more than I thought I would today. They ask questions about my life and share their own stories.

They don't talk much about Emilio, which is disappointing, but I have a feeling it's because he's in the room with us.

For the first time ever, I feel friendship with someone other than Dasha.

I feel like I belong.

A knot forms in my chest, and I chug my mimosa.

This will end when I have to kill my husband.

Emilio is their family. They hold a loyalty to him.

I doubt they'll be as forgiving as Neomi was with Gigi's *dead* father-in-law.

22

EMILIO

I watch Liliya while pretending to pay attention to what the other men around me are saying.

I nod and make comments when needed.

Liliya throws her head back, laughing with the other wives. Her laugh echoes through the room.

Surprisingly, it doesn't grate my nerves like most do.

It's cathartic, almost—like a favorite song that dissolves the static inside your head, calming you.

For a moment, I look at the men around me.

All bosses, underbosses, or capos in our Mafia families.

This group of men kills without regard and doesn't shy away from committing crimes. While I share so many similarities with them, there's one large difference. They're all happily married men who love their wives.

None of their relationships began like that. Like mine, they all carried conditions with either contracts, force, or blackmail.

Cristian, Severino, and Antonio discuss the fastest way to move illegal weapons. Severino is considering ridding himself of his dealer and taking over the business. Cristian said they'd have his support both financially and with manpower. Antonio nods, saying he's interested as well.

If you'd asked me years ago if I believed any of them would find love in their hearts, that'd be a quick no. Yet, somehow, they found a fucking sliver of it for their wives.

Their stories don't give me hope for my marriage though.

There's no softness inside my chest to heal.

Only a decaying heart, rotting from the inside.

I welcome that rot—can't wait for it to happen.

The day I feel nothing will be the best day of my life.

Cristian leaves the group to make a phone call as the other men engage in a side conversation.

I turn to Benny. "How long did it take for Neomi to stop being a pain in the ass?"

The men around me stop. Antonio tightens his hand around his glass. Damien inches to my side, unsure if this conversation will be good or bad.

Benny stiffens, mid-sip of his drink. "Excuse me?" His tone is sharp.

We're not friends, merely acquaintances. We also work for two different families who were once at war.

I quickly get to the point. "Out of every man in this room, our marriage agreement is the most similar."

Benny's shoulders slightly ease, and he takes another drink.

"Neomi didn't want to marry you," I go on. "Her father made that decision for her. The same with Liliya, only it was her brother."

Benny nods, now understanding my question. "Neomi hated me at first." He points at me with his half-filled glass. "What helped was making it clear I was just as inconvenienced and resentful of our fathers' decision. I was also robbed of deciding my own future and couldn't stand her ass either. We were both shoved in a shitty predicament we had no power over."

"Liliya knows I had no interest in marrying her." I knock

back my bourbon. "We're past that step, and she's still giving me a hard time. What's next?"

"Time and life are what's next."

I wait for him to elaborate. A fortune cookie could've given me better advice than that.

"We went through the ups and downs of marriage," he adds. "As time passed, we realized that our hatred toward each other was anger that we'd been forced together." A slow, rare smile spreads across his stern face. "It didn't hurt that I killed someone for her. They won't admit it, but women love it when you kill for them."

"Not always," Antonio says. "Gigi wanted to kick my ass when I murdered her fiancé."

"It didn't help that you told her fiancé to choose between his life and hers," Benny argues.

Antonio shrugs. "I like playing games before I kill. Makes it less boring."

I rub at my temples. "I've already killed someone for her."

Benny draws back. "That didn't relieve any of the tension between you?"

"She doesn't know I did," I reply.

He nods in understanding before simply saying, "Get her to fall in love with you."

I shake my head. "I want her to *behave*. Not fall in love."

"Getting her to fall in love with you is how you get her to behave." He sets his glass on the bar, leaning in closer.

"Nah." I reach behind the bar and pour myself another bourbon, knowing this is one of those times I need it. "That's too much trouble."

Benny shakes his head. "Man, you're in for a rude awakening."

Antonio, Damien, and Julian nod in agreement.

"You will fall in love with each other. Then she'll have your babies. You may think that sounds miserable now, but your wife will bring you the best damn days of your life." Benny's face softens an inch as his gaze slips to Neomi across the room. It turns smug when he looks back at me. "Now, that's all the free advice I have for you. The less I can help you goddamn Lombardis, the better."

"Thanks for the Marchetti words of wisdom," Antonio calls to Benny's back as he walks away, headed straight for his wife.

I was there the day Benny wanted to kill Antonio for kidnapping Gigi.

It was intense. Not only did I think I was about to lose my boss and friend, but also my own life. Had Cristian not stopped Benny, he'd have pulled the trigger, whether Gigi was pleading in the background or not.

Benny isn't our friend. All the Marchettis carry hatred toward us. They just look past it for Gigi and their wives, who've all become friends.

The door opens, and the servers shuffle into the room, carrying plates.

I follow the rest of the men to the table. Liliya tenses as I take the chair beside her. She doesn't look in my direction as she grabs her napkin. Before she can undo it, I grab it from her.

Biting into her lip, she doesn't say a word as I unroll the napkin and drape it over her lap.

I watch her swallow hard as I squeeze her knee before doing the same with my napkin.

"I'll have the braciole," Liliya says when the server stops behind her.

A lump forms in my throat, and I dig my fingers into the table, wondering if she ordered my mother's favorite meal to fuck with me.

Even though it would be impossible for her to know this information, my mind always travels to the worst-case scenario. I always think the worst of people because it's usually all I see from them.

I don't trust my wife.

She's a runner, a liar, a manipulator.

But, goddamn it, I want to.

I hold up my glass when the server reaches me. "Just a refill. Bourbon."

Leaning back in my chair, I listen to the conversation without contributing. I sip my drink, taking turns watching the people around me and watching Liliya.

She looks more comfortable in this room full of strangers than she does with me. The wives are doing a good job at hiding the fact that their husbands have probably killed men in this very room.

She participates in the conversation more than I do, and people throw questions at her from around the table.

Natalia asks her, "How's married life, Liliya?"

Liliya pulls at her dress strap. "Married life is ..." She pauses, searching for a word other than *miserable*. Her head turns in my direction. "We're adjusting."

"You'll get there," Gigi says in assurance before pointing at me with her fork. "*Both* of you will."

For how much violence flows through the Marchetti blood, I don't know how she's always so goddamn positive.

I'm relieved when the focus shifts from my marriage to Genesis sharing updates for the Safe Hearts remodel. Together, everyone at the table helped her raise a million dollars to move the shelter to a new building and renovate it.

I had no issue writing a check then, nor do I now for my monthly donations. I only wish my mother had found Safe Hearts before her death.

When the servers return with the main courses, I glance over at Liliya's braciole and inhale the strong aroma of garlic, olive oil, and basil. My stomach rumbles, and I knock back my drink in one go to quiet it.

The braciole looks just like it did when my mother used to order it.

"Do you want a bite?" Liliya asks, leaning in toward me.

Fuck? Do I look like I'm salivating?

Shaking my head, I look away from her. "I'm good."

She grabs her fork. "Have you had braciole before?"

I nod. "Have you?"

"No, but it sounded good on the menu." She cuts a piece.

Resting my elbow on the chair's arm, I nudge closer to her. "You made a good choice."

A hint of a playful smile hits her lips. "Does that mean *you do* want a bite?"

I hesitate, not answering.

"Oh, come on," she says with a low groan. "Didn't you give me crap for *not* eating?" She straightens her shoulders. "How about this? You eat, and I'll eat."

I snatch the fork from her hand and shove the bite in my mouth. Closing my eyes, I savor the taste of slender, slow-cooked veal, homemade tomato sauce, and fresh Parmesan cheese. Liliya plucks the fork from me and takes her bite.

A small moan escapes her lips.

My cock jerks in my pants. It's the sexiest fucking sound, and it reminds me of her moans in the shower when I tasted her sweet pussy.

Maybe Benny is right. I should let *life happen*.

But one piece of advice I won't take from him: fall in love.

———

"Where are we headed now?" Liliya asks, buckling up as I pull out of L'ultima Cena's parking lot.

I shove my black Ray-Bans up my nose. "To get our marriage license."

She wrinkles her nose. "We don't have that?"

"No." I flick the turn signal.

"Where do we go to get the license?" She grabs her purse from the floorboard and rifles through it for her sunglasses. They're bright red, in the shape of hearts, and they look ridiculous.

"City clerk's office."

"If it's not signed yet, does that mean we're not *legally* married?"

I ignore her question, not wanting her to get any ideas, and check that the doors are locked.

"I'll google it then—"

I snatch her phone from her hand and roll down my window. She dives across my lap to grab it before I launch it outside.

"Rude," she grumbles, smacking her back against the seat and tugging her phone against her right side, as far from my reach as she can make it. "I just wanted to have a little chat with my friend Mr. Google."

"You're signing the marriage license. I don't give a fuck what *Mr. Google* says."

"Or what?"

"Or I'll kill every person in the clerk's office."

She rolls her eyes. "No, you won't."

I slam on my brakes. Her phone falls from her hand as she heaves forward.

She slaps her hand on the glove compartment to stop from hitting her head.

I peer over at her. "You want to test me on that?"

She rears back to glare at me. "What's up with you guys and murdering innocent people?"

I'm not someone who murders innocent people *ever*.

I only kill men who've wronged me or someone I care about.

If Liliya gives me a hard time signing the marriage certificate, I won't kill people there. I'll just hold a gun to her head until she signs.

I park the SUV, and thankfully, she doesn't give me a hard time during our walk into the clerk's office. Or when we sign the paperwork that officially binds her to me for the rest of her life.

She's a Lastro now.

God help her.

"All right, my turn," she says when we're back in the SUV.

I stare at her in annoyance. "Where do you want to go?"

"The bookstore. You said you'd buy me as many books as I wanted, remember? Pull out that credit card because my TBR is miles long."

23

LILIYA

The bookstore is calling my name.

Just Liliya—leave off the Lastro, thank you.

From now on, I'm going mononym.

Like Cher or Beyoncé.

Shockingly, Emilio kept our agreement of me signing my name on the dotted wife line and him taking me book shopping.

I'm all smiles while giving him directions to my favorite romance bookstore and coffee shop, Chapters and Coffee.

I shamelessly eye fuck him as he backs into a spot.

The way his strong arm flexes and his jaw is tense as he focuses on the task.

Something is so sexy about a man who can easily parallel park.

I parallel park like it's my first day having hands.

Taylor Swift—another argument I won—plays in the background as he peers over at me.

"Pick me up in an hour." I hold out my palm toward him. "A credit card or five hundred in cash, please."

He ignores my hand, steps out as traffic speeds past him, and circles the SUV to my side. My door whips open, and he back-tracks a few steps, giving me room to step out.

I frown and say, "I take it, this means you're coming?" in annoyance.

He nods, circling his keys around his fingers.

"I prefer to shop for books in peace."

"Either I come with you or you get your ass back in the vehicle."

My runner rep is seriously messing with my freedom.

I throw my arms up in frustration and stomp toward the bookstore. When I reach the door, I loudly huff while opening it and try my hardest for it to slam in his face. He shoots his hand out, stopping it.

The bell above the door jingles as we enter the small bookshop.

There isn't much room, and the selections are all limited to romance, but it's the comfiest place I've ever set foot inside.

Delaney, the store owner who's standing behind the counter, glances up from her book.

"Hi, Liliya!" She sticks a bookmark between the pages and sets down her book. When she notices Emilio behind me, she straightens her glasses, as if they could possibly be malfunctioning.

I normally only come here solo or with Dasha.

Rudely, I don't bother introducing Emilio.

I don't know how to.

Saying *husband* sounds too … weird.

She doesn't look at Emilio in fear. The way she bites into her pierced lip says she'd consider scribbling her number on his receipt before he left.

My body relaxes at the smell of a lit vanilla candle, coffee, and fresh book pages wafting through the air. *Heaven.*

Emilio steps to my side, slipping his hands into his pockets, and scans our surroundings as if looking for an enemy.

As we walk side by side toward the counter that acts as both the barista bar and checkout area, the height difference between us screams. He's almost as tall as the bookshelves.

A bookshelf I'd love to climb and—

I shake my head, trying to rid myself of lustful Emilio thoughts.

"Caramel macchiato," I say, ordering my usual.

"Extra vanilla and soy milk," Delaney adds.

I give her a thumbs-up before peering back at Emilio, raising a brow—a silent ask if he wants something. As soon as he steps in front of Delaney, her cheeks warm, and it takes her a few seconds to find the buttons on the screen.

"Coffee," he says. "Black."

I stick out my tongue, making a very immature, grossed-out face.

Emilio pays, and I smile at the generous tip he leaves.

Takes me to a bookstore and *a good tipper?*

Don't threaten me with a good time, devil husband.

Delaney makes Emilio's drink first since it's clearly the most complicated. She slides it across the counter to him, but he doesn't touch it. It just sits there, as if he's waiting for mine to be ready as well.

I shuffle away from the counter and pretend to browse the shelves. Delaney's curious stares are making me too antsy.

Emilio follows closely, like an unwanted shadow.

"I didn't know you were a romance reader," I say jokingly, needing some kind of conversation. "What's your favorite genre?"

He says nothing.

I turn the corner, running my fingers along the spines. "If you say Mafia romance, I'm calling *cliché*."

His face is unreadable, but somehow, I know he's listening to my every word.

"Small town?" I tease. "Cowboy?" I pause, dramatically

gasping and snapping my fingers. "I know. You're a why-choose reader."

He raises his brow.

Finally, a reaction.

"The fuck is that?" he asks.

I stop to slightly face him. "It's a love triangle where the heroine gets *all* the guys." I grin from ear to ear. "I've always dreamed that's my future. Just little ole me and all the men." I spin on my heel and walk away, not bothering to wait for his reaction to my taunting.

The moment I turn the corner, out of Delaney's sight, Emilio crowds me. He wraps his hand around the back of my neck in a tight and possessive hold. I yelp as he yanks me back, pulling me flush against his chest.

His lip brushes my ear as he holds me in place. "I don't share."

I should pull away, fight him, and even scream, but I don't. "How can you hate something you've never tried?" I mutter, my voice raspy.

He slides his fingers to the front of my throat, tightening his hold, as if wanting to feel my pulse heighten.

Stupidly, I keep pushing him like I'm begging for him to punish me. "You ever heard the phrase, *Don't knock it till you try it?*"

Anger radiates off him.

His voice turns menacing. "I'm a territorial man, Liliya. What's mine stays *fucking mine.*" He scrapes his fingers along my neck, adding pressure, as if wanting to mark me as *his territory.*

I pant out a breath. Heat zips through my stomach, straight between my legs. I squeeze my thighs together to keep from pushing him down and straddling him.

"My wife is *my wife.*" His free arm wraps around my waist, and as he shifts, I feel something hard against my ass and sweep my tongue along my lower lip. "If another man even thinks about touching you, there isn't a single author twisted enough to write the kind of hell I'd unleash on him."

Holy motherfucking shit.

The husband I hate isn't supposed to turn me on like this.

"Caramel macchiato is ready, Liliya!"

Emilio slowly releases me, like he knows I need a second to remember how my legs work.

As bad as I want to glance down at his pants, to see if I felt what I thought I felt, I resist.

I rush toward the counter, my heartbeat thundering.

My hands tremble as I grab my drink, my fingers clinging to it like it's hard to hold.

Emilio emerges from behind a bookshelf, all cool and composed, like he didn't have me pinned against him and panting only seconds ago. He walks with confidence and no shame.

I lift the cup to my lips but quickly pull it away.

There's no way I can drink a hot drink right now.

I need something to cool me off, pronto.

"I'm so sorry, Delaney," I rasp, struggling to get the words out. "Can I swap this for an iced macchiato?"

"Of course," she says brightly. Her gaze keeps darting between Emilio and me, full of curiosity.

Emilio walks to the counter to pay for my new drink without a word.

Again, he leaves her a good tip.

I retreat a few steps and relax against a wall to ease my pulse before I have a heart attack.

Emilio grabs his coffee, strolls toward me, and settles in a bright pink armchair.

"Go shop," he says, taking a sip of his coffee.

I nod, unable to meet his eyes, and scramble toward the shelves. I grab every book that's been on my TBR list.

My arms are overflowing, and I've already dropped a few books as I make my way to the counter.

"Can I start a pile?" I ask Delaney.

"Pile away." She grins and slides my iced macchiato toward me.

I take a quick drink and hand my cup to Emilio. He raises a brow, and without a word, I return to my shopping.

I don't stop until I've cleared nearly half the shelves.

My arms and brain hurt.

It's been a day, and I'm officially exhausted.

———

"I need to leave," Emilio says, coming into the bedroom when we're back home. "For the love of God, please keep your ass in this house."

I'm spread across the bed, and I hold up the book I'm reading in response. My eyes feel so heavy that I doubt I'll be able to make it through the second chapter—I read the first one on the drive back—let alone create and execute an escape plan.

"If she has enough books, she'll behave," he mutters, as if preaching to himself.

Or maybe she won't kill you, is what I think in my head.

24

EMILIO

When I'm a mile away from the estate, I pull to the side of the road, open the glove compartment, and grab the burner inside.

I input the code and go straight to the only saved number. Hannah's.

It rings repeatedly before going to voicemail.

I hang up, curse, and toss the phone back into the glove compartment in frustration.

Chicago is so far away, but I need to make the drive soon.

I just need to find a babysitter for my wife first.

———

I didn't choose this lifestyle.

It was chosen for me by blood.

I held my first loaded gun at five.

It upset my mother, and she complained. In return, my father threatened to have me use it on her, even putting his hand over mine and forcing me to aim at her head.

This lifestyle instilled an addiction to violence toward those who'd wronged us.

Therapy was never an option.

Neither was forgetting nor forgiveness.

It's always *vengeance*.

I cut off my headlights and turn into a back alley behind a dark warehouse.

"I don't trust this motherfucker," Julian says from my passenger seat.

I almost punched him in the face when he got in thirty minutes ago. His cologne was too fucking strong and taking over the smell of Liliya's perfume that still lingered there.

"Me neither," I tell him.

"At least the warehouse won't trace back to us." He takes off his baseball hat and rubs the back of his arm over his forehead.

We park across from a black sedan. As soon as we step out of the vehicle, the driver's door opens. A tall man gets out, walks our way, and greets us in a thick Russian accent.

"Do you have him?" I ask, cutting straight to the point.

He nods and pops the trunk.

A light turns on, putting the man inside the trunk on display.

Mozart Rocko. He should've been tied down and killed a long time ago just for having that stupid fucking name. The same with his parents for choosing it.

If it hasn't become clear, I'm a name judger.

Mozart's eyes widen at the sight of us. He rocks from side to side, struggling to break free from the restraints. A rag is shoved in his mouth so he can't scream.

"I already know this fucker will get on my nerves tonight," Julian mutters as we drag him from the trunk.

I laugh when his head smacks into the taillight.

When Mozart's resistance becomes too aggravating, I punch him in the face. He whimpers but calms his ass down. Mission accomplished.

The Russian unlocks the warehouse door and flips on the lights as we drag Mozart inside. I drop Mozart on the concrete as if he were a sleeping bag and I was a pissed-off kid whose parents had just dropped him off at camp.

The warehouse smells like mildew, chemicals, and gasoline. Random furniture is scattered throughout, and a fridge is in the corner.

A butcher's hook hangs from the ceiling. As I get closer, I notice specks of blood on the chair beneath it and the ground.

Julian fists Mozart's collar and drags him across the floor to a chair under the hook. He pushes Mozart into the chair as the Russian ties him to it using a rope.

"Hello, Mozart," I greet when they're finished.

Mozart whimpers against the rag and shakes his head to get his long hair away from his eyes.

Julian and the Russian stand behind me as I casually stroll toward Mozart and tug the rag from his mouth.

Just for a moment, I want to hear his screams.

Savor them.

It's exactly what he does.

It's rather disappointing though. My victims' screams were once my favorite song, but that's now been replaced with Liliya's laugh.

I backhand Mozart in the face. "If you shut the fuck up, I'll let you live."

He slams his mouth shut.

"Where's your phone?"

He motions toward his front pocket.

I grab it. "Passcode?"

"Sixty-nine, sixty-nine."

The Russian chuckles behind me, and I motion him forward.

He does, and I hand him the phone.

"You do all the talking," I instruct. "Tell him what we

discussed earlier." I clasp him on the back as if I were the coach and he was a Little Leaguer.

He eagerly nods.

I hit the contact for Dad and FaceTime him.

No one picks up.

I try again.

Voicemail.

"Boy, does your dad really love you," I say to Mozart, who's staring at us with a pale face and crying.

On the fifth FaceTime call, Fredricko finally answers.

Fredricko Rocko—apparently shit naming runs in the family —has the weapons connections we want.

"Say hello to your son," the Russian says, aiming the camera at Mozart, following my earlier instructions perfectly.

"Dad!" Mozart yells, sounding like a fucking panicked teenager instead of a man my age. "Please! Tell them you'll do anything if they let me go! Tell them we have money!"

"What do you want?" Fredricko asks, sounding almost bored.

"All your weapons connections," the Russian replies, keeping the camera pointed at Mozart so Fredricko doesn't see us. "We want to know how you're getting so many unmarked weapons, so fast. You're getting shit even the military doesn't have."

"I'm afraid to tell you that's private information that I don't share," Fredricko replies.

"You'd better turn it into public information if you want your son to stay alive," the Russian says.

"You are one dumb motherfucker," Fredricko replies, his tone now more amused than bored. "You have a strong Russian accent. It's clear who's behind this."

"Fuck you," the Russian says.

"I won't give you my connections," Fredricko says. "Now, like my son said, I will pay you whatever you want to let him go, unharmed."

I tap my foot against the concrete, letting the Russian know he needs to hurry and close this deal.

"Not even for the safety of your son?" the Russian asks.

Fredricko chuckles. "My son has disappointed me plenty of times. You know what hasn't?"

None of us answers him.

Mozart continues to bitch, moan, and plead for his life.

"Money. Wealth. My legacy." Fredricko leans forward and lights a cigar. "Whoever you are behind the phone, will you at least do me one favor?"

None of us says anything.

"Leave a few limbs for me to bury. My wife will be heartbroken about this and want a proper funeral."

"I'll leave you his decapitated head," the Russian says.

"At least she'll be able to look into the eyes, she says look so much like mine," Fredricko comments. "I'll text you the address where to send his remains, should you see fit to kill him. It's in your best interest not to because there aren't many Russians who'd be interested in my weapons in this country. I'll easily find out who you are and kill everyone. You let my son go, and I'll forget this ever happened."

The Russian glances over at me, as if the severity of his actions is finally sinking in. I give him a nod of reassurance that he's doing the right thing.

He's not.

Rats and traitors always die, but it's not like I'll tell him that.

It's common fucking knowledge. Go to the bookstore like my wife and read about it.

As seconds pass, I notice the Russian overthinking this.

I pull my Glock from my blazer and shoot Mozart in the forehead.

To further prove my point, I pull the trigger and watch another bullet hit his cheek. I keep doing it until he has enough holes in his body to play Peg Solitaire with it. The Russian has no choice but to play by my rules now.

The Russian hurriedly ends the call.

"Clean this up," I demand.

I don't care how sloppy a job he does.

It's not my warehouse.

Like Julian said, nothing here will trace back to us.

Lev nods. "Sure thing."

I grin, loving that Aleksy's easiest person to turn was his own underboss.

———

On the drive home, I pull over. I throw the door wide, hang my head out, and vomit until my stomach is empty.

A wave of dizziness hits me, and my body aches.

Somehow, I make it home without wrecking.

I drag myself up the stairs, feeling like I've been drugged.

Sweat drips from my forehead like a faucet.

For the first time in my thirty years, I don't bother to change out of my clothes or lock my gun up before collapsing into bed … right beside my sleeping wife.

25

LILIYA

Either I'm dreaming of puking or someone is puking, is my first thought as I open my eyes.

I sit up, groggy, and peer over to find the sheets behind me messy, but no Emilio.

The sound of retching comes again as I stretch.

Definitely not dreaming.

I slide out of bed, head toward the bathroom, but stop when I notice Emilio's gun on the nightstand.

It's right there.

My golden ticket out of this marriage.

All it'd take is me squeezing the trigger and *let freedom ring*.

No way would he leave his gun out in the open like that.

Is this a test?

Probably.

Shaking my head, I chicken out and walk to the bathroom. The door is shut, and I ease it open to find Emilio bare-chested and crouched over the toilet. His skin is pale and shiny with sweat, and his hair is stuck to his forehead.

He stares at me with glossy eyes before slumping against the wall.

Is he hungover?

Sick?

Now would be the perfect time to kill him.

I'll never find him in a moment of weakness like this again.

But can I?

I rush over, and when I kneel beside him, he looks away.

Scooting closer, I rest the back of my hand against his forehead. "You're burning up."

"I came from hell," he says, his voice hoarse. "I'm always hot."

"Ha-ha. Funny, Satan."

He goes quiet, like his last reply took all his energy.

"Do you think you're done getting sick?"

He tiredly nods.

I hook my arm under his and start to stand. "Let's get you back to bed then."

"Can't." He shakes his head, mumbling, "I have shit to do."

"Emilio," I say as gently as I can, "you're going back to bed. End of discussion."

I tug on his arm, but he doesn't move.

Groaning, I use all my weight to try to drag him away from the toilet, as if playing tug-of-war. He doesn't move an inch. After a few more failed tries, he gives me a break and slowly stands. I'm at his side as he stumbles out of the bathroom toward the bed. I pull the blankets back, and he drops onto the mattress like a dead body, not even bothering to adjust his pillow.

As he settles, his gaze drifts from me to the gun on the nightstand, then back to me. Without saying a word, he pulls himself up, grabs the gun, and tucks it into the drawer.

He doesn't lock it.

If he falls asleep, it's mine.

I'm sure though, even half dead, Emilio would still stop me from getting it.

I pat his head. "Stay." *My turn to boss him around.*

His heavy eyes close, and he relaxes. I count to twenty, making sure he doesn't get up, before going to the bathroom to change clothes. When I'm finished, I check on him again, then walk downstairs.

It's already ten, and Maggie usually shows up around nine.

"Good morning," I greet her as I step into the kitchen.

"Morning," she sings back in her dainty voice before glancing past me to the doorway. "Is Emilio still home?"

"He left a few hours ago. One of his Mafia friends picked him up." I grab a banana from the fruit bowl and peel it. "Said I could use the Range Rover for the day."

"Nice try," she says around a soft laugh. "Emilio texts me with any daily changes."

"Like a true babysitter." I frown, biting into the banana.

"Being called a babysitter is an upgrade from prison guard. I'll accept that promotion."

"He's upstairs." I use the banana to point at the ceiling. "He was puking his brains out. I made him get back in bed."

Her eyes widen. "You *made* him?"

"Yep. I wear the pants in the relationship now." I take the final bite and toss the peel in the trash.

She shakes her head in amusement.

"Do you know if there's a thermometer somewhere around here?"

She pauses, thinking. "I had one in my old bathroom. If no one cleared it out, it should still be there."

She exits the kitchen, and without asking for permission, I follow her. After Emilio kicked me out of the library, I stopped exploring my new home, scared of what I'd find or Emilio finding me somewhere I shouldn't be. I also told myself this wouldn't be my home for long, so I didn't need to grow attached to it.

But as I trail Maggie, I admire all the beauty of the parts I haven't seen. The intricate details and family portraits still hung along the walls. The benches with books and coats. It was once lived in, not abandoned.

This is my home until I get the nerve to kill Emilio.

Maybe I should start making it feel more like it—brighten it up, bring its life back. It'd give me a distraction, something to do.

We turn a corner and walk down a dim corridor to a tucked-away wing that resembles a small apartment with a living room, kitchenette, and bedroom. Like the rest of the home—minus the kitchen and bedroom, since I helped Maggie clean those—it's coated in dust.

"Is this where you stayed when you lived here?" I ask as she moves into the bedroom.

She flips on the light, and it flickers a few times before illuminating the room.

Her shoulders drop with a sigh as she slowly nods, taking in the room. "Nothing has changed," she says, her voice tinged with sadness.

I linger in the doorway, unsure if I should step inside or let her have her space.

"It doesn't surprise me," she murmurs, almost to herself. "Emilio moved out the same day I did, and Nuncio never set foot in this room before. I doubt he did after. He didn't love this home the way Evalina did."

My chest aches at the pain in her voice.

I want to wrap her in my arms, hug her tight, and never let her go.

She sniffles, turning toward me. "I've lost so much. This is the one place I could've kept. Nuncio would've let me stay. But I couldn't. I left and chose to be a lonely old woman instead."

I step inside. "Do you have children, Maggie?"

She brushes her hand along the bed before sitting on the edge. "My son died when he was seven."

My chest tightens more, and I cross the room to sit beside her. "Maggie, I'm so sorry." I gently rest my hand over hers.

"He and my husband were in a car accident," she says, voice shaking. She squeezes her eyes shut as a tear slips free. "Both families I loved were taken from me in the same way." Her hand trembles beneath mine, and I squeeze it tight. "Evalina had taken me in when I had no one. She even paid for my family's funerals."

I slide my arm around her, pulling her into a hug.

We sit there, silent.

Tears fall down her cheeks as she looks around the room, memories spilling in from her past between these four walls.

"All right," she says, patting the bed. "Let me go find that thermometer."

Without meeting my eyes, she stands and quietly disappears into the bathroom.

This time, I don't follow. I stay where I am.

A few minutes later, she returns, holding an old digital thermometer. "Still in the same drawer."

I stand, hug her again, just because, and take the thermometer from her. We haven't known each other long, but in the short time, she's shown me more love than my mother ever has. Sadness rushes through me. She's another person I'll lose after I escape Emilio.

As we walk back to the kitchen, I make a decision—I'm going to restore this home.

Bring light back into it for Maggie.

She deserves that.

She grabs her purse from the island. "I'll run to the store and get some things for Emilio. Text me if you need anything." She pauses mid-zip. "I can't believe he listened to you and didn't leave."

I grin and flex my arm. "Told you, I'm the boss now."

"Keep it up." She cracks a smile. "Take care of him while I'm gone, okay?"

I salute her.

"No one ever has, you know," she adds after a pause.

"What do you mean?"

She swings her bag onto her shoulder. "I mean exactly that. Emilio's spent his whole life taking care of others. Putting himself last. It's ... nice to see someone finally care about *him*." She sighs. "Evalina tried, but Nuncio said she was *babying him*. He wouldn't even let Emilio rest when he was sick. Nuncio called it *being a man*."

Her lip curls in disgust.

She wants to punch Nuncio in the face as much as I do.

No, probably more than I do.

My shoulders fall, my heart sinking. "That's horrible."

She nods. "It is, but it also made Emilio who he is. He's guarded, cold, and far from perfect, but once he loves someone, he'll protect them until his last breath. You may think otherwise at the moment, but I promise you, Liliya, you're always safe with him."

I hold in my breath to stop myself from saying I'm not sure I believe her.

"Do you know our marriage is ... contractual?" I ask in almost a whisper.

"I do," she says softly. "He told me. That's why I'm here. He wants you to be happy here, Liliya. He just doesn't know how to make that happen. It's hard to create something you've never had before." She wipes at her eyes, pulling in quick breaths.

"I'll be back soon," she adds, starting to go but stopping. "And, Liliya, please don't run while I'm gone. This house, Emilio, *I* ... we like having you here." She turns to kiss my cheek before leaving.

I hear the front door close, walk upstairs, and tiptoe into the bedroom.

Emilio is sleeping. I grin at the slight snore coming from him.

Out of instinct, my attention goes to the nightstand.

The gun.

With my eyes on it, I walk to Emilio's bedside.

"Hey," I say, nudging his shoulder to wake him. "Let's check your temp."

His eyes crack open, and he blinks, as if trying to remember where he is.

I hold up the thermometer, and he reaches for it.

Shaking my head, I pull it back. "I'm a nurse, remember? Say *ahhhh.*"

He scowls. "I need my phone."

"Later. Now, open up."

His scowl deepens as he pushes himself up and leans against the headboard, and I stick the thermometer in his mouth.

I read the screen when it beeps. "Your temp is 101. You're officially benched for the day. Mafia work can wait." The memory of what Maggie told me—about him not taking sick days—will make me hold my ground even more now.

He pushes the blanket off. "I don't take sick days."

"You do today." I stop him from getting up. "Maggie went to the store to pick up some things for you and will be back soon."

"Maggie knows?" he groans as if that's his worst nightmare.

"She knows, and we made a pact. You're not leaving this bed until your fever breaks."

A long sigh leaves him as he sinks his head back down on the pillow.

He's back asleep in seconds.

I curl up in the corner chair with my book. I'm only a few pages in when his phone rings. I glance around, not seeing it on the nightstand, and decide to ignore it.

It rings again. Cursing, I set my book down and hunt for his phone, finding it in his pants on the floor. Antonio's name flashes on the screen.

Not now, Mafia boss.

I hurriedly silence the call.

It rings again.

Another ignore.

The next call comes from Damien.

I stomp toward the door and toss the phone into the hallway.

Emilio needs to rest, and doing Mafia things is not good for men with fevers. He can go back to killing and committing crimes when he's feeling better.

I grab my MacBook on the way back to the chair and decide to research restoring old homes while also keeping an eye on him.

I've never felt so torn in my life.

Do I nurse my husband back to health … or smother him with his pillow?

"Shit," I whisper, my heart skipping a beat as I hear banging on the front door.

It can't be Maggie. She has a key.

They're going to wake Emilio if they don't stop.

I spring off the chair and run downstairs, taking two steps at a time. My feet skid to a stop at the front door, and I stare through the peephole.

My stomach flips.

I reach for the doorknob but suddenly stop, rethinking my decision.

"Open the fucking door," the voice on the other side barks. "Or I'll break it off the fucking hinges."

26

LILIYA

Antonio Lombardi isn't lying.

He's really about to knock the door off its damn hinges.

The pounding echoes through the home like gunfire.

I press my eye to the peephole again. Antonio's face is bright red, his lips curled in a snarl, and his fist pounds against the door.

My heart slams against my rib cage.

I wasn't even this scared with Emilio.

My hand shakes as I unlock the door and open it.

Antonio forces his way inside. "Where is he?" He storms through the house without waiting for a response, checking rooms and calling out for Emilio.

I run after him, somehow managing to slip into his path, and stand in front of him.

I hold a finger to my lips. "Shh!"

"Shh?" He looks at me, stunned I'd even dared to say that to him.

What'd he expect from me? A roundhouse kick or punch in the face?

He stares me down, as if ready to murder me at any second.

While Antonio is terrifying, I understand Gigi's attraction to him. There's no warmth to his face; it's all darkness and intimidation, like how they say the devil is beautiful. A jagged scar runs along his forehead, and his hair is a touch darker than Emilio's.

Hot Mafia boss, yes, he is.

Still, my husband is hotter.

I lean in closer. "Emilio is sleeping."

Antonio's jaw tenses. "Emilio doesn't sleep."

"First, yes, he does," I say, for some reason sounding panicked, stressed, and pissed, all at the same time. "He's not a damn vampire. Second, he has a fever and is resting. I'll write him a nurse's note if you need one."

Antonio narrows his eyes at me. "Sick?" he huffs out, as if thinking I'm bullshitting him.

"Yes!" I shoot back, struggling to keep my voice low. "He's in bed, sleeping."

He moves in closer, tipping his head down to glare at me. "I don't fucking trust you."

I cross my arms, matching his stare while my pulse speeds. "Yeah, well, right back at you."

He takes a step back, surprised by my response. "You have no reason not to trust me."

"You have no reason not to trust me," I counter.

"I have a book of reasons not to trust you." He pushes past me. "I want to see him, and he'd better be fucking breathing. If he's not, you won't be in the next five fucking minutes."

I scoff, following him close. "Geesh. Does your wife know you talk to women like this?"

"My wife knows everything about me."

"She'd probably kick your butt if she knew you were behaving like this."

He ignores me, heading straight for the stairs.

We both stop when the door opens, and Maggie walks in, juggling grocery bags in her arms.

Her worried gaze pings from me to Antonio. "What's going on?"

"Emilio isn't answering anyone's calls," Antonio explains, not having near the same attitude with her as he did with me.

"Yes, because he's sick," she replies while setting the bags on the floor.

"Did you see him *sick*?" Antonio asks.

"Well ... no ..." Maggie stutters and then finishes, "But Liliya said he was."

"I want to see him," Antonio demands.

"Fine." I slap my arms to my sides. "But you'd better not wake him up, Antonio. I swear to God."

"Or what?" He raises a thick brow, pausing for only a second on his way up the stairs, going straight to Emilio's bedroom.

I'm behind him.

Maggie is too, only moving slower than us.

Antonio bursts into the room, stalks straight to the bed, and presses three fingers to Emilio's throat. I hold in a breath, waiting for Emilio to wake and freak out, but he doesn't.

"See," I say, walking backward until we're both back in the hallway. "He has a pulse." I cross my arms. "You happy?"

His eyes burn with hatred. "Be smart about the choices you make, Liliya." He taps his temple with a hint of smugness in his voice. "Don't do something stupid and get yourself killed. I have no problem getting rid of those who are a threat to my family."

I stare at him, silent and stunned.

Oh my God. He knows.

27

LILIYA

"There's no way Antonio can know," Aleksy says calmly, lounging behind his desk as if there were no problem. "You're being paranoid. We're the only ones who know about this plan."

I place my hands on the arms of the cracked leather chair, leaning forward. "What *is* the plan?"

He scratches the back of his neck, not saying a word.

For the past five days, dread has been my closest friend. My appetite is gone again, sleep is a stranger, and I'm almost positive Antonio Lombardi has painted a target on my back.

Emilio's fever broke that same night. He muttered a simple, "Thanks," before leaving and not coming home for two days.

I've barely seen him, and when I do, he's quiet and distant. I've caught him talking on the phone behind closed doors again, but at this point, I'm too scared to even question him about it.

What little connection we made is gone now.

After Antonio left that day, Maggie asked what he was talking about.

I told her the truth. "I have no idea."

While not as much as Emilio, Maggie has also become

distant. She still shows up every day, makes small talk, and helps clean the home. So far, we've mopped and swept all the floors, cleared out all the cobwebs, and cleaned all the windows.

Emilio said he could hire a company to do it, like he does the outside, but I told him I wanted to do it myself. It gets my mind off the mess that is my life.

The night of Emilio's fever, I texted Aleksy, telling him we needed to talk.

He never replied. Jerk couldn't even give me a thumbs-up emoji.

We're only speaking now because my mother called and demanded I attend Uncle Yaroslav's birthday memorial party. She also insisted I bring Emilio.

He told me he'd rather drink bleach.

I throw my arms out, waiting for Aleksy to speak.

Someone knocks on the door, and Aleksy rocks back in his chair, relieved at the interruption. Anything to prevent him from answering my life-and-death question.

"Come in," he calls out.

Lev steps inside, standing tall and straightening his suit collar when he notices me. He jerks his chin up and winks in my direction.

I shrivel in my chair, looking away from him, and hold back the urge to roll my eyes. If he'd done that prior to Aleksy becoming boss, I'd have flipped him off.

But now that Aleksy has given him power, I don't know what he'd do if I did.

I'm not a Lev fan. Not only because he was the first boy I made out with, via a dare. He used *soo much tongue*, traumatizing me enough to avoid kissing a boy again for a solid year.

He also asked Yaroslav to marry me, which my uncle promptly said no to—thank God. It was the only time I ever appreciated a decision he'd made.

Aleksy stands from his chair. "Come on. The party is waiting."

I do the same with a disgruntled sigh.

Lev is the first to leave, then me, and Aleksy. We walk straight outside to where the party is.

Not many people showed up to celebrate a man who was truly hated. A few kids are in the pool, a group in the corner is singing karaoke, and others are seated at tables.

I ignore Lev trying to talk to me and slump in the chair beside my mother.

She pinches her lips together.

When I don't ask her why she's giving me that look, she does it even more exaggerated, scooting closer to my face.

I turn to her friend, Rita, and start a conversation.

My mother taps my arm. "I think it's very disrespectful for Emilio not to show up."

I peer over my shoulder at her and roll my eyes.

"I bet he wouldn't allow you to miss a Lombardi event," she adds, swatting a wasp away from her face.

I sink deeper into my chair, not answering to avoid an argument.

"Well?" she pushes. "Do you go to them?"

"Emilio is sick," I grumble.

"Not too sick to drop you off."

"Would you have preferred I walk the twenty-five miles?" I fold my arms across my chest, leaning back to pin my glare on her.

"He could've at least come in and said hello."

"I'm sure he'd have felt *so welcome*," I say, rolling my eyes again.

Luckily, Rita chimes in on the conversation, asking my mother about the sale of the house. I jerk forward. So much has happened that I forgot she'd sold our home.

"Why'd you sell?" I ask her.

"It's too big a house to live there alone," she replies, playing with the gold bracelet on her wrist. "You know how people downsize when their children move out."

I mirror her pinched expression. "Where do you live now then?"

She's quiet for a moment before saying, "Here, of course." A breath leaves her. "Well, the pool house."

"Aleksy wouldn't even give you your own wing?" I bring my glass to my lips and hold back a smile. "This home has, like, fourteen of them."

"Your brother needs his privacy to focus on work," she argues.

I set my glass down to prop my chin up with my fist. "I overheard three women—one of them Dima's favorite hooker—bragging that Aleksy moved them in and gave them their own wing."

My mother has always wanted to be the matriarch of the Bratva. She complained to Uncle Yaroslav about it regularly. She wanted the respect he received from other members.

While she may have their so-called respect now, she'll never have mine, especially after not stopping Aleksy from forcing me down the aisle.

Aleksy cuts the music, stands, and raises his glass to make a toast. I slouch in the chair, rolling my head back, as he rambles on about loyalty, pride, and how the Morozovas will be the most powerful family in the city soon. I start to tune him out until I hear my name.

Everyone turns to look at me, and I grind my teeth.

"And to my dear sister Liliya," Aleksy says with fake sincerity, "who's made the ultimate sacrifice for this family. We appreciate everything you have done and *will continue* to do."

I rub at my elbows as my ears ring.

"To Liliya," everyone says, raising their glasses.

I don't bother with mine.

I don't even smile.

He's right about one thing: I have made the ultimate sacrifice for this family.

But what he's wrong about? The Morozovas will never be the most powerful family in the city, even if I succeed in killing my husband.

The Bratva will die under my brother.

I have to make a choice. Am I a Morozova or a Lastro?

28

EMILIO

As much as I wanted to stay away from Yaroslav's memorial shit show, I didn't want one of the other men to have to endure it either. No one deserves that hell.

Which is why I agreed to drop Liliya off and pick her up.

At first, I hadn't wanted her to go, but as I thought about it, if she did try to escape while in Bratva custody, it'd give me a great reason to murder Aleksy.

Right now, that's all I need—a reason to end his life.

I don't bother stepping out of the Range Rover when I arrive. I just shoot Liliya a quick text.

> Me: I'm outside.

A few people pass, eyeing me, but I ignore them.

It's dark, and I flash my headlights when I spot her walking in my direction.

She yanks open the door, drops into the passenger seat, and throws her bag onto the floorboard before slamming the door. Groaning, she rests her head against the window and lets out the longest breath I've ever heard.

"Rough day?" I ask.

"You have no fucking idea," she snaps, massaging her temples.

"Aw, come on. Celebrating your dead Bratva uncle wasn't fun?"

She scoffs. "No, and *someone*"—she pauses, lifting her head to glare at me—"took their sweet time picking me up."

I pretend to check my watch. "My bad. Lost track of time."

"Your *loss of time* put me through hell. Aleksy started drinking at noon. I had to endure three slurred speeches. Then, when the alcohol really hit him, he cried to my mother and me, saying he felt we didn't respect him like we should. If you'd been another twenty minutes, I'd have drowned myself in the pool."

It's reckless for any boss—I don't care if it's Mafia or Bratva —to get shit-faced drunk. Further evidence that someone needs to get rid of him.

I don't reply to her, only leave the party and head home.

We're about twenty minutes out when a ringing comes from the glove compartment.

"I'll get it," Liliya says. She tugs on the handle, but it's locked.

She jiggles it, as if it were a vending machine that stole her money.

"Don't worry about it," I say as my pulse spikes.

I can feel her glare on me as she says, "You know, it's really sus to keep a phone hidden from your wife."

I glance at her sideways. "Sus?"

"Suspicious. Would you like me to read you the definition?"

"In this life, we keep certain things private. It's only to keep you safe."

"Still sus." She taps her lips. "Very, very sus." She groans, throwing her head back. "I have a husband with a burner. Classic cheater behavior."

My jaw tics as I tighten my knuckles around the steering wheel.

I don't bother correcting or arguing with her.

A few minutes later, my phone in the cupholder rings.

Liliya snatches it before I can. "Hannah's calling," she announces loudly. "Is Hannah calling both phones?" She's being sarcastic, but I don't miss the hurt in her tone either.

I try to grab the phone, but she yanks it out of my reach. She yelps when I pull the car to the edge of the road.

She wouldn't call both phones unless it was an emergency.

She calls my phone again.

Again. And again.

Each call makes my heart pound faster.

Liliya holds the phone in her lap. I can tell she wants to answer, but she's also scared to.

Then, it stops ringing.

Seconds later, it pings with a text.

Liliya reads it out loud. "Hannah says, *Casserole. Casserole. Fucking casserole.*" She clicks her tongue against the roof of her mouth. "Unless she's taking our dinner order, that's code for something."

I snatch the phone from Liliya and return the call.

It only rings once before she answers, sounding panicked. "It's time, and I need to get to the hospital!"

I shift the car back into drive and stomp on the pedal. "Did your water break?"

"Did your water break?" Liliya repeats before lowering her voice. "Oh my God, did you knock a woman up?"

29

LILIYA

I've always known affairs were the norm in this world.

My father had mistresses. So did Uncle Yaroslav.

Dasha and I made a bet on how many Emilio would have before their first anniversary. Three was my guess. Hers was four.

Knowing it'd happen is one thing.

Living it right now? It feels like a knife through the chest.

Even if I never wanted to marry Emilio or if we hadn't had sex, there's still a storm raging inside me. One filled with anger, betrayal, and heartbreak.

I breathe through my nose, trying to relax.

"Where's Andre?" Emilio asks Hannah.

I lean closer to him, trying to make out their conversation, but the volume is too low.

"I know you're scared," Emilio says, a comfort in his tone I've never heard. "But we need to find him."

My gut clenches with a twinge of jealousy that she gets this part of him.

But also concern for the woman.

"If she's in labor, she needs to get to the hospital," I say tightly.

He doesn't look at me or acknowledge that I even spoke.

Covering the phone's speaker with his hand, he says, "No one," into it.

That sure as hell stings.

"I'll get a flight." He cuts the wheel into a hard U-turn. "Keep calling Andre. If he doesn't answer, call Angelica. Have her drive you. Stick to the plan, okay?"

When he finally ends the call, I ask, "What's going on? Where are we going?"

Before he can answer, the sound of tires screeching interrupts us.

I whip around my seat just in time to see two blinding headlights barreling straight toward us.

"Emilio!" I yell.

Bam!

The impact of the car rear-ending us hits us like a punch.

The Range Rover jolts forward, throwing me halfway off my seat.

Emilio shoves my head down with one hand and reaches into the console with the other, pulling out his gun while controlling the steering wheel with his knee.

"Stay down and cover your head, Liliya!" he yells.

Gunfire explodes.

The rear window shatters.

Emilio stays focused and calm, bracing his arm across the seatback and firing out the broken window.

Then, he floors it.

My pulse races, and I wish there were something I could do to help.

The car behind us picks up speed.

But then comes another problem.

A second person on a motorcycle drives up beside us.

Great. We have two vehicles behind us now.

"Hold on," Emilio says, jerking the wheel.

We hit the motorcycle.

The motorcycle spins out, crashing on the side of the road.

My heart pounds against my ribs as I grip the seat.

"As soon as I stop, you run," Emilio instructs, his eyes on the rearview mirror, watching the other car.

He veers off the road, and plunges us into the trees. The Range Rover crashes through branches, and he slams on the brakes.

I throw open the door and run.

My adrenaline pumps, and the wind smacks me in the face as I sprint away from the SUV and road.

Emilio is right behind me, gun in hand, watching our backs.

The other car's headlights shine through the trees, and they honk their horn.

"Keep going, *guaio*!" Emilio shouts as we hear shots being fired. "Ignore them!"

My legs burn, but I push harder.

I gasp for air, and eventually, my legs give out. Kneeling forward, I catch my breath. Emilio doesn't say a word as he scoops me up and throws me over his shoulder.

He moves us faster than I could, and neither of us says a word. I don't know how much time passes until he slowly drops me to my feet against a tree.

"I think we're good," he says, fighting off his exhaustion. "I doubt the lazy bastards even got out of the car."

I slide down the trunk, falling on my ass. "Who were they?"

"No idea." He starts pacing in front of me.

"You still need to get to the hospital," I whisper. "You have a baby on the way."

He abruptly halts and crouches in front of me. Grabbing my

chin roughly, he gets in my face. "If you tell anyone about that phone call or what we're about to do, I'll kill you, Liliya." His voice is raw, drenched in real threat. "And this time, it's a promise."

30

LILIYA

After Emilio's threat, do I even want to know the truth? Ignorance is sometimes bliss.

Emilio stands and pulls his phone from his pocket. I stay slouched against the tree. My legs couldn't stand even if I begged them to.

"Hey," he says into the phone. "It's Emilio. No one can get in touch with Andre, and we have an emergency."

He nods, scratching his jaw, and moves out of earshot.

Who the hell is Andre?

He paces between two trees before finally shoving his phone back into his pocket and returning to me.

"Come on," he says.

"Where are we going?" I eye him warily. "How are we getting home?"

"We're not going home."

"Then where are we going?"

"You'll find out when we get there."

I sigh, still not moving. "Are we walking?"

"We have a ride coming, but we need to meet them in a neighborhood about half a mile away."

My shoulders curl forward as I use the tree to brace myself and stand. My body screams in protest.

"Do you want me to carry you again?" There's an unexpected sincerity in his tone.

I shake my head. As exhausted as I am, he has to be even more so.

We walk silently under the full moon. When we meet a narrow road, I look each way, as if expecting the men who chased us to appear.

Emilio leads us into a neighborhood and straight to a parked black Suburban. He opens the back door and gestures for me to get in. I sink into the seat, my body relaxing. He slides in beside me.

"Emilio," the older man behind the wheel says as he pulls onto the road. He has a deep smoker's voice.

Emilio gives him a single head nod and tugs his phone from his pocket. His jaw tenses as he texts.

I stare at the back of the driver's head, debating on asking if he knows who Andre is, but don't.

The ride is quiet. The only sound is the occasional slurp from the driver taking a drink of his slushy.

I run my fingers through my knotted hair before lowering my head and whispering, "I forgot my purse in the Range Rover," to Emilio.

He doesn't look away from his phone. "Leo will get it."

I nod, turning my head to stare out the window. My eyes grow heavy as I drift into a light sleep. I jolt awake when the SUV rolls to a long stop.

Emilio opens the door, steps out, and offers his hand. "Come on."

His palm is warm as I take it. As my feet hit the pavement, I look around, noticing my surroundings.

We're at a private airstrip, surrounded by small planes and jets.

Emilio leads me straight to a compact jet. A man with a long ponytail stands at the base of the staircase.

"Good evening," he greets, his voice deep like gravel.

Emilio gestures for me to enter the jet first.

I don't know how safe it is, flying to who knows where with this man, but I also don't know how safe I am staying behind either.

So, with a nod, I walk up the stairs.

———

I wait until we're in the air before I start my questioning.

The inside of the jet is sleek and clean, and everything looks almost new.

Dark leather with a monogrammed *R* stitched into each seat, food and drink bars, fresh flowers, and *soo* much legroom. I could do a full-on Pilates workout in the aisle and still have plenty of room.

I'm seated, buckled up beside Emilio. "Who's Hannah?"

He doesn't flinch or say a word.

Just stares straight ahead, working his jaw.

"Who is she?" I stress.

Silence.

I repeat the question ten times.

Each time, I'm met with more silence.

I finally stop wasting my breath.

My phone is in my purse in the Range Rover, so I'm in for a boring flight since my company sucks.

Thankfully, the flight is short.

I'm yawning every three seconds by the time we land. Emilio hands the ponytailed man, who I learned was the pilot, a stack of hundreds. The pilot hands him a car key and tells us good night. I follow Emilio into a small parking lot.

He stops at a black sedan, pops the trunk, and tosses me a black baseball cap. "Put this on."

I shove it over my hair as he does the same.

We get into the car, and as Emilio drives, I realize we're in Chicago from the street signs. By this time, I don't even have the energy to ask him why we're here.

He drives to the back of a neighborhood until we're at a street with only one two-story brick home.

Emilio cuts the engine and turns to me. "I don't trust you, but right now, I don't have a choice. What you're about to see never happened. You'll never repeat it to anyone." He grips my shoulders, giving them a shake. "Do you understand me, Liliya?"

"I ..." I inhale a controlled breath. "I understand."

We get out of the car, and I follow him to the front door. My heart rattles with each step we take.

Emilio collects a set of keys from his pocket and hurriedly unlocks the front door. As soon as we walk in, I hear screaming.

"I'm here!" Emilio yells, racing into the living room.

A pregnant woman is doubled over on the couch, clutching her belly.

"Oh my God," I gasp, dropping beside her. "What happened?"

"I'm either dying or ..." She stops to inhale deep breaths, and I can tell she's having a contraction. "Or I'm in labor."

"How far along are you?"

"Full term," she says, clenching her teeth in pain. Tears fall down her cheeks, hitting the already-dried mascara on her face.

I glance at Emilio. "We need to get her to the hospital."

"Did you try to call the midwife?" Emilio asks the woman.

"Yes," she says. "Her phone is going straight to voicemail."

"Goddammit," Emilio screams, clenching his fist, as if stopping himself from driving it through the wall.

"We have to go to the hospital," the woman says. "We have no choice."

Emilio scrubs a hand over his face, staring at me in a pain I've never seen from him. "Can you deliver a baby?"

I slowly shake my head. "I think we need to get her to a hospital."

"It'll be okay," the woman tries to assure Emilio, but from the fear on her face, even I don't believe her.

I'm missing *something* here.

We help the woman into the car. I climb in beside her in the back seat, holding her hand and telling her everything will be okay, while Emilio speeds toward the hospital.

When we arrive, I assist her inside while Emilio parks the car.

"She's pregnant and bleeding," I tell the woman at the front desk.

She immediately leads us to an exam room. "The nurse will be right with you."

As I help the woman onto the bed, she studies me curiously.

"You're his wife," she says, so certain of herself.

I nod. "I am. Who are you?"

We both look up when the door opens, and Emilio enters.

He'll have no choice but to answer my questions now.

31

LILIYA

T he moment Emilio shuts the door, the woman cries out and bends forward, a contraction hitting.

My guess is that the baby is coming soon.

Glancing at the bed, I take her in.

Something about her looks so familiar, but I can't put my finger on it.

Her dyed red hair is piled back in a messy bun.

She grabs her purse, squeezing her face in pain as she rifles through it. "I need to get a hold of Andre."

"Liliya." Emilio's gaze cuts to me. "You can go to the waiting room."

I stubbornly stay in my chair.

It's childish and rude. I wouldn't want a random woman in my labor room.

A gentle knock on the door interrupts us.

"Hi there," a nurse softly greets, entering the exam room.

Emilio moves toward my chair, callously staring down at me as the nurse talks to Mystery Pregnant Woman.

He keeps his tone low, so only I can hear, "Waiting room. *Now.*"

Not wanting to create a scene, I stand and quietly slip past the nurse on my way out. A few other people are in the waiting room, and the kid behind me watches *Peppa Pig* at full volume.

All eyes rise to Emilio as he storms into the waiting room.

He fixes his tired stare on me. "Let's go."

I jump to my feet and follow him through the parking lot, straight to the sedan.

"We're leaving her?" I ask as he unlocks the car.

"We're going to find her husband."

"Husband?" I stress, blinking at him.

"Yes, the father of her baby."

"Oh." I press a hand to my heart, silently saying, *Thank God*, to myself.

I can at least cross *secret love child* off my list of possible marital problems.

As soon as we're in the car, Emilio inputs an address into the GPS and drives off. After a short drive, he pulls into an empty warehouse parking lot.

He cuts the engine. "Get out."

This day just won't end.

First, I had to deal with my mother and Aleksy.

Then, we had the whole car-chase, shoot-out situation.

Now, I'm in Chicago, hunting down a pregnant woman's husband and about to walk into a shady warehouse.

The wind hits me as I follow him inside, and as soon as we enter, I notice two men. One slouched in a chair at a table, and the other standing beside him.

The standing guy reaches for his gun. "Emilio?"

He doesn't relax until he's certain it's him.

Emilio stalks toward them. "Where the hell is your phone, Andre?"

I struggle to keep up, halting when I reach them. The man in the chair is shirtless, and blood soaks the towel pressed to his shoulder. His lip's split, and his cheek is turning purple.

"Lost it somewhere in the middle of *getting shot*," the man sitting mutters, gesturing to his shoulder.

"She's in labor," Emilio snaps, not even caring about the man's wound.

"Fuck!" Andre tosses the towel aside, trying to stand, and blood pours from his wound.

I stumble back to avoid getting splattered.

Before he can fully rise, Emilio shoves him back into the chair by his *injured* shoulder.

The man curses and punches Emilio's ribs.

Neither of them flinches.

It's like watching two cousins fight.

Emilio jerks his chin at me. "She'll get the bullet out. Then, we'll go to the hospital."

"You took her to the fucking hospital?" the man screams, his face turning almost as red as the blood coming out of him. "Are you out of your mind?"

"Neither the midwife nor Angelica answered their phones," Emilio snarls at him. "And it seems you were out playing target practice—you being the fucking target."

"You're lucky she'd care if I murdered your ass," Andre says, flexing his jaw.

"Same," Emilio says. "We're wasting valuable time arguing." He whistles, pointing at me. "Bullet. Out. Now."

Andre pushes to his feet again. "She can do it on the drive to the hospital."

I quickly shake my head.

Not freaking happening.

I'm not about to play Operation while Emilio swerves through traffic.

"If we're going to the hospital, they can stitch him up there," I say, suggesting the obvious.

"No," the man grinds out. "If they stitch me up, I won't be

with my wife. And I don't like hospitals." His face hardens as he eyes me down. "Who are you?"

I shift from one foot to the other. "Liliya."

"Russian." His gaze flicks to Emilio. "This the wife?"

Emilio tensely nods.

"Andre," the man introduces before pointing at the burly guy. "This is Opal."

"Now, let her get that bullet out of you," Emilio tells Andre. "If you waste another minute, I'll have her push it in you deeper."

Andre nods, and I eye the first-aid kit on the table.

They clearly planned to take care of the gunshot hole themselves.

Andre is sweating bullets as I dig the tweezers inside his wound, trying to find the bullet.

"There," I whisper to myself when I find where it's lodged.

I'm surprised he doesn't wince or scream as I carefully pull the bullet out.

It's covered in blood as I drop it onto the table.

He snatches the bullet, slipping it into his pocket.

As soon as I'm finished stitching him up, he stands. "Now, take me to my wife."

32

EMILIO

When we arrive at the hospital, I pull up to the entrance.

"Keep us updated," I tell Andre as he steps out. "Don't you fucking leave her side."

He scoffs, as if it's an insult to even tell him that.

He limps toward the entrance, looking a hot mess, all bloody and bruised.

I don't know what they'll do when he walks into the hospital like that, but I'm sure with what I've seen from Andre, he'll make them bring him straight to his wife.

I appreciate the way he cares for and protects her.

I could never repay Andre for what he's done for me.

I check the time.

Four a.m.

Peering at Liliya in the passenger seat, I can tell she's close to passing out. She could hardly stay awake on the drive to the hospital.

My phone vibrates with a text from Antonio.

Antonio: You good?

When we reach a red light, I reply to him.

Me: All good.

Earlier, before we left the woods, I called to give him a rundown of what had happened on the drive from Aleksy's. I texted Leo, telling him to have our tow guy pick up the Range Rover and for him to watch over the area.

After we ended our call, my next goal was to find Andre. I called his older brother, Gabriele. While he didn't know Andre's whereabouts, he did offer the family jet to get me to Chicago.

I accepted the offer with no hesitation.

Liliya keeps nodding off as I drive to the small condo building. She hasn't said a word since Andre got in the back seat.

"We're staying here tonight," I say as I park.

She doesn't question me as she slowly unbuckles her seat belt and follows me into the second-floor unit. I flip on the light, noticing it's just how I left it—cheap furniture, no decor, the bare minimum.

"Emilio," Liliya says, moving like a zombie across the room before collapsing on the couch. "I need answers."

Ignoring her, I move to the kitchen and collect a knife.

When I return to the living room, her body stiffens when she notices it. She curls inward, tucking her knees to her chest.

I slam the knife onto the coffee table in front of her.

She flinches, gaping at me before slipping her attention back to the knife.

It stays frozen there for a minute, as if she can't look away.

I unholster my gun, placing it beside the knife.

"Pick one," I demand.

Her eyes go wide, fear replacing her sleepiness.

She's now fully alert.

"Pick one!" I roar, slamming my fist on the table. The knife bounces, and the gun shifts from the force.

"What …" Her voice breaks as she takes deep breaths. "What's going on?"

I step closer, like the predator I am, until I'm close enough that I can practically breathe in her fear. Hostility burns through my blood.

"Your job is to kill me, *guaio*," I say, my tone controlled. "Isn't that what your brother told you to do?" I gesture to the table. "Go ahead. Pick your weapon." I lean in close again, my nose brushing hers. "*Kill me, Liliya.*"

33

LILIYA

"**K**ill me, Liliya."

I'm frozen in place—unable to move, to speak, to *think*.

Emilio lifts the knife, turns it in his hand, and holds it out to me like an offering.

When I don't reach for it, he clamps his strong arm around my elbow to drag me off the couch. His hand slides down my arm until it finds mine.

"Stop it," I say, fighting against him as he forces my fingers around the knife handle.

Both of our hands are on the knife, and he raises it to his throat. It brushes along his Adam's apple, and in my mind, I'm imagining one wrong move, and we'll slit his carotid artery.

"Do it," he snarls, pushing the blade into his neck. "Do what your brother is too spineless to do himself."

Pain shoots through my arm as I try to break free.

He outpowers me in every single way.

I lock my elbow, trying to get some control.

"Come on," he taunts. "Make your family proud, *guaio*. Kill me so they can pass you off to the next bidder."

I halt, the truth in his words a slap in the face.

I stumble forward when he releases the blade from his throat. I suck in a breath of relief, but that's only temporary.

He captures me from behind, shoving me against his chest, and I cry out when he lowers the knife to my throat. I shudder at the cold, sharp metal against my sensitive skin. I jerk back when he nicks me with the blade.

"Let me go," I say, struggling to break free.

"Maybe I should kill you instead."

He slowly drags the blade along my throat. The pressure is light as a feather, and all I can think about is how close I am to being dead.

As if to further antagonize me, he rests his chin on my shoulder and bites into my neck, *so close* to where the blade is.

"You said vows you never planned to keep," he says into my ear, his tone so sinister that chills spread through my body. "Now is the time for that death to part us."

I squeeze my eyes shut, waiting for the blood to flood from my throat.

He digs the blade in deeper, and I hiss in pain.

Tears hit my eyes, and I squeeze them shut.

Do not die crying, Liliya.

I betrayed him, and just like in any story of betrayal, someone must die.

It was clear that the chance of survival wasn't in my favor to begin with.

He keeps the knife to my throat for *one second, two, three ...* all the way to ten before lowering it. He shoves me forward, but I don't get the chance to flee before he catches my wrist and spins me to face him.

Our eyes meet like a fatal attraction.

I stare at him, terrified.

He stares back, menacing.

Only inches separate me from my murderous husband holding a knife.

Regret washes over me. He gave me plenty of chances to kill him, and I didn't take them. This is on *me*.

His strong chest rises and falls with harsh breaths while he clutches the knife. His knuckles hold it so tight that they're turning white as he stares me down.

I'm there, unable to move, and my body shakes.

He slowly reaches out to drag the pad of his thumb along my throat, tracing the path the knife went only seconds ago.

A desire that shouldn't burn cracks through me.

I run my tongue across my bottom lip. He bites down on his, so tight that the muscles in his jaw twitch.

Without warning, he slides his thumb between my lips. I sink my teeth into it.

He doesn't flinch, only smirks.

My shoulders shake as I gasp for breaths. His thumb slips free from my mouth. He sweeps it over my lips before clamping his hand around my jaw. His fingers bite into my skin.

Not once does our eye contact break.

His gaze finally drops to my mouth, and my eyes travel with it.

When his eyes rise again, so do mine.

As he inches closer, I do the same.

The knife clatters to the tiled floor, echoing off the four walls like a warning, telling me to run. I jump but don't look away from him.

He's a room full of red flags, and I'm about to wave my white one.

I gulp as he comes closer, the toe of his shoe meeting mine.

It happens so fast that I'm not sure who moves first. For a short second, our lips brush against each other's.

That's all we need.

That simple spark, the match, to light our fire.

As if suddenly brought back alive, Emilio grips the back of my neck and drags me in for a kiss.

A *real kiss* from a man like him.

It's rough, no tenderness or patience.

All desperation and teeth and anger.

I kiss him back, just as carnal and punishing.

Everything our marriage is.

My head spins as he fists my hair to tug my head back, exposing my throat, just like he did when he was holding the knife.

I cry out in both pain and desire.

He drives me backward, and I stumble over the knife before he slams me against the wall with a heavy thud. If there were any pictures on these bare walls, they'd be on the floor from the impact.

"You fucking drive me insane," he growls against my mouth, grinding his hips into mine.

He curls a hand around my throat, giving enough pressure to trap a few breaths.

"I should hate you," he whispers, his tone rough and low. "You've been plotting my death, yet here I am, so fucking hard for you that it hurts." His grip on my throat tightens before easing some, and his thumb strokes the side of my neck. "I should be squeezing the life out of you, but instead, I'm going to fuck you so good that you'll want to die alongside me because no man will ever be able to pleasure you like I do."

A moan tears from my throat. "Please," is all I can say in desperation.

I claw at his shoulders and fist his shirt—my way of *making a move*.

Lord knows I don't exactly know how to.

"Please what, *guaio*?" He loosens his hold just enough for my lungs to inhale a full breath. "Would you like me to die tonight or spend the rest of my life fucking you, giving you pleasure every single day?"

Lifting my leg, I hook it around his waist. "Option two, please. I want my husband to pleasure me."

He groans, a gravelly sound climbing straight from the bottom of his throat.

From his goddamn soul.

"First, wife, I want you to answer a question," he says, his voice rough and ragged.

Of course he does.

This man can't do anything simple.

"What?" I stutter out.

He releases my throat, and I take deep breaths as if I'd been underwater for hours.

"Why haven't you killed me like you were told to do?"

I rear my head back, hitting the wall, not wanting to look him in the eye as I whisper, "I couldn't."

"Why?" He drives his hips forward, slamming me against the wall. "Why couldn't you put a fucking bullet in my head?" I stay silent, refusing to look at him, so he grabs a fistful of my hair to force me to meet his eyes. "Answer me."

I hiss in pain, my scalp on fire. "Because I'd rather die at your hands than cause you pain!" I scream at the top of my lungs.

He freezes, losing a breath and dropping my hair at my admission.

I'm just as shocked as him.

A growl leaves his throat as he pulls me away from the wall and drags me across the room. I nearly lose my footing as he turns us. We collapse on the couch. Him below me, and I am straddling him.

"Kill me or fuck me, Liliya." His intense stare is locked on mine. "Put me out of my misery either way."

I lower my gaze, dropping my hands to his shirt.

He flexes forward as I start working the buttons. As soon as I finish, I run the top of my hand over his waist, feeling his hard erection. He eases back, stretching out his arms, and his shirt falls open.

In awe, I trail my hand across his muscular chest before stopping at his heart. I leave it there, waiting to see if this man is human or just as much of a devil as they say.

There's a beat.

The rhythm is uneven, but it's there.

He relaxes his head back, drawing in heavy breaths before tilting his head forward when I grind against him.

He grips my hips, stopping me. "Take your panties off. If you're going to slide your pussy against my lap, I want to feel it."

I slowly rise, and his eyes are on me like a hungry madman as I hook my thumb into the waistband of my shorts. I peel them off, along with my panties, and they fall to the floor.

He stares at me in what resembles worship, as if I'm the one thing he'll forever cherish.

I pause, taking my husband in.

A scarred man, a killer, but also the one to whom I swore loyalty to at the altar.

He stares back, as if I were holding the breath he needs to live.

His shirt hangs open, and his hair is messy. As my eyes travel down, I make out the outline of his cock.

"Your pussy is glistening for me," he says. "Beautiful. I'm sure it tastes like fucking heaven." He licks his bottom lip.

I reach for his belt, but before I can undo the buckle, he scoots to the edge of the couch. His arm circles around my waist, and I gasp as he pulls me forward until my thighs hover in front of his face.

He brushes his nose along my lower belly, breathing in my scent before placing a single kiss there.

My body is on fire as he lifts one of my legs, places my foot on the couch beside him, and opens me wider for him. He drags a single finger through my wetness. The way he does it is so slow yet possessive, like he owns me and has all the time in the world to play.

I'm growing wetter and wetter.

The need for him is becoming too much.

"Please," I whimper.

"Please what, *guaio*?" he asks, his voice rough yet also teasing. "You want me to finger your sweet pussy like this?" He plunges his thick finger inside me.

I grip his shoulders. "Yes."

"I can't wait to hear you begging me to fuck you while I have my tongue buried so deep inside your pussy that you forget your own name." He shoves another finger inside me. "No, scratch that. You'll forget your first name. But you'll never forget you're a fucking Lastro. That you're *mine,* branded with my last name."

A shiver ripples down my spine. My thighs twitch as he pushes another finger into my pussy.

He curls his fingers inside me, making my hips buck forward.

His fingers drive in me, fast and deep, as he lowers his mouth to my core.

My entire body tightens as pleasure takes over.

Aleksy was stupid if he thought I'd choose his vendetta over *this*.

My husband will win.

Emilio's tongue pleasures me in ways I never thought possible.

Being this good at oral should freaking be illegal.

He groans, and in seconds, his fingers are no longer between my legs. He grips my waist, flips me, and shoves me onto the couch.

I barely have time to breathe before he drops to his knees and spreads me wide to make room for himself.

He lowers his head and buries it between my thighs like he's starving for me. His nose nudges my clit, and he drags his tongue slowly through my slick heat.

"You're dripping for me, baby." He pulls back just enough to show how wet his lips and chin are from my arousal.

He doesn't wait for a response before disappearing back between my legs, curling his tongue around my clit and sucking it with just the right amount of pressure.

My knees buckle, and my back arches.

I moan his name and beg him for more.

He keeps working me with his expert tongue, sliding it along my slit before taking breaks to plunge it inside me. He alternates between licking and touching, making me a desperate, trembling mess.

"That's my good girl," he says. "Relax and let me take care of your beautiful pussy."

It doesn't take long *at all,* unfortunately, before I'm falling apart.

Pleasure rolls through my body as my orgasm takes over.

"That's it." He fingers me harder while sucking on my clit. "You going to come for your husband? Soak me with your juices. You're all I want to taste for the next fucking century."

His tongue circles inside me, and his fingers drive in so hard I'm shocked he hasn't ripped something.

My thighs tremble, my stomach tightens, and then it happens.

An orgasm shatters through me.

My hair falls in my face, and my body shakes like a hurricane.

I cry out, moaning his name.

My hips lift off the couch as I give in to the best feeling of my life.

But Emilio doesn't stop.

He moans into my pussy, his tongue and fingers still at work and not even slowing down. He wants to steal every bit of pressure he built up inside me.

God, I never want this to end.

My head is spinning by the time he finally stops.

He releases my thighs from his shoulders, holding them to make sure they don't drop to the ground since I'm pretty much powerless.

He stands, and my mouth waters at the sight of his cock at full attention beneath his pants.

I lick my lips, just as hungry for him as he was for me.

Somehow, I gain the energy to slide off the couch and fall to my knees on the carpet in front of him. His abs tighten as I reach for his belt, unbuckling it.

As if on instinct, his hips buck forward when I unzip his fly and undo his pants. I shove his pants and briefs down. His hard, huge cock springs free, only inches from my face.

I lick my lips as he curls his hand around his cock. He strokes himself once slowly before rubbing the tip against my lips. I happily open my mouth, welcoming him, but he doesn't give me much.

I suction my lips around him, sucking, and he tsks me.

"As bad as I want to fuck that mouth, I need to feel your tight pussy wrapped around this cock first." He slaps my cheek with his cock. "But you haven't begged me yet, have you?" He grabs my elbow, pulling me to my feet, and shoves his hand between my legs again. "It seems I'm going to need to keep pleasuring my wife's pussy until she gives me that."

I suck in a deep breath as he drives his blunt finger inside me, stroking me hard before adding three more fingers. My head drops back as I moan.

"Let me hear it, Liliya," he groans, his lips brushing my jaw as he finger fucks me. "I won't fuck this wet pussy until you beg."

I reach for his cock, my goal to stroke it, but he smacks my hand away.

"Please," I whimper.

"Please what?"

"Please ... fuck me."

I don't have to ask him twice.

His hand leaves my pussy, and he's pushing me into the bedroom and turning on the light.

I moan as he drags my shirt over my head, unclasps my bra, and immediately pushes my breasts together. He shoves them up, groaning before sucking on a nipple and biting into one.

My body is on fire, burning for him.

I've never felt so ready to explode.

It's like he's torturing me like he does his victims.

I manage to break free from him, fall on the bed, and scoot to the head. I open my legs, ready for him to put me out of my misery. He pulls his shirt over his head, flinging it across the room, and kicks his shoes off before removing his pants.

My breaths come out ragged as he climbs between my legs. The warmth of his body is another relaxant, yet it also sends more heat through my body.

He guides his cock between my folds, dragging it teasingly through my wetness.

"Tell me this is what you want," he says. "Tell your husband you want him to fuck you because you want this marriage."

I grip his wrist, stopping him, and settle the head of his cock right at my opening. "I want my husband to fuck me tonight, and tomorrow, and for the rest of our lives ... *until death do we part.*"

He thrusts his hips forward, so deep that my body inches up the bed.

I cry out in pain.

I bite into my lower lip and dig my nails into the comforter.

He stops, what just happened dawning on him as he stares down at me in shock. "You haven't done this before?"

I slowly shake my head, surprised I'm not embarrassed telling him this.

Some of the tension releases from his body, as if he's telling it he needs to be gentler.

What looks like pride or ownership spreads across his rough face.

He gradually pulls his cock from me and slowly dips it back inside, not going as deep as he did before.

His strokes are gentler, only moving a few inches more with each one.

He's helping me adjust to his size.

To make this more comfortable for me.

Lowering his head, he kisses me, keeping his steady pace. I feel like I'm on top of the world as our hips meet each other's, and he cups my breast.

"Your pussy feels perfect," he says against my lips. "Everything about you is perfect, Liliya." He raises his hand to my face before raining kisses along the other side of my jaw.

His body presses mine into the mattress, and as each minute passes, our breathing grows heavier.

His strokes grow faster.

I start meeting him thrust for thrust.

Lifting my gaze, I stare up at my husband as he grinds into me.

He's not a hero in a tale, but he isn't the monster either.

He's a flawed man who grew up in a dark world.

It's what gave him the gray parts.

But it's what makes my husband who he is.

Just like before, it's as if he knows my body so damn well that it doesn't take long for me to lose control again. I dig my nails into his back as waves of warmth flood through me.

"Emilio," I say, moaning into his shoulder as he shoves his face into mine.

I bite into his skin as I orgasm.

A few more thrusts from him, and he collapses all his weight on me.

We take a moment to catch our breath, and he slowly pulls himself up. He stares down at me and lightly presses a kiss to my lips.

Then, to my nose.

Then, my forehead.

It's a side of Emilio I've never seen before.

He slowly pulls back, easing the weight of his body off me, until he's settled at my feet. His hand reaches between my legs, and when he draws his fingers back, I see the red painting his skin.

"Blood has never looked so beautiful," he says, his eyes locked on mine. He pushes them into his mouth and sucks hard. "Nor has it tasted so fucking delicious."

I should be embarrassed by this.

Grossed out.

But I'm not.

I'm glad this didn't happen the night of our wedding.

He waited until we *both* were ready.

My husband didn't just fuck me.

He made sure to fuck all the hate I had for him gone.

Or really, was there any there to begin with?

34

EMILIO

L iliya's breathing is steady beside me.

She's tangled in the sheets, looking so peaceful as she sleeps.

I didn't just sleep with my wife tonight.

She gave me a part of herself no one had ever had.

A part of her so fucking precious that I didn't deserve.

A twinge pulls at my heart that she handed it over willingly, like she'd been waiting for a person worthy and found me.

Do I find myself worthy? Fuck no.

But pride swells that she did.

Being a virgin wasn't something I demanded in a wife. I'd never base a woman's value on that.

I ease out of bed, grab my phone from the nightstand, and tug on a pair of shorts from the dresser.

This condo is my secret. I bought it under a dead man's name and in a neighborhood that no one talks about.

Only a select few know I have it.

No one in New York.

I unlock the sliding balcony door and step outside. The wind nearly blows the door shut. I lean on the railing, scanning the parking lot and cars, looking for anything suspicious.

All is clear.

I call Lev, and unsurprisingly, the rat doesn't answer. I'll break his nose for that later.

Antonio is my next call.

He answers after one ring, not even sounding tired. "Where the hell are you?"

I rest my arm on the railing, looking down. "Chicago."

"The fuck are you doing in Chicago?"

"I'll explain when I'm back."

"Where's Liliya?"

"She's with me."

"Be careful with her."

I blow out a breath. "Did Leo find anything when they picked up the Range Rover?"

"A dead asshole and a wrecked motorcycle."

"Let me guess. Dead asshole was Russian?"

"Bingo."

"Fuck," I mutter.

"Watch your back, especially with the wife."

I pinch the bridge of my nose. "For some reason, I halfway trust her."

"That's stupid. You don't trust anyone. Not to mention, your *wife's* family told her to kill you."

"The family that gave her to a man rumored to have helped his father kill his own mother and sister. You think she holds any loyalty to them?"

He pauses for a moment. "Let me know when you're on your way back to New York. Don't make it longer than another day. We don't fucking vacation."

We end the call, and I crack my neck before throwing my head back.

It doesn't release the tension like I hoped it would.

My next call is to Andre.

"How's she doing?" I ask him.

"You're an uncle," he says with a grin in his voice.

I smile for what feels like the first time in a long fucking time.

"She's resting. Tired as hell." He whistles. "My wife is a fucking trooper. I damn near fainted when the baby came, and I fucking gut men regularly."

"I'm happy for you two."

"Appreciate it. Stop by and visit us later."

"Unless shit goes south, that's my plan."

"You bringing the wife?"

"Her name is Liliya, asshole." I'm quiet for a moment before saying, "We'll see."

Do I trust her enough to show her all my secrets?

The cobwebs I keep hidden?

"Tell her thanks for digging that bullet out of me," Andre says. "I owe her one."

I nod, though he can't see me, and tell him, "Go get some sleep and nurse that wound," before ending the call.

I spend another thirty minutes outside, soaking in the fresh air as the sun rises. Then I trek back into the condo and check on Liliya.

She mutters something in her sleep as I kiss her forehead.

How much will I tell her when she wakes up?

35

LILIYA

A noise in the kitchen stirs me awake.

I relax in the soft sheets, stretching out my arms, and smile at the ceiling.

Flashes of last night run through my mind, replaying like a movie.

Sex with Emilio wasn't gentle, sweet, or lovey-dovey.

It was messy, chaotic, and fueled with frustration.

Just like our marriage.

Last night, I didn't only learn that Emilio was amazing in bed, but I also learned where my loyalty was.

It's not with Aleksy.

Not with the Bratva.

But with the man who protected me from bullets.

Who carried me through the woods when I was too tired to run.

Who maybe murdered the man who'd assaulted me.

My loyalty is to my husband. No one else.

I slide out of bed, wrapping the sheet around my naked body. Goose bumps coat my skin as the cold air hits it, and I leave the bedroom.

Emilio is seated at the kitchen table, a coffee mug in one hand and his phone in the other.

"Morning," he says, setting both down to provide me his full attention.

He's shirtless, his dark hair tousled, and his eyes heavy.

Both of us are in dire need of a good night's sleep—or five.

Doubt those five nights will come anytime soon.

"Coffee?" he asks.

I shake my head, walking into the kitchen. "Just a glass of water is fine." Holding the sheet with one hand, I open cabinets with the other until I find a glass, fill it, and settle in the chair across from him.

Questions swarm my mind, but I'm not sure where to start.

I lift the glass, take a sip, and finally murmur, "Soo ..."

The word lingers between us.

Emilio takes a drink. His gaze drops to the table, and when he lifts his head, his eyes lock with mine.

I hold my breath.

"The woman we took to the hospital last night ..." He pauses for a moment, biting into his bottom lip before slowly releasing it. "That was my sister, Aurora."

I draw back in shock. "Your sister?"

"I keep her listed in my phone as Hannah."

"So ... she's not dead?" It sounds stupid to ask, but I need to hear him say it, to make sure I'm understanding correctly. "Everyone thinks she died with your mother in the lake."

He smooths a hand over his jaw. "That was the plan."

"Is your mom also alive?"

He leans back in his chair, pain spreading along his features. "No. She's really gone."

"All the reports say Aurora died with her."

"That's what she wanted everyone to believe."

I swallow. "Why?"

"The day my mother died, she'd tried to leave my father. He

beat her, told her if she ran, then he'd kill her and Aurora. My mother escaped, loaded Aurora in the car, and took her to their favorite hiking spot. She called Maggie, asked her to go get and hide Aurora, and said to give me the letter she'd left in Aurora's bag."

The hairs on the back of my neck stand as chills hit me.

"She kissed Aurora goodbye, left, and drove her car into a lake."

That chill spreads down my entire spine.

"The letter asked me to tell everyone Aurora was in the car with her. My mother figured if my father thought they'd both died, then he wouldn't go looking for Aurora and hurt her. She didn't trust anyone but Maggie and me to protect her. Maggie had a family friend in Chicago, so we took Aurora there. For a year, we didn't contact Aurora once. We completely cut her off for her own safety. After my father's death, we started visiting, but it's still very limited. The past year, I've tried to make it more regular though."

A mother who died to protect her daughter.

A brother who's keeping that secret for her.

Emilio lowers his voice. "That's your husband's biggest secret. Don't make me regret telling you."

I inch closer, resting my elbows on the table. "Your secret is safe with me." I draw back and run my hand through the tangles in my hair. "How'd you know Aleksy asked me to kill you?"

The corners of his mouth form a smirk.

"Your brother is an idiot," is his answer that really isn't an answer.

"That much is obvious," I grumble. "But that doesn't answer my question."

"I already told you a secret today."

"Is there some kind of limit?"

"If we're going to spend the rest of our lives together, we might as well spread them out. Learn something new each day, you know?" He stands, takes a long draw of his coffee, and winks at me. "Now, I need to shower. While I won't share any more secrets with you now, I have no problem sharing a shower."

I stand, undoing the knot holding the sheet up and allowing it to fall to my feet. "Are you saying I'm dirty, husband?"

"I'm saying that I'm ready to fuck my wife again."

36

EMILIO

A rush of adrenaline hits me as I admire Liliya's naked body when she enters the bathroom.

Last night, I left no part of her untouched.

I tasted her like a starved man.

Doing that for the rest of my life is my newest goal.

Liliya smiles at me, a little too smug for my liking.

I take one step, grabbing her by the hips, and spin her around. Her palms hit the wall as I press into her, dragging my hand down her spine and the dip of her ass.

"You're making a face that looks like you're up to trouble," I murmur into her ear.

She glances at me over her shoulder. "I was hoping you'd be my trouble."

I draw my hand back and slap her ass.

She yelps but tilts her hips toward me, like she wants more.

"Are you going to behave while we're in Chicago, *guaio*?"

She doesn't answer, just bites into her lip.

I give her another whack.

This one stings my hand, and I can already make out my handprint on her skin. Her moan tells me she's loving this.

I inch back and push down my shorts. My cock bobs forward, throbbing and hard as a rock. She peeks over her shoulder, eyes dropping to my cock, and presses her thighs together, rubbing them.

"Come here, Liliya," I say, stepping away from her and stroking myself. "You want to play games and tease me? Get on your knees and suck my cock."

She saunters toward me, being so obedient.

Such a contrast to my normal runaway bride.

She sinks to her knees in front of me and rakes her nails up my thighs. My fist clenches around my cock. The pain feels so good.

I buck my hips forward. "Deep throat me."

Her lips part, just barely, but she pauses.

"I've never done this before," she says shyly.

I stop stroking myself at her admission and stare down at my perfect wife on her knees before me. She looks up at me, vulnerable but also trusting.

"You're joking?" I ask before realizing my response was an asshole one.

When she shakes her head, something inside me shifts.

She gave me her virginity last night.

I saw the blood with my own two eyes.

That monster inside me awakens more, burning for her.

Never did I think I'd be one of those men who got off, knowing this woman had only been and would ever be mine.

I lower my hand, brushing her cheek, then slowly cup her jaw to raise it.

"*Guaio*," I say lightly.

Her eyes meet mine, a touch more confidence in them at how softly I said her nickname.

"You were made to please me, Liliya," I tell her, my tone low. "You already know how. It's instinct."

Grabbing the base of my cock, I piston my hips forward.

She opens her mouth, and I guide my cock inside.

I ease into her mouth and admire the sight of her lips stretching around my cock. She's the most beautiful woman I've ever seen in my life.

Her throat tightens as I bottom out. She gags, and I back out a few inches. As I do, I groan at the sight of my cock coated with her spit. I wipe the corner of her mouth with my thumb.

"We'll work on that gag reflex, baby," I say with a hint of praise.

Spit drips from her lips, trailing down her chin. I fist her hair and push myself in deeper. She adjusts herself on her knees, making herself more comfortable, settling her thighs against her ass.

My balls draw tight, pressure building as I fuck her face.

So slow, so gentle, so unlike me.

Hell, at this pace, I'm *making love to her face*, if I had any romance inside me.

My cock twitches in her throat as I buck my hips. Shutting my eyes, I allow my head to fall back as she sucks me.

"Add your hand," I rasp out. "Stroke me, *guaio*."

My body shakes, as if my veins were on fire, and her fingers wrap around my throbbing cock. She sucks harder, moaning around my dick, and tightens her grip around my base.

"Good girl." I tip her chin up. "Look at you, right where you belong. On your knees for your husband. Sucking his cock. Not running off."

I thrust deeper, harder, and she eagerly welcomes it.

The pressure in my body builds fast.

Too fucking fast.

I pull back, stopping her before I fall apart. "I'm finishing inside your pussy." I release her hair and draw my cock from her mouth. "Up. Shower. *Now*."

Her cheeks are flushed, and her lips swollen and slick as she scrambles to her feet.

As she passes me, I drag my finger down her spine, and she shivers.

She steps inside the shower, water cascading down her perfect curves and full breasts.

My wife is a vision.

Her nipples tighten, and I stroke my cock, watching her. She drags her hand down her body and then crooks her finger at me in a silent invitation. I step in, shutting the door behind us.

The shower space is small, but cramped or not, I'd fuck her in a mop bucket if I had to.

Nothing will stop me from having my wife.

My cock presses against her stomach as I back her up against the wall.

Ownership and need flare through me.

She's mine.

My fucking wife.

I make eye contact with her. Water clings to her lashes and beads on her lips. I lean in, brushing my lips over hers and collecting the droplets before shoving my tongue inside her mouth.

Our bodies tense, pressing into each other's as we kiss.

Fuck, how I want to wreck her.

To shove my cock inside my wife and take what's mine.

But I don't.

I force myself to go slow.

And it's motherfucking torture.

My thumb strokes her cheek as my other hand tangles in her hair, curling in the wet strands.

One day, I'll have this fistful of hair as I fuck her from behind.

My cock jerks when I think about it.

I breathe against her lips, "Last night, when I buried myself inside your pussy, it was nothing I'd experienced before." I trail my hand from her face down to her thighs to cup her slick heat.

"You were made for me, Liliya. While you might not have been the first bride in the contract, you were the one who was supposed to show up at the altar."

Her sharp nails dig into my arms.

I nudge my nose against hers and then rain kisses down her jaw.

"I won't be the perfect husband," I whisper, my throat sore and voice hoarse. "But you'll always come first with me. You'll wake up with a kiss to the forehead and go to sleep with an ache in your pussy from how hard I fucked you. That's my added fucking vow I didn't say at the altar."

I slip my hand behind her to grab a handful of her ass and pull her against me.

She gasps, and I catch her moan in my mouth. Her thigh lifts and wraps around me. I grind against her, my cock sliding against her folds, but I don't give in to my desires yet.

At least not with my cock.

Her body arches as I thrust three fingers inside her, spreading her for me.

She moans against my neck as I finger-fuck her. Her heat clenches around me, and I'm close to losing my goddamn mind.

Her hips slap against the shower wall as she rides my hand.

She's on the brink—her pussy tightening around my fingers, pulsing, and her body trembling.

I bend my knees to line up my cock with her soaked entrance. With one hard thrust, I enter her tight pussy. The longest groan of my life leaves my lungs.

I don't move for a moment.

Just stay there—deep inside her pussy—before torturously drawing back.

A breathy moan leaves her lips as I pull all the way out.

"More," she begs, tilting her hips forward like she's trying to pull me back in. She kisses the corner of my mouth. "I want all of you, always."

I crash my lips into hers and thrust back inside her.

I lift her thigh higher on my waist, slam her against the wall, and catch her hand in mine, threading our fingers and pinning them to the shower wall.

I fuck my wife good, hard, and so fucking deep.

"How does my cock feel inside you?" I whisper against her throat before biting it.

"So good," she moans, her voice breaking as I suck on her neck. "I've never felt so good."

I rotate my hips, rolling them slowly, finding her G-spot.

When I do, her body jolts forward, and I smirk.

Her moans turn into whimpers. I release her pinned hand and slide my thumb between us, circling her clit as I pound into her. Her nails claw at my shoulder as our bodies smack against each other's.

"Yesss," she cries out, dragging out the word as her pussy pulses around me.

"Come for me, Liliya," I grit out. "Tighten your pussy around my cock and squeeze every drop out of me. I want to know how good my cock makes you feel."

A moan of desperation leaves her lips, and her orgasm rips through her. Her body spasms, her legs giving out. I catch her before she collapses, flip her around, and hike her ass up.

With one hard thrust, I'm back inside my wife.

I slap her ass and run my finger down her spine, feeling her tremble beneath me. It only takes a few more deep strokes, and I lose it, groaning her name.

As I slowly release her, she drops to the shower floor and catches her breath.

I kneel beside her, slide my hand between her thighs, and gather my cum leaking from her.

I smear it over her lower stomach, rubbing it in. "I'm putting a baby inside you."

———

Liliya hops on the vanity, tugging my robe tighter around her body. "So ... do we have a niece or nephew?"

I stop mid-towel-drying my hair to peer at her in question.

"Did Aurora have a boy or a girl?"

I hang my towel on the hook and smooth back my wet hair.

She gasps. "You didn't ask, did you?"

"She had a healthy baby. That's all that matters. Andre said she was sleeping and they needed to rest."

She throws her hands up. "Next time you talk to them, you hand me the phone to ask all the important questions."

I open a drawer for my deodorant and swipe it on. "Andre's the one who called. We'll find out today."

"Speaking of Andre, what's his deal? Guy screams serious Mafia vibes."

"That's because he is Mafia. Somehow, my sister escaped one mob family, only to fall in love with the son of a Chicago mob boss. Guess it's in our blood to be attracted to this life." I shake my head, remembering how against it I was when I found out.

But at least with Andre, I know she's well protected.

No one can hurt her.

"What's the plan today?" she asks. "Besides finding out if I need to buy a pink or blue onesie."

"We need to get you a new phone and clothes."

I should've taken her off Aleksy's phone plan the night of our marriage. He could easily track her location. Big mistake on my part.

I wait for her to argue, but she surprisingly doesn't.

"You'll also get a new number," I add, knowing *this part* may be a problem for her.

She bites into her cheek. "Is that so I can't call Dasha?"

"No, so Aleksy can't track you." I step into her space, and she parts her legs, giving me room to stand between them.

"Fair point," she says around a long breath before lowering her voice. "Are you still not going to tell me how you knew he'd asked me to kill you?"

"Nope. Just know, in this world, talking too much gets you killed."

"Ah, so that's why you're always so quiet." She presses a light kiss to my chest. "Aleksy is going to think I'm the one who told you. They called my father a rat. He could easily say I'm just the same."

I slide a strand of wet hair off her cheek. "No one would dare hurt you." I run my hand along her cheek. "Do you think you could've killed me?"

"Do *you* think I could've killed you?"

"It'd have been fun, watching you try." I smirk, sliding my hand beneath her robe to stroke her bare thigh.

"I could've done it when you were sick, you know."

"Yet here I am, still standing."

"That day, when Antonio came over, did he know what Aleksy had asked me to do?" She gnaws at her bottom lip.

I slowly nod, kneading her thigh with my knuckles.

"Does he want to kill me?" Her body trembles, as if Antonio is the big bad wolf, coming to destroy her.

"No," I say around an amused lie. "He told me to keep an eye on you. We wanted to see where your loyalty was."

I raise a hand from her robe, and she shivers as I brush my knuckle along her jawline.

She rests her hand on mine. "I chose you. I will always choose you."

I kiss her forehead. "Good girl." I pat her thigh, then retreat a step. "Now, get dressed. Either grab something of mine or what you wore yesterday. We'll run all our errands and then visit Aurora and the baby."

"That sounds wildly domestic." She playfully elbows my stomach. "Look at us, being so husband and wife. Showering, shopping, not wanting to kill each other."

I help her to her feet and smack her ass.

As she walks away, I notice something.

My entire body isn't as tense as usual.

My jaw isn't tight. My neck isn't strained.

I feel light, and for the first time in a long fucking time, I smile.

37

LILIYA

This arranged Mafia marriage has veered more into the domestic category.

Emilio said he liked to keep a low profile in Chicago, so we slipped on the baseball caps from yesterday before shopping. He didn't flinch at a single price tag as we shopped for a new phone and clothes. He also paid for everything in cash.

We ate tacos for lunch in the car, and now, we're on our way to meet the baby. He called Aurora earlier, and she said they had left the hospital and were at Andre's family's estate.

When we reach the *family estate*, I'm reminded that while the locations and organizations may be different, so many of these crime families are similar. Like now, we're stopped at a wrought-iron gate when we arrive.

These men aren't only armed; they're also wearing full tactical gear and masks. Security cameras watch us. The masked guards grip their rifles as one motions for Emilio to roll down his window.

Instead of doing that, he grabs his phone and texts.

At his lack of cooperation, a tall guard approaches us and bangs on the window with the butt of his gun.

I jump, slapping at Emilio's shoulder, as if he suddenly went deaf and blind, not noticing the madman looking ready for murder.

To further prove his homicidal point, the man points the rifle at Emilio's head.

"We're outside the gate," Emilio says into the phone. "Tell these fuckers to stand down." He ends the call and tosses his phone in the cupholder.

The guard retreats a step seconds before the gate slowly opens.

A decked-out, bright blue golf cart with gold rims comes speeding through. Blinking, I notice Andre behind the wheel. He slams on the brakes and jumps off the cart, casually strolling toward us. You wouldn't think the man was shot only a day ago.

Emilio waits until Andre is at his window before rolling it down.

Andre's heavy gaze bounces from Emilio to me before returning to Emilio. He gestures to the right. "Park there. You know the drill. And *no guns*."

Emilio nods, turns the wheel, and parks on the side of the isolated road.

"Don't tell anyone your name unless I introduce you first," Emilio says to me, opening his door.

Okay.

Sounds very un-women's rights, but whatever.

"What if someone asks me?" I throw out before he steps out.

He peers over his shoulder, and with a slight annoyance in his tone, he says, "I'll do all the talking."

"Do I pretend I'm a mute then?"

"Just let me do all the talking. Okay?"

"Okay." I click my tongue against the roof of my mouth.

"You do all the talking. I act like I don't know words. Got it." I wait until he's out of the car and at my door before getting out.

We walk to the gate, where Andre is waiting in the golf cart. We climb in, and he guns the gas, driving down the long drive. The property is massive, sprawling with fountains and more weeping willows than I can count. Benches of different colors are beneath each tree.

It's like we're in a park that was designed when someone was tripping on LSD. Every few yards, I notice another armed guard. I scoot in closer to Emilio.

To get my mind off them and since Emilio still hasn't asked, I lean forward and shout, "Niece or nephew?" to Andre.

"Niece," Andre yells back.

I smile, peering over at Emilio, and notice a slight smirk on his lips.

Andre makes a sharp right, and Emilio wraps his arm around my shoulders to stop me from flying out of my seat.

Jesus. He's a new dad.

Someone needs to teach him about safe driving.

My jaw drops as the home comes into view.

It's *huge*. Bigger than the Morozova estate, than Emilio's, than any home I've ever been inside. It's all stone, reminding me of an old-time castle. Straining my neck to look up, I notice more armed men on the roof, perched up like birds.

We don't stop at the front door. Andre speeds past the men and landscapers, only slowing when we reach a set of double doors tucked in the back.

He brakes, throws the golf cart into Park, and hops out.

Emilio and I follow him through the doors, landing in a large living room that screams just as much wealth as the exterior of the home. While the furniture and decor look expensive, the space also feels cozy and comfortable. Family pictures hang on the wall and are displayed on the end table and coffee table.

A tall woman—my guess, in her mid-fifties—stands from the

couch. Her dark hair is pulled into a sleek bun, and she's wearing a Chanel pantsuit.

She barely pays a glance at Emilio before her eyes cut to me in suspicion. "Who's she?"

"Ma," Andre says, sounding tired, "I told you Emilio was bringing his wife."

Her gaze lingers on me, still untrusting. "Does she know what'll happen if she tells anyone about Aurora?"

"She won't talk," Emilio says flatly, stepping slightly in front of me in protectiveness.

"She's who dug the bullet out of me last night," Andre adds. "Be nice to her." He turns to look at me. "She's protective of my wife."

I understand Aurora's attraction to Andre.

His face is strikingly handsome with a natural tan complexion, high cheekbones, and a sleek jaw. Eyes and hair the color of straight coffee. His body is lean and muscular. He also has the whole *serial killer with a smile* vibe going on.

"Rightfully so," Andre's mother says, still eyeing me like I'm about to pull out a gun and shoot the place up. "You know the wrath I'd force your father to unleash if anything were to happen to Aurora or the baby."

So, they call her Aurora, not Hannah?

Emilio brushes his hand along my back to put me at ease. "Angelica, I promise, you can trust Liliya."

"Liliya." She repeats my name.

I shift uncomfortably, not sure if she's saying it so she'll remember the next time she sees me or so she doesn't forget the name she'll put a hit out on if needed.

Her smile is half sincere, half patronizing. "Pretty name."

"Angelica," Emilio warns at the same time Andre groans, "Ma."

"No arguing or violent threats when the baby is around," a sweet, tired voice calls out.

Aurora appears, looking exhausted but on top of the world, carrying a baby bundled in a pink blanket. Her hair is pulled back in a tight braid, and she's dressed in pajamas and UGG slippers.

She grins when she notices us. "She's ready to meet her uncle Emilio."

All eyes are on my husband as he steps forward, his gaze locked on the little one in Aurora's arms.

Aurora rocks her in place. "We named her Evalina."

Emilio freezes for a moment, scratching the back of his head. "You named her after Mom?"

"I did." Aurora looks down and softly runs her finger over Evalina's cheek. "She has her eyes." She motions toward the couch. "Sit down. You can hold her."

Emilio's steps are slow, and the other woman slides to the other end of the couch to give him room. He reaches out, gently taking Evalina in his arms, as if she were made from glass.

As she's tucked in his hold, for a moment, his body goes still.

Everyone tries to pretend their attention isn't fully on him.

He stares down at her in affection, like she's already everything to him.

"She does have Mom's eyes," he mutters, staring deep into them.

The same man I feared to marry, who saw bloodshed as a daily hobby, cradles his niece with tenderness.

We give him a moment, allowing him to meet his niece.

"Would you like to hold her, Liliya?" Aurora asks.

"I'd love to," I whisper.

I don't look at Angelica, but I almost expect her to stop Aurora, as if I still can't be trusted.

She doesn't.

Instead, she tells us she needs to get to her nail appointment and will be back soon. I'm surprised when she tells me goodbye and says it was nice meeting me. As I sit down next to Emilio,

I'm not sure if I should take Evalina from him or wait for him to hand her over.

Aurora steps forward, as if reading my mind. She gently takes Evalina from Emilio's arms and places her in mine.

"She's perfect," I whisper, hugging Evalina close.

Evalina purses her lips in her sleep and is smaller than I imagined. She stirs, a sigh escaping her before nodding back off. My heart has never felt so warm and happy.

When I peer at Emilio, his gaze is fixed on me, his features softer than I've ever seen.

Could this be our future one day?

A child. A home. A life built on love.

Reality settles through me.

I want this. I'm done running.

I want us to build a family and have a home filled with happiness.

38

EMILIO

"You're not upset I named her after Mom, are you?" Aurora asks, leaning against the kitchen counter.

Evalina is in her bassinet, sleeping, exhausted after everyone took a turn holding her.

Liliya is on the patio with Angelica, who's now back from her nail appointment and most likely asking Liliya a hundred questions. Angelica means well. She's just cautious about who she allows in her home and around her family. Her husband is king of Chicago's underworld, so she has every reason to see every new face as a threat.

I shake my head as she plops down in a chair in exhaustion. "Not at all."

"I know she'll have Andre's last name—"

It's rude, but I talk over her. "That's for the best. The Lastro name is tainted. Evalina Ricci is a beautiful name."

She frowns. "The Lastro name isn't tainted."

I give her a look.

"Seriously, it's not. I hope you have lots of babies to carry on our family name."

I don't say anything, only look out the window to check on Liliya. She's sitting in a chair, posture perfect, nodding and listening to Angelica.

"I like Liliya," she comments. "She's good for you."

I turn my attention back to her. "She's a pain in my ass."

"Andre said the same about me plenty of times." She laughs around a sigh. "You wouldn't have brought her here if you didn't trust and like her."

I flex my fingers and straighten my watch. "You needed me, and I didn't want to waste my time figuring out what to do with her. So, I made the choice to bring her. I just pray it wasn't a mistake." I take a slow sip of the fancy water that Angelica said was filtered through pixie dust or some shit. "Who put a bullet in Andre?"

"He won't tell me." She rolls her eyes. "I'm sure he pissed someone off."

"I wish you hadn't married into this world. It puts you in too much danger."

"Andre and his family would take a bullet for me without blinking. They're like the Lombardis on steroids when it comes to bloodshed over people they love."

"His father is a don. That makes your life more in danger than it was, being the daughter of a capo."

She holds up a finger. "Or *more protected*." She perks up. "I like to look on the bright side of things, dear brother."

"At least Andre isn't next in line to be the boss."

Andre is the youngest, and his brother, Gabriele, is set to be the boss when his father either steps down or dies.

While I've only met Gabriele once, he's the perfect candidate to take over. Their father, Constantino, has taught him well. He'll continue to run a great empire.

"Just stay safe, okay?" I chug the remainder of my water and toss the bottle into the recycling bin.

"Are you going home today?" she asks around a long yawn.

"Yeah. Gabriele said we can use the jet again."

"I love that jet," she says around a sigh before yawning again.

As much as I'd rather stay here and spend time with her, I need to get back to New York and find out who tried to kill me and my wife.

The list of possible suspects who'd want me dead is long.

Could be the Russians, a rival family, or some entitled prick who lost money at the poker table. Hell, it could be all of the above.

If I had to place my chips, I'd stack them against the Russians.

Whoever it is, they won't live to try again.

———

"Why don't the Lombardis own a private jet?" Liliya asks while we're in the air.

It's all she's done—*ask questions.*

One after the other, over and over again.

I'm half tempted to find a parachute in here, strap it to her back, and tell her we're skydiving back to New York.

"Because they're expensive as hell," I reply.

"Tell them they need to make more money then." She motions toward the jet. "Clearly, Andre's family has it figured out. Maybe you should switch sides. Andre's Mafia fam looks like they pay better."

I massage my temples, a headache pounding so hard that my ears ring. "Let's play a game."

"Monopoly?"

"No, it's called Liliya Goes Five Minutes Without Asking a Question."

She tilts her head to the side, thinking. "Best I can do is, Liliya Goes Three Minutes Without Asking a Question."

I groan, going back to rubbing my head.

She dramatically slumps in her seat. "What am I supposed to do during those three minutes then?"

I remove my fingers from my head, one by one, and smirk in her direction.

Her eyes widen, and she slaps my arm. "Yeah, right. They probably have cameras in here, and I'm pretty sure Angelica would slit my throat if I were caught being *naughty on her plane.*" She makes a slicing motion across her throat. "She's probably already plotting my murder now."

"Angelica doesn't want to kill you," I state.

"She probably doesn't want to see me suck your cock on camera either. Sorry, hubby. One thing I've yet to find as a turn-on is voyeurism."

"We'll work on that." I ruffle her hair.

"Buy us a private jet, and I'll give you a blow job whenever you want." A full-on smirk spreads across her face. "Now, did you mention Monopoly somewhere?"

I shake my head, not having any interest in a board game. "You just sit there. Ramble. Whatever."

She exhales slowly. "Guess I'll just read on my phone. Can't go wrong with a guaranteed happily ever after."

She turns quiet, losing herself in her book.

I pull my phone from my pocket and open the Lombardi group chat.

I have a lot of shit to figure out.

Starting with the fact that none of them know Aurora is alive.

I swore I'd tell Antonio and the other men after my father's death.

But when that happened, I still stayed silent.

In this world, every secret you share is a risk.

The more people who know she's alive, the less protected she becomes.

They attended her funeral and mourned her alongside me.

Stood at her grave, not knowing she wasn't in it.
Planted a tree in her name.
Antonio hosts a dinner in her memory every year.
My keeping this from them isn't just a lie.
It's betrayal.

39

LILIYA

Julian picks us up from the airport, and as much as I want to ask Emilio where we're going, I keep my questions to myself.

It's only a short drive until we pull into Lucky Kings' private back parking lot.

I've never been inside the casino. Like with the restaurant, Uncle Yaroslav said that's a Mafia business and we needed to stay far away from it.

I silently follow them into the building.

Julian makes a right, disappearing into a room, and I keep trailing behind Emilio.

We stop in front of a set of glass doors. He opens one, gesturing for me to go inside.

The room is empty and looks like an upscale employee break room with a couch and TV.

There's a food area with pizza, pastries, chips, and cookies.

A fridge with a glass door I can see through is stocked with rows of drinks.

"Stay in here. Eat a snack. Just don't leave, *please*," is all Emilio says before leaving the room.

I grab a Dr Pepper from the fridge, snatch a doughnut, and plop down on the couch. As I drag my phone from my pocket to finish my book, I notice a new email notification on the screen.

Dasha emailed me five minutes ago.

I check behind my back, looking from left to right, before opening and reading it.

Liliya!
WHERE THE HELL ARE YOU? I've been calling and texting you! Please get in touch with me. I need you!

I hit Reply.

I got a new phone/number. Where are YOU?

I keep my phone in my hand and take a bite of the doughnut, and my attention drifts to the TV.

A reality dating show plays, where women compete for one man's heart. I nearly snort out my bite when one says that she's going to drag another woman down the hall by her hair if she stops her from winning a *date night*.

My phone pings with a new email from Dasha.

What's your new number?

I reply to her.

Give me yours.

She doesn't waste time before replying.

You know I can't. Just talk here. I need money.

I set the doughnut to the side, suddenly nauseous.

Money? How the hell am I supposed to get her money?

Emilio made it clear. Right now, we're all in danger.

That could include Aurora and the baby.

Another email comes through. This one has her phone number.

I swallow hard, my hand sweaty around the phone.

Can I do this?

Risk our lives and safety?

She's my sister. My blood.

I shoot up from the couch, chug the Dr Pepper, and toss everything in the bin.

I stare at the door, as if it's daring me, and tiptoe toward it.

I could sneak out, find an ATM, meet with Dasha, and no one would notice, *right?*

Sounds easy enough.

40

EMILIO

I walk into the conference room and lower myself onto a black leather chair. Antonio's already seated at the head of the table, his face unreadable. Julian, Leo, and Damien are also here.

I texted them during the flight, asking them to meet with me here.

My chest feels heavy as I say, "I have something to tell you."

None of them speaks. Just wait for me to continue.

It takes a good five seconds before I can get, "Aurora is still alive," to leave my mouth.

It's about time I'm honest with them.

The room explodes in response.

"You're fucking joking," Damien snaps.

"How long have you known about this?" Antonio slams his fist on the table.

"Man," Julian says, shaking his head.

"Explain—*now*," Antonio roars.

I blow out a long breath, and then that's exactly what I do.

I tell them how my mother called that day, hysterical. She said she didn't have much time, but needed me to promise that I'd protect

Aurora. I tried to talk her down and ask where she was. She wouldn't say. Only said she loved me and would see me in the afterlife.

Then, I heard it.

The impact of her hitting the guardrail.

Glass shattering.

The splash as the SUV went underwater.

She didn't scream once.

On the phone, I kept yelling her name, but she never answered.

She drowned in the lake before I could even help her. It killed me to end the call and dial 911 for help.

Later, Maggie called me, crying. She said my mother left a letter for her to give to me.

Shutting my eyes, I clear my throat and repeat her words in the letter.

Her handwriting was the sloppiest I'd ever seen—so unlike my mother. She didn't have the letter locked in some drawer, waiting for the right moment. Her last words were written in a rush.

And I've had them memorized for years.

> *Emilio,*
>
> *I'm so sorry, honey, but I have to go.*
>
> *Your sister will never be safe from your father as long as I'm alive. By the time you read this, the Range Rover will be at the bottom of Lake George.*
>
> *You need to tell them Aurora was in the car with me.*
>
> *Maggie knows to do this as well.*
>
> *We must keep Aurora safe. This has to be kept a secret. Only the three of us know.*
>
> *Aurora's life depends on it.*

And if the day comes and you're given the opportunity to kill your father, you have my blessing.

May he rot in hell.

Burn this after reading.

I love you. I'll be waiting for you on the other side.

Mom

Tension is on every man's face as they listen.

When I'm finished, Damien leans forward, resting his elbows on the table, and steeples his fingers. "Why the hell would you keep this from us?"

The betrayal and hurt bleed through his voice.

We're brothers.

Family.

And I've been lying to them for years.

I drag a hand across the back of my neck, guilt clawing at my spine, and shake my head.

Antonio studies me, not saying a word, as if calculating how to deal with the situation.

How to deal with *me* and whether I'm someone he can still trust.

"Where is she now?" he finally asks.

I keep my tone neutral as I say, "Chicago."

"Chicago?" His eyes narrow. "What the fuck is she doing in Chicago?"

"Maggie's family friend took her in."

"She's with that friend now?"

"She *was*."

Antonio leans forward slightly. "Where is she *now*?"

"She married into the Ricci family."

His chair scrapes back as he pushes up from the table. "Excuse me?"

I expected that piece of information to make him the most reactive.

"And since I'm laying everything out," I go on. "She just had Andre Ricci's baby. My niece. Named her Evalina."

Antonio freezes, his face softening at the memory of my mother.

The other men have similar reactions.

Antonio drops back into the chair and drags a hand over his face. "I assume that's why you were in Chicago?"

I nod.

His back straightens. "You brought Liliya? Knowing what this secret could cost you? We still don't know if we can trust her."

This is why I chose to follow Antonio and not his uncle when his father died.

He's worried about Aurora's safety.

Even after finding out I've been lying, he still has that loyalty toward my family.

"I trust her," I say, my voice deep with certainty.

His jaw is tight, and he breathes through his nose while checking his watch. "You guys get home to your wives. Let me speak to Emilio alone."

I rest my elbow on the armrest and lean into it as the other men filter out.

Each one of them says something before leaving the room.

"I'm glad she's okay," Damien says. "Tell Aurora we'd love to meet little Evalina."

"She made the best pumpkin cookies," Julian adds. "Tell her to make us a batch."

"Dude, how the hell did you keep a secret like that?" Leo says. "You're a lot better at keeping a straight face than me." He laughs, clasping me on the shoulder as he leaves.

When they're gone, Antonio stares at me like a disappointed father.

"Keeping something like this from me is bullshit," he spits. "It could get you killed. Me killed. *All* of us killed." His voice is bitter yet controlled. "This also makes me stop and wonder if you're hiding anything else from me."

I throw out my arms. "That's my only secret. You can be pissed, make me suffer consequences, whatever. But I don't regret protecting my sister. My father made it clear to my mother —if she ever did anything to piss him off, he'd kill Aurora. Every day, she had to deal with that fear." I slam my hand on the table as the pain of that memory seeps inside me. "Every. Fucking. Day!" I relax in my chair, telling my heartbeat to chill out. "I should've told you after my father died, but I'm still always worried one of our enemies will use her to hurt us."

Antonio scrubs his hands together. "And now she's involved with the Riccis?"

"They love her and aren't a threat to us."

"Constantino Ricci is a cold-blooded bastard. He's the Cristian Marchetti of the Chicago underworld, not some elderly grandfather who wants to rock Aurora's baby to sleep at night."

"They aren't a threat to us," I state again, making myself as clear as possible. "I'm not saying we should fucking brunch with them, but if shit ever hits the fan? I guarantee they'd make a damn good ally."

He exhales, rubbing the back of his neck. "Fair point, and speaking of allies, what's going on with Aleksy? I'm ready to get rid of that pain in the ass."

"Liliya is aware we know he asked her to kill me."

He rears back, surprised. "How'd that play out?"

"I gave her the option of a knife or a gun to kill me with."

He smirks in amusement. "We're all so fucked up." His smile broadens. "I did something like that with Gigi. At the cabin, when I kidnapped her and she was making a fuss." He flicks his hand through the air like taking her was nothing but a misunderstanding.

"We have Liliya's loyalty," I say, going to bat for my wife.

He cocks his head to the side. "How sure are you?"

I hesitate—a big fucking mistake.

He slams his hand on the table. "Get back to me when you know it's guaranteed she's with us *and only us*. In the meantime, take your wife home. It's late, and I need to get back to mine. She doesn't like it when I stay out late anymore."

We leave the room, and Antonio doesn't turn toward the exit.

"Maybe I should go say hi to Liliya," he says, walking along-side me.

I peer over at him. "You don't think you scared her enough when you barged into my house and threatened to kill her while I was sleeping?"

"I had to send a message," he says with no regret. "It's what we do." He slaps my shoulder. "I can't have you murdered on me."

We round the corner, and I walk into the room, fully expecting to find my wife.

41

LILIYA

I nearly drop my phone when I glance up to find Emilio and Antonio entering the room.

That doesn't look suspicious or anything.

Antonio's gaze pings from me to Emilio. "Innocent?"

"I'm emailing my sister," I blurt. "She needs money."

I clutch the phone tight, hoping they don't think I'm up to no good.

I want to prove to them that they can trust me.

Emilio said he didn't want to hurt Dasha. I believe him.

Aleksy, on the other hand? I'm not so sure.

"The runaway sister?" Antonio asks.

My throat is dry as I nod.

Antonio peers at Emilio. "Good luck with that. I want to see you first thing in the morning."

He leaves the room, and Emilio strides toward me.

"She doesn't have my new number," I say in a rush. "We've emailed. That's it." I jump up and thrust the phone into his hands.

His brows draw together as he scrolls through our emails. Exhaustion is clear on his face.

A twinge of guilt hits me when I say, "If you can just take me to the ATM and then somewhere I can wire her the money, I promise, I won't do anything stupid."

He hands me back my phone. "Why does she need it?"

My tone turns somewhat harsh. "Uh, because she's on the run from my brother and the freaking Bratva."

He scratches his cheek, ignoring my attitude. "How much?"

"All the cash I can get her." I make a swooping motion toward the door. "I have plenty in my savings."

"My wife doesn't pay for anything." He looks at me as if I've offended him in the worst way. "Has that not been understood since the beginning of our marriage?"

"But it's not *for me*. It's for my sister. The woman who ditched you at the altar."

"Exactly. And for that, I'll throw in an extra ten grand for her." He smirks. "I wanted you anyway, so her running worked out in my favor."

I blink at him. "You *what*?"

He takes a step toward me, closing the distance between us. "The night of our wedding day, before you made escape attempt number one, you asked why I made you move in with me when I hadn't enforced the same rule with Dasha."

"In the kitchen," I whisper, leaning into him as goose bumps form. Memories of that night sweep through my thoughts.

His stance is wide as he stares at me, not breaking eye contact. "I never wanted her. Never even entertained the idea of living with her. But you?" He reaches out and brushes his knuckles over my cheek. "I did. That's why I made it the only change in our deal when I could've made Aleksy give me a hell of a lot more."

"We hardly knew each other," I rasp out, nuzzling into his touch.

"Trust me, I'm the last fucking person to believe *in the moments.*

It wasn't love. I don't do love. But it was *something*. Something I only felt *with you*." He tilts his head down to kiss the top of my head and pulls away. "Now, come on. I'll call the number she emailed you from *my phone*. We'll get her the cash, and then we're going home."

I show him the number, and he dials it.

Dasha answers right away.

Emilio talks to her, setting up arrangements.

I look at the time on my phone.

It's nearly one in the morning.

After he ends the call, he runs his hand through his hair. "This night is never-fucking-ending. Come on." There's frustration in his tone, but it's not toward me.

It's toward Dasha.

The day.

All his problems.

I eyeball him skeptically. "Are you serious?"

"Yes, and if this is some kind of setup, she'll regret it."

"It's not; I swear it."

———

Emilio was right.

This night *is* never-ending.

When we exit Lucky Kings, there's a new car waiting for us with the darkest-tinted windows I've ever seen. I ask who it belongs to, and he says it's for whoever needs it. Then he drives us to a high-rise building that turns out to be his condo in the city.

"So, you're selling this place, right?" I ask, eyeing the living room and calculating how easy it could be used as a mistress spot.

I'd hate to have to burn this entire building down if Emilio got that idea.

"If that's what you want," he says before disappearing into a room.

When he returns, a large duffel bag big enough to fit a body is slung over his shoulder.

Our next stop is a run-down twenty-four-hour diner just past the city limits. Emilio pulls into a space under a light and beside an older baby-blue Escalade.

I recognize the vehicle immediately.

It's David's, the guy who lived across the street from our family home. He and Dasha had a thing years ago.

She used to sneak out with him during her teens, and he took her virginity. But as far as I knew, it was never anything serious between them.

"Stay here," Emilio says, reaching into the glove box. He pulls out his Glock, shoves it beneath his waistband, and steps out.

The Escalade door opens.

David climbs out, looking stressed, and walks toward Emilio.

They start talking.

I lean forward, craning my neck, searching for Dasha.

The second I see her, I fling the door open and run toward her.

"Dasha!" I choke out, wrapping my arms around her. "Oh my God, you're okay." I pull away, gripping her shoulders, and look her over. "Where have you been? Are you safe?"

She gives me a tired smile.

Her eyes are dull. Her hair matted.

But she's alive.

I ignore Emilio's warning glare as we walk over to them. It's clear from the way his voice drops that he's hurriedly ending whatever conversation they're having so we don't hear.

Without a word, he walks to the sedan, and we follow. He pops the trunk and pulls out the black duffel bag.

"Fifty grand," he says.

Dasha reaches for it, but he yanks it back just as her fingers touch the strap.

"You take this, and you're done calling my wife for money. No more dragging her into your problems."

He drops the bag on the ground, and it falls at her feet with a heavy thud.

"You want to call her to talk? Fine," he goes on before thrusting his finger into his chest. "But if you need money, you call *me*." He moves his finger to point at me. "*Not her*."

"Damn," Dasha whispers, staring at Emilio in awe.

The complete opposite of how she looked at him at their engagement dinner.

My husband is standing on business *for me*.

To protect me but also help someone I love.

David grabs the bag from the ground and swings it over his shoulder.

Dasha hugs me again. "Maybe I should've married him," she whispers into my ear.

"No take-backs," I say, staring over her shoulder at my husband.

He's all mine.

Emilio's eyes meet mine and soften.

I smile in satisfaction and happiness.

He meets my smile and jerks his head toward the car.

Time to go home with my husband.

The lights are on in the house when we walk in, but my tired mind doesn't think to wonder why.

The second Emilio shuts the door, I launch myself at him.

I loop my arms around his neck and smash my mouth against his.

He tastes like cinnamon.

Soo good.

I love it.

Moaning against his lips, I start fumbling with his belt.

Desperate and needy.

He grabs my wrist, stopping me. "Wait."

I whine, my breathing labored as I inch back and frown.

"Does this mean I'm good to go?"

I turn slowly, mortified to find a man around Emilio's age emerging from the dining room. A laptop is in one hand, and his phone is in the other. He glances between us, amusement clear on his face.

My cheeks flame, and he smirks.

Kill me now.

Emilio releases a heavy breath. "Liliya, this is Franko. He's one of our security guards. He was keeping an eye on the house."

I shyly wave at him, unable to meet his eyes. "Hi."

"No, you're not *good to go*," Emilio says to Franko. "You can wait in your car."

I peer out the window, now realizing I missed that there was another vehicle in the driveway. All that was on my mind was fucking my husband.

Franko salutes us. "You two have a nice night."

He's out the door in seconds.

The courage to become a sex kitten and attack my husband is gone.

I glance around, biting into my lip and scratching a nonexistent itch. "So, that's why you stopped?"

"Yes." Emilio steps closer, and my breathing hitches. "If another man saw you naked, I'd have to pluck their fucking eyeballs out." He brushes hair from my face before stroking my cheek.

Such a gentle touch while his words are so murderous.

"You're for *my eyes only*," he says, emphasizing each word.

I trail my fingers down his chest and whisper, "And the same with you? For *my eyes only?*"

He smirks. "Are you saying you don't want another woman touching me?" He dips his head, lips running over my jaw.

I tilt my head, giving him better access. "I doubt I can stomach the whole eye-plucking part though. So, how about we just don't risk it?"

He groans. "I love it when you ramble."

His mouth moves to my neck, sucking gently, and heat surges through me.

My thighs clench.

I giggle when he lifts me off the ground and tosses me over his shoulder. He rushes up the stairs, taking two steps at a time, and my body bounces with each one.

He kicks open the bedroom door, turns on the light, and lowers me to my feet. "Let's finish what you started downstairs."

I smile innocently. "What did I start?"

He closes the distance between us, roughly shoving his hand down my shorts without bothering to unbutton them. "Oh, now she wants to play innocent?"

I shut my eyes, squirming as he tries to nudge his fingers beneath my panties. The space is too tight.

"If you want more," he says, his voice deep and dark, "lose the fucking panties."

I grin before slowly peeling off my shorts and panties and stepping out of them.

Emilio is back on me in seconds.

Our mouths crash together, messy and breathless.

We claw at each other's clothes.

He throws my shirt and bra across the room.

I fling his against the wall.

When I fumble to unbuckle his pants, he bats my hand away and does it himself.

We're tired, our movements frantic and messy.

"Does my wife want her husband's cock?" Emilio asks, stroking himself, staring straight into my eyes.

My gaze drifts from his eyes to his cock.

Both my mouth and pussy are drenched for him.

He looks so beautiful, standing there and stroking himself.

Perfection carved with sin.

Even if I did kill him, like Aleksy had asked, and chose my own new husband, I'd never be satisfied. No one could measure up to Emilio.

Emilio strokes himself lazily, his thumb teasing the head. "Tell me you want my cock, Liliya." His voice is almost pleading. I've never heard him sound so desperate.

He sways closer, caressing and cupping my breast. He stops stroking himself and lowers his head to suck on my hard nipple.

Pleasure rumbles through my entire body.

"I … I want your cock," I say, my pulse skyrocketing.

His mouth moves to the other nipple, and I shudder at the feel of his facial hair, rough against my sensitive skin.

"Tell me how you're going to make your husband's cock feel good." Grabbing my hand, he guides it to his erection.

Without delay, I wrap my fingers around him. "I'm going to make your cock feel so good," I say, slowly stroking him.

He grips my waist and pulls me up. My hand falls from his cock as he wraps my legs around his hips and charges toward the chair in the corner. He drops down, taking me with him, and gives me time to adjust as I straddle him.

I drag my hips forward, running my wetness around his hard cock. My insides are on fire. With one arm, Emilio holds me up, and he uses the other to line his cock up with my entrance.

I don't even wait for him, and he falls back in the chair as I impale myself on his cock. I throw my head back, thrusting my chest forward, as he fills me.

It's perfection.

So good.

Emilio's mouth moves back to my breasts.

He tugs on my nipple with his teeth.

Sucks on it.

Kisses between them.

All while I grind on his cock.

He holds my hips as I bounce on it.

The sound of us—moans, the wet smack of our bodies meeting, and my pants—fill the room like the perfect song.

Emilio grunts beneath me, calling my pussy perfection, and when I'm so close, I collapse my head and kiss him.

He slides his tongue into my mouth, dancing it with mine, and my body trembles as my orgasm washes through me.

I shove my face into his shoulder, biting into his sweaty skin as he clutches my waist. I have no energy to move, so he holds me tight as he thrusts his hips up, fucking me.

With each thrust, he releases a louder grunt.

Tells me how much he loves my pussy.

How he's going to fucking destroy it every day, then kiss it better.

Then, my husband comes inside me.

The following morning, I wake up to an empty bed, as usual.

I smile, stretching beneath the sheets, and remember all the dirty things we did in this room last night. After I rode him on the chair, I figured we'd be exhausted.

Nope.

It was like our orgasms gave us energy that was the equivalent of a Red Bull.

Emilio bent me over the bed and fucked me again.

Then, after that, he ate my pussy until I fell apart.

I slip out of bed, put on my robe, and slide my feet into my slippers before shuffling downstairs to find Emilio in the kitchen. He's shirtless, standing behind the island.

"It's not a Maggie-level breakfast," he says, nodding toward the open doughnut box in front of him, "but it's breakfast."

I stroll into the kitchen, rubbing the sleep from my eyes.

The doughnuts look like something I'd choose when I was a kid, wanting a sugar high.

"Are these Lucky Charms?" I ask, picking one up. "On a ... doughnut?"

He shrugs. "I told Franko to get one of everything." He nudges the box closer to me.

I grab a napkin, drop the doughnut on it, and then motion toward the box. "I got one. Now, your turn. You need a full stomach to do all the murderous things on your to-do list for today."

He shakes his head. "The only thing that I'll murder is myself if I eat this shit."

I narrow my eyes at him. "But you want *me* to die from it?"

"Terrible argument from me." He grabs his own napkin. "Pick one for me."

I scan the options before pointing at one with gummy worms.

"Fuck no," he says around a grimace. "What's option two?"

I point at one with toasted marshmallow and graham cracker crumbs.

"That'll do." He drops it onto his napkin.

I wait until he takes his bite before doing the same. I cringe at the shot of sugar that just entered my bloodstream.

After swallowing his bite, he wipes his mouth and says, "I need to do some things today. You have a few options to keep you busy."

I pluck a marshmallow off my doughnut, toss it into my mouth, and raise a brow.

"You can volunteer with Genesis at the shelter, hang out with Gigi at Antonio's, or sit in on one of Pippa's dance classes."

I tap my nails on the counter, remembering one of my conversations with the girls at Gigi's brunch. "Genesis mentioned they'd lost their nurse at the shelter. Maybe I'll help them out until they find a new one."

"Finish up and get dressed, and then I'll drop you off." He smiles.

Yes, an actual smile from my husband.

I freeze mid-chew, dropping my doughnut, and almost make a joke.

But I stop myself.

I don't want to mention it and risk him holding back his smile. He looks too handsome when he does it.

42

EMILIO

T hank God Liliya took it easy on me today and decided to spend her day at Safe Hearts.

Genesis has volunteered at the women and children's shelter for years. After she was kidnapped, Julian hired full-time security there. No more rotating volunteers. It's twenty-four hours a day—even when Genesis isn't there.

The women and children there deserve that protection.

Most women at the shelter have escaped domestic violence. I can't help but think what would have happened if my mother had gone to Safe Hearts. She could've saved her life. Deep down though, I know my father would've found a way to hurt her, even there. Possibly putting other women's lives at risk.

He always won, and no one dared to ever run from him.

My goal today is to find out who tried to shoot Liliya and me.

"A million will be wired to each of your offshore accounts," Antonio informs us.

We're back in the same room from last night—Antonio, Damien, Julian, and me. As soon as they came in this morning, they all asked about Aurora.

How she and the baby are doing.

Whether they'll see her again.

I doubt Andre will allow her to return to New York.

I nod at Antonio's words.

We all prefer to keep our money in offshore accounts. They're untraceable and protected. The feds can't get their grimy hands on our dirty money.

I have a fair share in stocks, bonds, and investments. Genesis's father used to sell Julian insider trading, and he'd give us tips. We all made a fucking killing. Between that, my inheritance money, payouts from our illegal ventures, and the casino, I live comfortably and want for nothing. I also take a few contract killings when I'm feeling bored.

Antonio turns to me. "I'm coming with you to meet with Aleksy. Not only do I want to hear what he knows about you being chased by armed men only miles from his home but we also haven't seen our share of his profits." He slams his laptop shut. "That's a fucking problem."

I nod, following him from the office and outside.

The other men go their separate ways, and Antonio and I slide into the sedan.

My phone rings before I start the engine, and Aleksy's name flashes on the screen.

I hold up the phone to show Antonio.

He nods, and I answer, putting the call on speaker.

"I have a serious fucking problem!" Aleksy yells on the other line, sounding nearly out of breath.

"What's that?" I ask in annoyance.

I don't give a shit about his problems.

I want to solve my problems *with him* first.

"Fredricko, that crazy fucking arms dealer—"

"I know Fredricko," I cut in dryly.

"Well, he just burned down my goddamn bowling alley!"

I grin wide, adjusting the AC vents to blast me in the face.

"He said it's payback for killing his son. He claimed I'm trying to steal his weapon contracts!"

I crack my neck. "Are you trying to steal his contracts?"

"No!" Aleksy snaps before lowering his voice, as if about to tell me a secret. "Would I love to have them? Of course. But I wouldn't even know where to start."

Is this him subliminally asking me?

I rub my chin, dragging my hand slowly down my throat. "Did you know your sister and I were shot at after leaving your house the other night?"

I couldn't care less about whatever bullshit he's dealing with.

I caused it and know why Fredricko is coming for him.

It was all a part of my plan.

"What?" he stammers. "No. Who did it?"

"That's what I'm trying to find out."

He goes quiet.

"You're not going to ask if your sister is okay?" I hiss.

If the roles were reversed and Aurora had been shot at, I'd be demanding to kill whoever it was.

"Is … is she okay?" he finally asks, and I hear Antonio mutter, "Fucking pathetic loser," in the background.

"Yes," I snap.

"Then what are you making a big deal about me asking for?" He scoffs. "You're her husband. You should be the one more concerned."

I grit my teeth, wishing I could punch the fucker in his face. "Any idea who could've been behind it?"

"No idea, man."

"Don't fucking lie to me, Aleksy."

"You think I'd do something to put my sister's life in danger?"

I hold in the urge to tell him he already did when he told her to kill me.

But I'm saving that for when we're face-to-face.

"We need to talk," I tell him.

"About what?"

"Business."

"In case you forgot, I have a fucking bowling alley problem!" he screams.

"Great." I shift the car into Reverse. "I'll meet you at the pile of ashes. Have some fucking nachos ready for me." I end the call and leave the casino's back parking lot.

"Man, you should've at least told him two nachos," Antonio comments, rolling down his window for fresh air.

———

We're ten minutes into the drive to the bowling alley when Antonio says, "We have company. A black SUV has been tailing us since we took our first right after the casino."

I peer into the rearview mirror.

Fuck.

Sure enough, there's a black SUV.

The windows are tinted so dark that I can't make out the driver.

I cut the wheel, and the tires squeal as I make a sharp right.

The SUV does the same thing.

Adrenaline storms through my blood as I slam my foot on the pedal. We launch forward, and I pick up speed as we weave through cars.

Horns blare.

I run a red.

The SUV stays on our ass the entire time.

Antonio turns, shoving off the seat, and grabs the AK-47 from the back seat floorboard. He undoes the safety and shoves the barrel toward the rear window.

My hand grips the steering wheel tight as I make another turn, nearly clipping a car and bouncing over a curb. Sweat builds along my hairline as sirens fire off behind us, but I don't slow my speed.

I can't, and I won't.

Not until we lose these fuckers or kill them.

The SUV's driver is trained.

This isn't their first fucking rodeo.

"I'm going to take out the driver," Antonio says. "Stupid son of a bitch."

Antonio grunts when I swerve to the right, barely missing a jaywalker. Leaning forward, he teases the trigger with his pointer finger, waiting for the right moment.

He won't miss.

He's one of the best snipers I know.

I wait for the sweet sound of a bullet firing.

But it never comes.

"What the fuck?" Antonio shouts, curving his shoulders as he leans in to get a better look through the rear windshield.

I check the mirror and mentally repeat his words.

Lev is standing through the sunroof of the SUV, waving his arms in the air, and motions for us to pull over. I check my phone, seeing missed calls from him.

"Should we stop?" I ask Antonio, easing off the gas some.

He doesn't lower the gun. "Sure. I've had a boring day. Might as well try to punish the fucker who made us go on a high-speed chase before I've had my second coffee."

I turn into a side alley.

The SUV slides in behind us.

I slam the car into park and glance at Antonio.

I kill the engine, wishing I were killing Lev or Aleksy instead. Antonio and I each shove a Glock in our waistband. He keeps the AK in his hand as we step out. Both of us are wary of what the fuck we're about to walk into.

My blood boils as Lev hops out of the passenger seat of the SUV, all smiles, as if this were all just a game.

"What the fuck is this, Lev?" I demand.

Before he can answer, the SUV's back door opens.

A large man in a striped navy suit steps out, calm and collected.

My jaw tightens. "Who the fuck are you?"

Antonio stiffens and mutters, "Fuck."

The man looks at Antonio first. "Lombardi." Then he nods toward me. "Emilio."

His Russian is thick enough to choke on.

He coldly smiles at us. "We have important things to discuss."

43

LILIYA

I study the space around me, impressed with the shelter's clinic room that smells like lemon disinfectant.

It's not like I expected something *bad*.

But this is hospital-worthy.

I shouldn't be surprised.

It seems when the Lombardi men help their wives, they go all out.

There's no giving the bare minimum with them.

From what I learned, Julian helped fund Safe Hearts to move into a different building. Somewhere with more square footage, better privacy, and higher security.

Genesis beams proudly. "Do you think you can make this work?"

I nod, opening the drawers and taking in the surplus of supplies. "I can definitely make this work."

She hoists herself onto the clinic bed. "Thank you again for doing this."

"It's no trouble," I tell her. "I loved being a nurse. Plus, it gives me something to do."

She points at me, her nails bright red. "You used to work at the hospital, right?"

"I did ..." My words trail off as nervousness hits me. "I was, uh ... fired."

Volunteering or not, being terminated from a job, especially one as serious as this one, never looks good on a résumé.

Genesis raises a brow. "For what?"

"The attending physician put his hands where they didn't belong. I kneed him in the balls."

A grin stretches across her face. "Niiiice." She cringes, holding up a finger, and her dark brows crush together. "Wait. You got fired, not him?"

I nod.

I'm reminded of that day, and anger knots in my stomach. I thought I could trust HR to do the right thing. I went to them straight-away. I cried and told them the situation, and they swore they'd fix it.

Their *fixing it* was firing me.

Genesis shakes her head, disgust lining her flawless features. "That's some bullshit."

I nod in agreement, a hint of sadness mixing with that anger.

She studies me for a second, kicking her feet back and forth. "Did you tell Emilio about that?"

I rest my back against the counter and stretch out my legs. "I think he already knows."

She smirks. "Is the doctor alive?"

I slowly shake my head.

"Then he knows." She does a mocking clap of her hands. "Nice job, Emilio."

Even though I most definitely shouldn't laugh at the murder of a man, a small hiccup of a chuckle leaves me.

"How are you adjusting to your marriage?" she asks.

I fake excitement. "Perfect. Like a honeymoon that never ends."

She laughs. "It'll calm down. I promise."

"I hope so," I grumble, massaging the space between my brows before motioning toward the doorway. "Is that why you spend so much time here? To get away from the craziness?"

She stops swinging her legs and shakes her head. "I've volunteered here for over a decade. It's one of my favorite places." Her posture tenses as she squeezes her eyes shut. "It's always been more of a home than mine ever was, if that makes sense. Now that my parents are gone, it seems even more so."

"Both of your parents are dead?" I suck in a deep breath. "I'm so sorry."

"Just my father is … well, dead. But my mother might as well be."

I see her visibly gulp as she tries to make herself more comfortable.

"My mom fled the country just before my father committed suicide. She knew the feds were coming for them. She didn't tell me goodbye or ask me to go with her." She scoffs. "She couldn't. They'd sold me to your cousin."

I scrunch up my nose, hating that I had some connection to that pain she suffered. "I'm so sorry, Genesis."

She offers me a simple smile. "You have nothing to apologize for. It's the people who see us as currency who need to apologize."

I return the smile. "I'm glad you're with Julian. Not my crazy-ass cousin."

"Yes, I witnessed his craziness firsthand." She looks up, as if reliving a memory of him. "The man planned to sneak me into Russia." Her voice turns a tinge more playful. "Now, I consider myself a smart person, but it'd take me a good ten minutes to find Russia on a map. How the hell would I have made it back to the States? But I'd have stolen a canoe and rowed here if it had come to that."

I throw my head back and laugh.

She hops off the clinic bed. "I have a class to teach." Her hand brushes my shoulder on her way to the door. "You let me know if you need anything, okay?"

"Okay," I reply softly as she disappears from the room.

I turn, looking through the drawers to take inventory, but stop when someone lightly taps on the door. A blond woman wearing a yellow jumpsuit stands in the doorway. A little girl with a sparkly Minnie Mouse headband stands between her legs, peeking through them at me.

"Hello," I greet, smiling at the mom before sending the girl a friendly wave. "I'm Liliya. Come on in."

The little girl waits for the woman to move before she follows, nearly at her heels.

"I'm Renea," the woman introduces herself.

"And I'm …" The little girl starts to say but then slaps her mouth shut, glancing up at her mother like she did a moment ago.

"Go ahead, honey," Renea urges.

"I'm Nova," she whispers shyly.

"Hello, Renea and Nova. It's so nice to meet you." I point at the door. "Do you mind if I close this to give us some privacy?"

Renea nods and waits until I shut the door to say, "Nova's throat is swollen. I was hoping you could take a look."

"Of course," I say, patting the clinic bed. "Can you hop up here for me, Nova?"

Nova waits for Renea to give her the okay.

When her jump is too short, Renea helps her.

As I slip on gloves and grab a penlight, I listen to Renea list off Nova's symptoms. I ask Nova to open her mouth wide and say *ahhh*.

She does, her *ahhhh* super long as I examine her throat.

All the classic strep signs are there.

I open a few more drawers, muttering, "Yes," when I find a rapid strep test.

Nova squirms as I swab the back of her throat.

"Now, just give it a few minutes, and we'll have the results to see if it's strep," I tell Renea as I toss the wrapper and start the timer.

Renea ducks her head toward me. "Thank you, Liliya."

I smile in response.

As we wait, I notice Renea's gaze keeps drifting to my ring.

Nova starts singing the ABCs when Renea leans toward me and says, "I'd say your husband must love you a lot. That's a beautiful ring."

I raise my hand, admiring my ring for what feels like the hundredth time since Emilio slipped it on my finger.

"Thank you," I say brightly.

She frowns, her shoulders caving forward. "I had a nice ring too. Big diamond." A sarcastic laugh escapes her. "Big house. Everyone thought I lived the perfect life."

I'm speechless for a moment.

"He used to beat me," she says, making sure to keep her voice low enough that Nova's singing drowns out her words. "Broke my fingers. Left bruises."

My chest tightens. I reach for her hand and squeeze it gently. "I'm so sorry, Renea."

A tear slips down her cheek.

I swallow, holding back my own.

"You're safe here," I assure her. "You and Nova both. We'll take care of you. Your husband will never touch you again."

It's at that moment that I decide this is where I'll stay.

Working at the clinic isn't temporary for me.

Like Genesis, I want to help these women and children.

Not everyone is lucky enough to have a husband who'd rather suffer every ounce of pain than for you to feel even a pinch of it.

And if needed, I'll have my husband hurt the men who hurt these women, like he did to the one who had hurt me.

Tears prick at my eyes as I give her hand another squeeze. "You'll find happiness. A love that cherishes you. Until then, you have us."

44

EMILIO

"Rurick Morozova," Antonio says, taking a step forward, meeting the old man's stare.

Ah.

While I've never met Rurick, I've heard of him plenty of times. He's Liliya's grandfather. Head of the Bratva out of Moscow. He ran things in Russia while his son, Yaroslav, controlled the Bratva in the States. He's also the one who approved for Aleksy to step in after Yaroslav's and Dima's deaths.

The SUV's back doors open again, and two other men step out.

Both in sharp black suits and wearing thick gold chains around their necks.

One is nearly seven feet tall, and the other hardly hits five-five.

Rurick gestures toward the SUV. "Can we speak privately?" His English is somewhat broken.

Antonio scoffs, not showing Rurick the respect he's used to, and shakes his head. "You just chased us down in your vehicle. I'm not getting in there with you."

Like me, Antonio trusts no one.

Rurick lifts a brow. "Then where? There aren't many places men like us can speak freely."

"There's a diner around the corner," Antonio replies. "We can talk there."

Rurick glances back at Lev and the other men.

"Just us," Antonio adds. "You and Lev. Me and Emilio."

"All right," Rurick says. "To the diner we go."

———

We get plenty of stares when we walk into the diner.

I've been here a few times.

Antonio's daughter, Amara, loves their pancakes.

They make them into smiley faces.

The hostess shows us to a red booth.

Antonio and I sit across from Rurick and Lev.

Lev looks nervous, and I'm surprised that, with his age and closeness to Aleksy, Rurick is even allowing him to be around.

It also makes me question Lev.

I had no idea he was scheming behind Aleksy's back with *us* and Rurick.

I glance at Rurick as the hostess hands us menus.

We all order coffee. That's it.

Rurick has to be in his late seventies. His face is wrinkled from a hard and violent life. It's a look I'm familiar with—seeing it on so many aged faces in the Mafia. He'll be unfit to lead soon and have to pass his corrupted empire down to someone else.

God help him if it's Aleksy.

God help every man in the Bratva.

He clasps his veiny hands together and rests them on the table.

No one starts the conversation until the server delivers our coffees and scurries off.

Rurick picks a creamer from the basket, cracks it open, and stirs it into his coffee before bluntly saying, "I want Aleksy gone."

I maintain my composure, holding in the surprise.

"That's your grandson," Antonio states as if Rurick somehow forgot.

I'd want the guy gone, too, but I'm not Bratva.

This isn't my business.

"I'm aware," Rurick says.

Lev repeats every motion Rurick makes.

From the creamer he selected to how he's stirring his coffee.

"Aleksy is ruining our organization. I won't allow him to ruin the decades of blood, sweat, and death my family sacrificed for our success."

Lev nods in agreement.

I lean in, cutting to the only thing I give a fuck about. "Who shot at me and Liliya?"

That's my priority for the day.

"Aleksy made the call," Lev says matter-of-factly.

I grind my teeth, rage barreling through me.

It takes all my self-restraint not to pick up the butter knife beside me and slam it into his jugular. Sweeten his coffee with his own fucking blood.

The idiot has my number.

He could've given me a heads-up.

I move closer, ready to get in his face, but Antonio blocks the move and asks, "Why would Aleksy put his sister in harm's way?"

Rurick scoffs. "We all know my grandson isn't the sharpest blade in the drawer."

My stare stays glued to Lev. "Why didn't you warn me?"

He turns to Rurick, a silent plea for him to answer the question for him.

Rurick doesn't back him up.

Just waits for him to speak for himself.

Lev pales some. "I didn't know about it until it was over."

I drum my fingers along the table's edge, still struggling to hold in my anger. "What do you want, Rurick? Why'd you chase us down?" I lock my gaze on him. "Are you here to apologize for ordering Aleksy to tell Liliya to kill me?"

Rurick shakes his head violently. "I told Aleksy to let that go, and I wasn't the one who called the hit. I told him we needed to start this on a clean slate." He picks up the mug, holding it tight in his chubby hand. "I've mourned my son's death. As for Dima, I'm happy the little fucker died. He had killed my son, so I don't mourn his death. Grandson or not."

Rurick gives no fuck about grandchildren. Noted.

"My goal with the marriage contract, for giving you my Liliya, was to build peace and a strong business partnership," Rurick says. "I didn't want any more violence."

Antonio leans forward, eyeing Rurick coldly. "Yet you're asking us to kill your own grandson."

"One death could save many lives," Rurick replies with no hesitation or shame. "So, yes."

Antonio scoffs. "Kill him your-damn-self then."

"We don't kill our own," Rurick counters.

I chuckle under my breath. "Sorry to break it to you, but we don't do the Bratva's fucking bidding." Spit leaves my mouth with the word *Bratva.*

Rurick raises a bushy brow. "Even after he tried to murder you and your wife?"

"Half the people I've met want to kill me," I counter.

I sure as hell plan to hurt Aleksy for ordering Liliya to kill me, but I need to figure out a plan. Everything I do is calculated.

Killing Aleksy is a slippery slope.

I need to see where Liliya stands before I pull the trigger.

Rurick ignores my comment, shifting his gaze back to Antonio. "Let's make a deal."

Antonio crosses his arms. "What kind of deal?"

"I'll give you a larger cut of our business profits—"

I interrupt him. "Do you mean the one currently burning to the ground?"

Rurick frowns. "What?"

I smirk, raising my mug. "Your bowling alley's burning as we speak." I make a *boom* gesture with my hand.

Rurick looks at Lev for confirmation.

Lev only lazily shrugs.

Rurick pinches his thin lips together. "Trust me when I say this: I don't like being in the States. I like the money from here —that's it. I'll give you a bigger cut, and Lev will stay here to manage things. He's low-ranking, no threat."

Lev immediately frowns at being referred to as *low-ranking*.

No underboss is low-ranking.

Rurick's attitude toward Lev shows he has no respect for him.

He's using him like a fucking puppet.

"Lev is good. Loyal," Rurick adds.

Lev perks up some.

"He also has no intention of ever becoming boss."

And Lev goes back to being depressed.

I grab a toothpick and point at Lev with it. "That true, Lev?"

Lev slowly nods, not even half convincing.

Antonio stands, collects a crisp hundred from his wallet, and drops it on the table. "We have Lev's number. We'll be in touch."

"It's a good deal, Antonio," Rurick comments, rubbing his stomach.

"We'll be in touch," Antonio repeats.

"It's a damn good offer," Rurick says. "A deal not to pass up."

"Didn't say it wasn't," Antonio said. "I said, we'll be in touch."

Rurick's jaw clenches as he watches us leave.

A lifestyle filled with violence will always put you in an early grave.

But the hotheaded ones with impulse issues? They die even younger.

That was another one of my father's lessons when I was growing up.

He spent years outsmarting death and then made *one* simple mistake.

He chose to side with a traitor, let his guard down, and became distracted by topless dancers. My father made the mistake of being too cocky and forgetting how brutal this world was.

"What's your take?" I ask Antonio once we're back in the car.

"We decide who stays breathing and who doesn't." He stares out his window, watching Rurick and Lev leave the diner and slip into the SUV.

"I don't trust either of the fucks." I glare as the SUV drives past us.

"Then it's just how we get rid of their bodies." He glances at me in concern. "This also puts you in a fucked-up spot."

I nod, starting the car.

If Aleksy wasn't Liliya's brother, he'd already be dead.

Letting him live despite his putting a hit on me paints me as weak.

I need to figure out how to put Aleksy in the ground without my wife hating me.

The Russian-owned businesses aren't exactly in prime real estate.

Most of them sit in the dying corners of the city.

Liquor stores, payday loan joints, and empty buildings surround them.

And now it's nothing but ashes.

The Bratva are sure having a rough year.

The bowling alley was their only semi-legit source of income.

All the other money Yaroslav brought in was dirty money from trafficking drugs.

We arrive just as the last fire truck leaves. Aleksy's in the parking lot, pacing, with his phone pressed to his ear.

When he spots us stepping out of the car, he mutters something, ends the call, and shoves the phone into his pocket.

"My *dedushka* is here," he says, his breath ragged and stressed, as if we care. "Lev just told me. That fat bastard hasn't left Russia in years. Something's fishy."

"I'd say he's here because you're fucking everything up," Antonio casually comments, as if that isn't the worst insult a boss could give to another.

Aleksy scowls at him, nostrils flaring. "I was handed a pile of shit. I'm doing the best I can to fucking fix it!" His voice rises, but still stays somewhat level. "Why are you two here? You couldn't give me one fucking day to handle *this* problem?"

"We haven't seen a dime from the profits we were promised," Antonio says.

Aleksy kicks at soot in the parking lot. "How am I supposed to figure out how much to pay you if the books are burned to ashes? On top of that, I now have to deal with fucking Fredricko!"

"You should've had our money weeks ago. Had you done that, you'd have known what the books said," Antonio replies. "I'll give you a number. Twenty grand. Tomorrow morning. Emilio will get it from you." His lips twist into a cruel smirk. "If you don't have the money, he'll set your house on fire with *you* in it."

Not giving two fucks about the bowling alley or Rurick, I step toe-to-toe with Aleksy. "Who shot at my fucking car the other night?"

"I told you, I had nothing to do with that," Aleksy fires back.

I hold his stare, allowing an uncomfortable silence to take over for a moment. Then, as I slowly pull back, I spit and then punch him in the face.

"What the fuck?" he yells, immediately reaching for his gun, and my fist comes into contact with his face again.

"I'll see you tomorrow," I say, turning and walking away.

Once we're back in the car, Antonio says, "If he doesn't pay, kill him. Rurick won't care. Hell, he wants us to." He calmly slips on his sunglasses. "Time to figure out a way to kill your brother-in-law."

It's been a long damn day.

It's after midnight when I pick Liliya up from Julian and Genesis's. She went home with them after they finished volunteering at the shelter.

She falls asleep on the drive home. I scoop her into my arms, and she curls into my chest as I walk us up the stairs.

"My husband," she mutters, her lips brushing my shoulder. "I'm so lucky I was forced to marry you."

I pause in the bedroom doorway, shutting my eyes for a moment.

She has no idea that I'm murdering her brother tomorrow.

No idea that she may hate me for it too.

45

LILIYA

N early every morning since saying *I do* to Emilio, I've woken up alone.

I've been okay with that.

My husband is a busy man—killing people, committing crimes, and all that. Apparently, it starts early in the day and ends late in the night.

Emilio just ruined that.

He's officially created a woman who wants to wake up with her husband every damn morning.

Especially if the mornings start like *this*.

Sunlight shines through the cracks in the curtains, giving me just enough light to see Emilio's head buried between my legs as he has me spread wide open for him.

Ragged moans slip through my lips as I open my eyes.

His mouth is hot as he flicks his tongue against my wet folds.

"Mmm," I murmur, lowering my hand beneath the sheets to fist his hair. "Good morning to you too."

I swear, I hear him lowly chuckle before he pushes his face deeper, tongue fucking me hard.

My body comes alive, and I buck my hips against his face.

His strong hand grips my waist, holding me where he wants me, as he thrusts his fingers inside me.

"God," I moan, biting into my lip. "*Fuuuck.* Right there."

Emilio excels at *everything*.

Killing, kissing, making me come apart with his mouth and cock.

I prop myself on my elbows to stare down at him while rotating my hips.

I take in his strong shoulders flexing as he holds me down and devours me.

The way his head moves in sync with my thighs as he laps me up.

The energy in my body builds, like a buzz that keeps getting stronger.

I drive my hips forward so hard that I'm surprised I don't break the man's jaw and collapse onto my back. He isn't fazed at my desperate need for him.

It only entices him to eat me out harder.

I'm whimpering.

Moaning.

Yelling his name.

Begging for more.

He draws my orgasm out, like a game.

As soon as I think I'm about to fall apart, he pulls back, giving me a break.

"Jesus, it's too early for games," I say, attempting to catch my breath.

He pauses, lifting his chin and resting it along my lower belly. "Let me play with you, baby. Let me start my morning off right."

Without waiting for my response, he lowers his head, tilts my hips up further, and gives me one swift lick from my ass crack to my pussy in one sinful motion.

This time, he doesn't hold back.

He devours me.

Fast. Hard. *Filthy.*

I buck against him, fisting the sheets, my knees shaking and toes curling.

"Yes, baby," he groans against my heat. "Soak your husband's face. Give me the best fucking breakfast ever."

He doesn't have to ask me twice.

Ecstasy rolls through me.

My body trembles, waves of pleasure shattering through me.

I'm shaking and breathless.

He patiently waits until I'm still before kissing one thigh, then the other.

It's almost like he's giving me a worship, a thank-you, for allowing him this gift this morning.

When he lifts his head, our eyes lock.

His gaze is wild and burning with heat.

He shifts, starting to move off my body, but I clamp my thighs tight to hold him in place.

"Nuh-uh, mister," I whisper, trying to lift my hand to waggle my finger, but I don't have the muscle strength to actually do it.

A smile pulls at his lips. He kisses my clit gently before sliding up and kneeling between my legs. "This morning was about you." His voice is raspy and thick with restraint.

My gaze drops to his cock. It's thick, hard, and slick at the tip with need.

My mouth waters, and I lick my lips. "If it's about me, then I want my husband inside me."

"So greedy, my wife." He brushes his thumb over my clit. "Always wanting her husband's cock, doesn't she?"

Electricity bolts up my spine.

I gasp when he shoves three fingers inside me.

He moves them fast and so deep.

"Please," I cry out.

I drop my eyes from his handsome, tired face to his tight jaw to his bare chest that's already gleaming with sweat. The muscles tighten under his skin as he moves.

I whimper when he pulls his fingers from my soaked pussy.

He hooks my legs over his shoulders, situates us, and then, with no warning, he slams into me.

"Fuuuck," he groans, throwing his head back. "So tight. So wet. So fucking perfect."

With each slam of his cock inside me, my body slips farther up the bed.

The sheets cling to my sweaty skin.

"Play with your tits, baby," he orders. "Rub those beautiful nipples."

I do as he said, smoothing my hands over them before tugging on a nipple.

"Fuck yes," he moans before leaning down to capture one in his mouth.

He sucks hard, like a starved man who didn't just eat my pussy like a full meal.

Sparks fly through me as my husband fucks me wild.

Deep.

Like we were meant for each other in every way.

Emilio is the only man I've ever slept with.

But I can't imagine anyone else ever making me feel like this.

Only Emilio.

My husband.

The man I was terrified to love.

That I thought would destroy me.

And now, I don't know if I ever want to live without him.

Stupidly, I verbalize those words when they were supposed to stay in my head.

"God, I love you so fucking much," I moan, breathless, digging my nails into his arm.

He freezes.

Oh shit.

Immediately, I start trying to correct myself. "I, uh—" My heart thrashes against my chest.

"Did you mean that, or was it only because I'm making your pussy feel good?"

"Uh ..." I turn my head to look at the wall.

He grabs my jaw, turns my face back to him, and forces my eyes to meet his.

He stares at me in desperation for the answer.

Like he's tormented, but he also needs to know.

"Both," I finally admit, my stomach twisting.

He doesn't reply.

Just drops my legs, crashes his mouth into mine, and pulls me tighter.

He fucks me slow, then hard, then deep.

Our bodies rub together, this position feeling so intimate.

And when he comes, buried deep inside me, he whispers, "I hope I just put a baby in the woman I'm falling in love with," in my ear.

I grin, feeling on top of the world.

This is what it feels like to be happily married.

———

"So, you know how Maggie and I have been talking about paint colors?" I ask Emilio as he fastens the last button on his black shirt.

After our bedroom sex came shower sex.

I'm curled up on the closet ottoman in my robe while he's getting ready for the day.

He nods, slipping a black blazer from its hanger.

"What do you think about repainting the bedroom?" I play with the belt of my robe.

The bedroom holds a lot of memories for him.

It was his growing up here.

His mother designed it and chose the paint colors.

But it's also outdated, and it needs revamping.

If I'm going to make this house a home—*my home*—I want to do it the right way.

There isn't one second of hesitation before he says, "Whatever you want."

All right, now onto the next subject that's a big one.

I draw in a breath, now tugging on the belt. "I was …"

He looks over at me, waiting.

"I was thinking of asking Maggie if she'd want to move back into her wing," I croak as if my throat is suddenly sore.

He crosses the room and presses a kiss to the top of my head. "That's Maggie's call. She's always welcome here."

I smile, my heart warming.

He kneels in front of me, adjusting my robe collar before running his rough hand over my cheek. "Does that mean you're ready to make this your forever home, *guaio*?"

I smile as his thumb runs over my lips. "I'm ready for this to be my forever." I slide my hand down his arm to clasp his hand. "With you."

———

The second I see Maggie over FaceTime, I squeal, "Maggie! God, I've missed you!"

I wish I could reach through the screen and hug her.

She waves to me, smiling bright, and I hear voices in the background.

"You make it to Chicago okay?" I ask, walking into the kitchen for a Dr Pepper.

"Sure did."

She turns the camera, and my heart squeezes when I see baby Evalina, cuddled in Aurora's arms.

"Hi, Liliya," Aurora says, giving me a tired wave.

Her hair is messy, strands going in every direction, as she rocks Evalina.

"My niece is still the cutest thing I've ever seen," I say, blowing a kiss through the screen.

Evalina coos, as if she heard me.

I smile wide.

I haven't known Maggie or Aurora for long, but I already feel like they're family.

I want to keep them in my life forever.

The camera shifts, and I see Angelica beside Aurora.

She narrows her eyes at me through the screen.

"Hi, Liliya," she says, crossing her arms. Her hair is slicked back in another bun, like she's ready for a business meeting.

I give her the friendliest smile I've ever made. "Hi, Angelica!"

"She'll warm up to you," Aurora says. "By the tenth time she sees you, she'll start treating you like family and ask you what your favorite meals are so you can have them when you visit."

I perk up and laugh, a rush of excitement hitting me at the mention of visiting again.

I planned to ask Maggie about moving in during this call, but I decided against it.

The timing isn't right, and I don't want to put her on the spot.

But once we talk alone, it's the first thing I'm asking her.

And maybe, now that the Lombardis know Aurora is alive, she can visit here too.

My heart hurts as Dasha comes to mind.

I swallow hard, hoping I haven't lost my sister forever.

We were supposed to stay close for the rest of our lives.

Have babies at the same time.

Raise them like siblings.

Celebrate all our holidays together.

Now, I don't even know when I'll talk to her again.

I stay on the phone with them for thirty minutes, talking and laughing, and when we finally hang up, I wander into the library.

I pull out paint samples and hold them against the wall.

I plan to remove every memory of Emilio's father here.

After narrowing it down to four shades, I curl onto the sofa and grab my book I brought down. I make myself comfortable and read, waiting for my husband to come home.

Not knowing when he does, it'll be complete chaos.

46

EMILIO

W hen I arrive at Aleksy's, the front gate is glitching.
Opening and closing, like it's caught in some
mechanical failure and stuck in a loop.

As I get closer, I realize what the problem is.

Two bodies lie motionless in line with the control sensor.

A convenience for me.

I drive, not bothering to swerve, and run over one of the
bodies. An SUV I'm almost positive belongs to Rurick is parked
crooked in the driveway. The driver's and back seat doors are
wide open.

When I walk up the steps, I spot Rurick's men, dead and
bleeding.

"Idiots," I mutter, walking inside.

The entry is empty. No half-naked women this time.

Screams and cries stream from Aleksy's office. Gripping
my gun, I head straight in that direction. The door is cracked
open.

I peek through the slit, taking in the scene, before walking in
without bothering to knock.

Aleksy stands before his desk, holding his gun like an executioner and pointing it at David, who's seated beside Dasha on a sofa. David's hands are raised.

Dasha begs Aleksy to put the gun down and listen to her. She apologizes for running off and tells him she'll make it up and marry any man he chooses for her.

Aleksy's attention whips to me when I step farther into the room.

Then, I almost trip over something.

Rurick's body.

Well, fuck.

I thought that'd be the other way around.

Rurick is flat on his back with a clean bullet hole between his brows. Blood pools around his head. His eyes are open, staring straight at the ceiling.

Aleksy half snarls, half grins like a rabid dog. "Emilio, look who I found." He steps forward to grab a fistful of Dasha's hair, yanking her up to her feet. He positions her so she's facing me. "My traitorous cunt of a sister." His smile turns more sadistic as he pushes her back down on the sofa. "Though, technically, my pathetic *Dedushka* found her first and brought her here. He thought he was making a point that I wasn't fit to lead. Old fucker didn't know he was signing his death wish, coming here and disrespecting me in my own home."

The words fall from his mouth fast and manic.

I just stand back, watching the scene unfold.

He shoves the gun barrel against Dasha's forehead. "You caused this, bitch. You ran and made him question me." He grinds the barrel against her skull while glancing at me. "Do you want the honors? It's you she bailed on at the altar."

I shake my head, completely unaffected. "I told you before, she didn't fuck me over. I left that wedding with a wife."

Aleksy snarls before moving the gun.

Bang.

The shot echoes through the room.

Dasha screams.

Blood sprays across the room, coating Dasha and the walls.

David slumps sideways as blood pours out of the side of his head.

Dasha scrambles to get as far away from David's body as she can. Blood soaks her face and white shirt.

Aleksy levels the gun at Dasha and looks at me. "You can have her." His nostrils flare so wide that I feel like I can peer straight into his stupid fucking brain.

He wants Dasha dead but can't pull the trigger himself.

"I'm only here for the money." I shake my head and push up my sleeves. "I don't give a shit about your family issues, but if you ask nicely, I don't mind paying for your therapy." I nudge Rurick's body with my shoe. "I do think you fucked yourself, killing this one. He controls all your business accounts. Your paycheck is now most likely gone. You dug your own grave."

Just like all the other hotheads, Aleksy will die young.

Footsteps come from the foyer, and my back straightens. On alert, I step away from the door. I press my body against the wall, giving myself a clear view of the doorway. Lev strolls inside, whistling, and he halts. He scans the room in a single sweep.

The second his eyes hit Rurick's dead body, his body tenses.

His jaw tics as anger flashes in his eyes.

"What the fuck did you do?" Lev asks Aleksy.

He crouches beside Rurick's body to check his pulse. Shaking his head, he stares at Aleksy in repulsion and stands.

"I killed the king," Aleksy says, booming with pride. "Which makes me the king of all kings. And you, Lev, you just got promoted."

Lev bares his teeth. "That was a mistake, Aleksy."

Aleksy is so caught up in his ego trip that he isn't paying attention to the real problem.

He throws his head back in laughter and says, "I'm the fucking king!"

Lev withdraws his gun and doesn't hesitate to point it at Aleksy.

Aleksy stops, and recognition dawns on his face moments before Lev pulls the trigger.

Aleksy drops to the ground.

Dasha desperately screams even louder as blood gushes from her brother.

Unlike him, I don't give Lev the chance to kill me.

I raise my gun and put a bullet through the back of Lev's skull.

He collapses on top of Rurick's body, like a blanket.

Dasha suddenly goes quiet as she stands and walks backward, falling into the corner.

I walk over to her.

Her eyes are wide in shock and fear.

I lower my gun and motion for her to stand. "Come on. Let's go."

47

LILIYA

"Liliya! Liliya!"

At first, I think I'm dreaming of hearing Dasha's voice.

Until it grows louder, almost a scream right in my face.

I blink, waking up from my nap. I dozed off while reading.

My book falls onto the ground, and I glance around the library.

When I hear my name again, I jump to my feet and sprint out of the room.

Dasha and Emilio stand in the foyer. My heart kicks up a beat when I notice Dasha covered in blood. Her breathing is ragged, and her body is trembling as she keeps yelling my name.

She doesn't even notice that I'm right here.

"Dasha," I say around a harsh breath.

She turns and stumbles in my direction. "Liliya!" Nearly falling into me, she throws her arms around my body.

I pull back, holding her at arm's length to give her a once-over.

Is the blood hers?

Is she hurt?

I need to know these things.

I scan her, looking for any injuries.

The blood isn't fresh, just dried and caked on her skin and clothes.

"Aleksy killed *Dedushka* and David!" she yells.

I tighten my hands on her shoulders. "What?"

I glance at Emilio, unsure if she's telling the truth.

"He came here from Russia to find me!" she adds. "They kept us in a fucking warehouse, hungry and freezing, before taking us to Aleksy this morning. *Dedushka* told Aleksy to kill me for running off. He said if Aleksy didn't, then Aleksy wouldn't be Bratva boss here any longer. He'd be in the ground."

My stomach twists, and I gulp.

"Aleksy just pulled out his gun and shot him!" she screams. Her words come out so fast that she doesn't even take a breath between them. "Then Lev came in and killed Aleksy!" Her voice rises. "Aleksy is dead, Liliya! He's gone."

I drop my arms, falling back a step, and glance at Emilio again for confirmation.

He slowly nods.

I whimper but stop myself from breaking down.

I need to be strong for Dasha.

Emilio comes toward me, and I notice the blood on him.

"Let's get her upstairs and cleaned up," he tells me, towering over Dasha to place a kiss on the top of my head. "I'll explain everything later. First, I need to make some calls." Surprisingly, he gently cups Dasha's shoulder. "You're safe here."

Emilio carries Dasha up the stairs, and I follow them into our bathroom. "I'll be downstairs." He shuts the door behind us.

Dasha stares straight ahead in a daze.

She moves like a zombie as I help her out of her clothes.

I turn on the shower, test the water, and guide her inside. I join her, fully dressed.

She cries.

Says everything is her fault and she wishes she had never been born.

I finally snap my fingers in front of her face and scream her name.

She flinches, her anguished eyes meeting mine, but is pulled back into reality.

"Nothing is your fault. Aleksy and *dedushka* are dead because of their bullshit. Not yours."

"But … but David," she says, her lip shaking as tears meet with the water running down her face.

"David died trying to protect you," I say, softening my tone. "I'm so sorry."

She chokes on a sob. "I loved him."

I pet her hair. "I know you did. And he loved you. I know it."

I lather a washcloth in soap and hand it to her.

She scrubs her skin harshly, as if trying to take off a layer.

The more she scrubs, the more she calms.

When she's finished, I step out of the shower, soaked, and change into sweats and a tee. She dries off as I throw my wet hair into a bun, ignoring the water dripping on my back.

She wraps a towel around herself. I pull her into a tight hug. She cries in my arms, her body shaking, and I rub her back while telling her everything will be okay.

But I don't know that.

I don't know what the fuck is going on.

―――――

An hour later, I walk downstairs.

I calmed Dasha down, gave her a melatonin gummy, and made her comfortable in Aurora's bedroom. It didn't take her long to doze off.

Emilio and Antonio are sitting in the dining room.

Their conversation stops when they notice me.

Worry lines their faces, though I see hints of happiness on them both.

There's no sadness from them that my brother is dead.

I stop in my tracks, that reality finally hitting me.

My brother and Dedushka *are gone.*

Emilio stands and helps me into the chair beside his.

Neither man says a word until I've made myself comfortable and Emilio sits back down.

Antonio clasps his fingers together, sitting across from me, and leans closer. "First, I want to say I'm sorry for your loss."

I bow my head and whisper, "Thank you." I glance from him to Emilio and back at him. "Are you guys going to tell me what's going on?"

"Your brother fucked up," Antonio says.

I can't stop the snort that leaves my mouth.

"Aleksy had asked you to kill Emilio," he states, and I heavily nod. "That request came directly from your grandfather in Russia. He wanted Emilio dead in revenge for Yaroslav's murder. Which is bullshit because we had nothing to do with that. We only killed Dima." He scratches his cheek. "When your grandfather learned Emilio was still alive, he came here to punish Aleksy for it."

"The night of the party, when we were run off the street, was that Aleksy or my *dedushka*?" I ask.

"We think it was both," Antonio answers. "Lev said it was only Aleksy's call, but I don't believe him."

"Wait." I raise a brow. "Lev? My brother's Lev?"

Antonio rubs his chin. "Lev was playing all sides. He was betraying your brother. Your grandfather wanted Aleksy dead, but knew he couldn't do it himself. So, he and Lev were trying everything they could to convince us to kill him. The hit on Emilio that Aleksy ordered from you? Lev told us about it, hoping we'd kill Aleksy. The car chase? Lev blamed it on

Aleksy. They wanted Aleksy gone, but knew it'd look bad if they did it themselves."

"And Dasha?" I stutter out. "How'd they find her?"

"Your grandfather did," Emilio says. "He brought her to Aleksy to prove that Aleksy was a fuckup. What he didn't expect was for Aleksy to kill him."

A pang forms around my heart.

My poor brother.

Another soul taken by violence.

"Has anyone spoken to my mother?" I ask.

They both shake their heads, showing no interest that they care to either.

"What happens now?" I whisper, and my shoulders fall with a long sigh.

"Someone will eventually arrive at your brother's," Emilio directs. "They'll find the dead bodies and call the police. You'll get a call. You and your sister will grieve over the loss and tell the police nothing."

I nod, completely okay with that plan. "And what about Dasha?"

"Your sister is free to decide her own future," Emilio says, his eyes focusing on me with deep intention. "You *both are.*"

Is he giving me an out from this marriage?

48

EMILIO

Thank God Lev was a traitorous bastard and killed Aleksy.

I didn't have to pull the trigger that could've cost me my marriage.

I saw the grief on Liliya's face when Dasha told her Aleksy was dead.

Aleksy might've treated her like shit and put her life on the line, but she still loved him. He wasn't always the monster the Bratva molded him into.

Like the rest of us, he had come out of the womb with a clean heart.

Bloodless hands.

But it didn't last long.

The world we live in doesn't allow us to be pure.

I told Liliya she had the choice to leave.

I saw the shock on her face, but she didn't answer at the table.

Instead, she kept asking Antonio questions.

He told her that Julian had connections with the feds, and she wouldn't be questioned about anyone's deaths. We had also made sure to gather all the video surveillance, save it on a hard drive for us, and then delete it from the estate's records.

Antonio is gone now, Dasha is asleep, and Liliya and I are in our bedroom.

I'm sitting on the edge of the bed, staring at the wall, wearing only a towel, post-shower.

Liliya climbs up behind me and starts massaging my sore shoulders.

I relax into her touch, inhaling the aroma of her sweet perfume.

Everything about her is sweet.

So perfect.

"Do you want me to leave, Emilio?" she murmurs to my back.

That useless organ in my chest stiffens. "No," I reply without looking back at her. I raise my hand and cup it over hers. "I want you to stay here forever."

"Then, why would you say something like that?" Hurt is clear in her voice.

I turn, helping her onto my lap, and scoot back until she's comfortable. "I only want you here if *you want* to be here. No longer is this a forced marriage. I want a willing wife who's happy. If you can't be that here, then I have no problem letting you go."

She peers down at my lap, not meeting my eyes.

I brush my thumb along her jawline. "What are you thinking, *guaio*?"

"I am happy here," she whispers. "I'm happy here, with you, in our home. This is the future I want. With you. Forever."

I place my thumb beneath her chin to raise her face until her eyes meet mine.

She gives me a warm smile.

One that melts some of that ice around my heart.

I drop my head, kissing her collarbone, and suck on it.

"I'm staying here because I love it here, and I love *you*," she says, sticking her thumb beneath my chin, mimicking exactly what I just did to hers, so our gazes collide.

My pulse soothes.

My muscles relax in a way I've never experienced before.

This woman calms my entire fucking system with one sweet look.

"Sure, we were brought together because of a crappy situation, but somehow, someway, we made it work." She leans into me and brushes her lips against mine. "I thought I was marrying the beast. The one who'd make my life miserable. Instead, I got the dark Prince Charming who gave me a fairy tale." She grins against my mouth. "I love my HEAs in my books, but I like getting my own even better."

———

"Here I thought we'd have to kill Aleksy and deal with the Russians, but the entire organization just killed themselves," Antonio says from the head of the table, displaying a huge-ass smirk on his face. "Easiest fucking takeout I've ever seen. It was also a plus that Rurick had killed Fredricko after he learned about him burning down the bowling alley. He handed the weapons connections right over to us."

I nod, lighting a cigar and leaning back in my chair. "Do you think any of the Bratva stragglers will come after us?"

"Nah," Damien says. "They're too busy slaughtering each other. There's also no bloodline left, except for Dasha, Liliya, and their mother. You think any of them wants to play Bratva queen?" He huffs out a pleased laugh. "I love when my enemies die, and I didn't even have to get my hands dirty."

"Fuck that," I say, exhaling smoke. "I prefer getting my hands dirty when it comes to my enemies."

Julian scoffs. "Then why didn't you cut off Aleksy's head when you found out he'd sent you a murderous bride?"

I jab my cigar toward each one of them. "Don't act like you all haven't been vulnerable with your wives and refrained from violence so they wouldn't get sad."

Antonio lifts his vodka glass. "Guilty as fucking charged."

We all follow suit.

"To our wives," Damien says. "May they drive us crazy, fuck us wild, and prove that our hearts actually fucking work."

EPILOGUE

LILIYA

Ten Months Later

"**W**hat do you think?" I ask Maggie, doing a dramatic spin to show off the freshly painted blue room. The ceiling is painted with fluffy white clouds and a sun. Painted hot-air balloons and animals adorn the walls.

This is the only room I didn't paint myself.

Emilio wouldn't let me.

And frankly, my artwork consists of stick figures and flowers.

"I love it," Maggie says, beaming as she takes in the room. "It's adorable!"

While she spent four months in Chicago helping with Evalina, we renovated her old wing of the house. By the time she returned to New York, it was move-in ready.

She lives with us now, and life has never been better.

But this room, I've kept it a surprise from her until now.

I'm just about to ask if she wants to go shopping when something warm and wet drops down my leg.

I freeze, feeling like I just peed myself.

"Oh my God," I say, taking a shaky breath before looking down.

Maggie, always one on her toes, is already on the phone. "Her water just broke," she says into the speaker before snapping her fingers at me. "Bag. Car. Hospital. You know the drill!"

I blink at her, my head feeling like mush as nervousness overwhelms me. "What was that plan again?"

Maggie grabs my arm, helping me down the stairs, and has me sit. I hunch forward as a series of strong cramps hits me. Maggie hitches my hospital bag over her shoulder, and I hear tires screech outside.

Maggie opens the door at the same time Emilio jumps out of the car and runs inside. He'd left only ten minutes ago to grab my favorite dinner. Since I'm so close to my due date, he hasn't been leaving my side much.

"Do you have the bag?" he asks.

Maggie holds it up. "Check! The car seat is installed?"

"Check," Emilio says as I double over when another cramp hits me.

"And baby is still in Mama," Maggie says, cracking a smile.

"Hopefully not in here for long," I cry out, doubling over at another contraction.

"All right, let's move," Emilio says, suddenly sounding like a drill sergeant.

He helps me into the car's back seat. Maggie slides in behind me. Emilio drives off, calling my OB as soon as he turns onto the road.

I ball my fists together, groaning as Maggie talks me through the pain. She tells me everything will be okay and we'll meet our little one soon.

The hospital isn't close.

I'm sweating, yelling, and ready to deliver this baby in the damn back seat.

When we arrive at the hospital, Maggie helps me out of the

car. Emilio drives off to find a spot. He must've found something front row because he sprints inside just as Maggie and I reach the front desk.

Emilio holds my hand, and the pain and cramps intensify as the nurse wheels me into the hospital room.

He doesn't leave my side as the doctor comes in and tells me it's time to have my baby.

When I'm in labor and scream that I don't think I can push any more, Emilio tells me I'm the strongest woman he knows and that I can do it.

My body feels weak as I cry out.

Emilio's hand doesn't leave mine as he encourages me to push and not give up.

He does this for eight hours, not even stepping away for a bathroom or drink break, and then it happens.

One final push, and I hear the cries.

My tears of pain turn into tears of happiness.

"You have a baby boy," the nurse says cheerfully.

I'm shaking as she places the tiny, wrinkled baby in my arms.

Emilio stares at us, speechless. He drops his head, kisses my sweaty forehead, and then softly brushes his finger along our son's cheek.

"I love you both so much," he whispers.

"And we love you," I say, sobbing and staring down at the little human we made out of love. Not out of duty or because of a contract.

When Emilio takes our son in his arms for the first time, nothing else matters but us.

Our little family that I want to keep growing.

We'll create a happy home.

We'll give our children everything we grew up without.

———

"Emeri," Aurora repeats, rocking my son gently while sitting on the hospital sofa. "Such a beautiful name."

"It means bravery," I say, struggling to fight off a yawn. "He wishes you'd brought Evalina to see him."

"She's at the house," she says with a smile.

I return the smile, happiness spreading all over my tired body, because *the house* means our house.

This will be Aurora and Andre's second stay with us.

Andre isn't a fan of the accommodations and brings his full security crew, but I don't care. They're here, and that's all that matters.

Emilio hovers over Aurora like she's never held a baby before.

For a man who swears not to have a heart, I keep seeing glimpses of it.

I'll never forget the way his entire face lit up when I showed him the positive pregnancy test.

And again, today, when he held our son for the first time.

I've never seen a happier, more at peace man than him in those moments.

Aurora stays for thirty minutes before saying goodbye. I'm pretty sure Emilio secretly texted and asked her to give me a break so I could take a nap.

Later that evening, Dasha and Leo visit.

They've been dating for three months now.

It's different, them dating and not being forced into a contracted marriage.

Antonio isn't thrilled about it, given his opinion of Dasha running from the last wedding and asking me for money, but he's slowly coming around. She still isn't invited to any Lombardi family gatherings yet though.

As for our family, no one has stepped up to claim the Bratva throne.

Everything went to my mother—the estate, money, and businesses.

I don't think she can handle it, but we don't talk much.

The Lombardis leave her alone and don't ask for any cuts in profits.

She doesn't know what really happened that day in Aleksy's office.

Nor will she ever.

She'd blame it on Dasha, and my sister doesn't deserve that.

Just like with Aurora, Emilio stands over Dasha as she holds Emeri.

He's going to be as protective of him as he is of me.

———

Those who wanted to give me time to rest at the hospital visit me when I'm home.

Maggie throws me what she calls a *Welcome Home, Mommy and Baby* party.

The other wives come bearing gifts and advice. They tell me they're only a phone call away and available, day or night, assuring me I'm not alone.

The men give me hugs and tell me Emilio will be a great father. Most of them call Emeri their nephew.

By the end of the night, I'm drained and can't wait to sleep.

Emeri's bassinet is in our bedroom. I check on him, making sure he's asleep, before undressing and climbing into bed. The soft sheets feel like heaven against my skin.

Emilio walks in, post-shower, wearing only boxer briefs. He pauses at the bassinet to kiss Emeri's forehead and then strolls toward our bed.

He pulls back the blanket and slides in. Propping himself up on his elbow, he stares down at me in admiration and softly runs a hand over my stomach. "I can't believe you grew our baby inside there."

I press my hand over his, interlacing our fingers. "And you helped make our beautiful baby boy."

"None of this would've happened without you, Liliya." He lifts our joined hands from my stomach and places them on his bare chest, right over his heart. "If you hadn't come into my life, this home would've rotted. It wouldn't be filled with love like it is now. I wouldn't know what it feels like to be *happy*. I'd still be the same heartless man I was.

"Before you, I was miserable. I wasn't afraid of death. In fact, sometimes, I welcomed it. But now, I fear death because it'll take me away from you and our son." His voice grows thick with emotion. "Turns out, maybe some hearts can be saved."

"Your heart never needed to be saved. It was always there," I whisper to him. "You just needed someone to show you the proof. Your heart is huge, Emilio. It runs full for all the people you love and protect."

"You did that." He tips his head down, kissing my lips, and pulls me close. "You proved that I have the heart."

As I lie there, the heat of him relaxes my body.

I smile.

Our hearts finally found a home with each other.

A place to feel safe.

Even the darkest hearts can find their happily ever after.

And usually, those are the best tales to read.

ALSO BY CHARITY FERRELL

Lucky Kings Series

Sinful Sacrifice

Sinful Ruin

Marchetti Mafia Series

Gorgeous Monster

Gorgeous Prince

Gorgeous Villain

Blue Beech Series

Just A Fling

Just One Night

Just Exes

Just Neighbors

Just Roommates

Just Friends

Twisted Fox Series

Stirred

Shaken

Straight Up

Chaser

Last Round

Only You Series: A Blue Beech Second Generation

Only Rivals

Only Fate

Standalones

Bad For You

Beneath Our Faults

Beneath Our Loss

Pretty and Reckless

Thorns and Roses

Wild Thoughts

Risky Duet

Risky

Worth The Risk

About the Author

Charity Ferrell is a Wall Street Journal, USA Today, #1 Amazon, and #1 Apple bestselling author.

She resides in Indianapolis, Indiana. When she's not writing, she's hanging out with her dog, on a Starbucks run, shopping online, or spending time with her family.

FIND HER ON:

www.ingramcontent.com/pod-product-compliance
Lightning Source LLC
Chambersburg PA
CBHW061644190726
48289CB00006B/1743